'Dark, compelling crime writing of the highest order'
DAILY MAIL

'Brilliant' *THE SUN*

'Exceptional… Mark is writing at the top of his game.'
PUBLISHERS WEEKLY

'A wonderfully descriptive writer' *PETER JAMES*

'A class act. Utterly original and spine chillingly good, when it comes to crime fiction, David Mark is in the premier league.' *ABIR MUKHERJEE, AUTHOR OF A RISING MAN*

'One of the most imaginative crime writers in the business, David Mark knows how to tell a good story – usually one that will invoke feelings of extreme horror and awe… in a good way, of course!' *S J I HOLLIDAY, AUTHOR OF THE LINGERING*

'Aector McAvoy, Mark's gentle giant, is one of the most fascinating, layered characters in British crime fiction. Mark is an outstanding writer.' *M W CRAVEN*

'Masterful' *MICHAEL RIDPATH*

'A true original' *MICK HERRON*

'To call Mark's novels police procedurals is like calling the Mona Lisa a pretty painting.' *KIRKUS REVIEWS*

'Mark writes bad beautifully' *PETER MAY*

THE GUEST HOUSE

THE GUEST HOUSE

David Mark

HEAD of ZEUS

An Aries Book

This edition first published in the United Kingdom in 2021 by Aries,
an imprint of Head of Zeus Ltd

A CIP catalogue record for this book is available from the
British Library.

ISBN (E) 9781800244023
ISBN (PB) 9781800246324

Cover design © Lisa Brewster

Typeset by Siliconchips Services Ltd UK

Aries
c/o Head of Zeus
First Floor East
5–8 Hardwick Street
London EC1R 4RG

www.headofzeus.com

Author's Note

Some of the locations in this book are real. Some of the houses actually exist. However, the events going on within are entirely fictitious. Any similarity to real people or genuine events are entirely coincidental, and a bit bloody worrying.

For Cal, whose spirit is mirrored in the land where she spent too short a life.
Raw, forbidding, darkly beautiful, Cal is forever Ardnamurchan.

Earth, that nourished thee, shall claim
Thy growth, to be resolved to earth again;
And, lost each human trace, surrendering up
Thine individual being, shalt thou go
To mix forever with the elements,
To be a brother to the insensible rock
And to the sluggish clod, which the rude swain
Turns with his share, and treads upon. The oak
Shall send his roots abroad, and pierce thy mould.

From 'Thanatopsis', by William Cullen Bryant

Prologue

January 18, 2.14am
56°44'07.0"N 6°32'17.0"W

A sea of smashed glass.

Snow and ice, ocean and darkness: a barbed frieze of ash and teeth and steel.

Five miles from the West Coast of Scotland, the elements become a maelstrom of power and violence. The Atlantic has saved its fury for this final stretch of water: a final, lethal punch thrown by a fading adversary. Here, nearing the wild, saw-toothed peninsula of Ardnamurchan, the sea and sky seem to conspire. The snow becomes a blizzard; the stormy waters now almost Biblical in their fury. Where the water meets land it attacks as if trying to claw great chunks of earth within its embrace.

A metal tube, crow-black, moves like a sluggish torpedo towards a serrated curve of land. Ahead, the glow of the lighthouse: yellow light transforming the tumbling snow into lace handkerchiefs and shredded bridal gowns.

Soft light bleeds in through dirty glass, illuminating a space that reeks of petrol and unwashed flesh; an assemblage of metallic squares, each black with shadow and grime. This is neither a ship nor a submarine; it is partly submerged, its single turret and tail visible above the foaming tide. The belly of the vessel droops below the waterline. It is fifteen feet from bow to stern.

A wave hits hard. Slaps at this tiny machine as if it were a tick burrowing into flesh. The craft rocks. Sways. Ploughs onward, rivets and plates shuddering as if beaten with hammers.

To the men within the belly of the black, Orca-like vessel, it is as if God has plunged His fists into the frigid waters and begun to stir.

Inside: four men. Sweaters, cotton undershorts and bare feet, shivering and grumbling, their lips moving around the butts of glowing cigarettes. They move with the gait of those more accustomed to the movement of the ocean than of the land. They are sure-footed, despite the ice and snow and the up-down-up-down surging of the sea. They have seen far worse weather than this. Have known nights so cold that each breath is an agony; nights when they have felt as though their skeletons had transformed into an assemblage of icicles and their skulls no more than packed snow beneath a layer of meat. Their limbs ache. Their bellies growl. They stink of fish guts and oil, of smoke and brine. They do not complain.

At the tiller is Aroldo. He's thin, but there is a strength to his wiry, featherweight physique. Beneath his scratchy, ill-fitting clothes, is a frame that is all ridges and hollows; muscles sliding over one another like the protective plates of a suit of armour. Here, in the darkness of the cabin, he is little more than two eyes and a glowing ember. He is smoking, pushing out lungful after lungful of grey smoke, pressing his lips to the crack in the glass so that the nicotine does not taint his cargo. It billows up to join the snow-filled clouds above. He sucks in a final drag then forces the butt through the hole. He cannot permit an untended flame within the craft.

The vessel lurches as it hits a gathering wave. Aroldo has time to steady himself. The three other men do not. They swear and grumble as they clatter, painfully, against the metal hull of the ship. He glances back at them and they fall silent. Despite their days and nights at sea, they are still strangers to one another. They have not formed a bond of shared misery. Though they have defecated in the same bucket and breathed in one another's foulness, there remains a hierarchy. Aroldo finds it better this way.

He carries a crew of three men. He does not know their names and they have been instructed not to tell. One is responsible for the shipment in the hold. Another is tasked with maintaining the engine and generator. The third is here to report back to their paymasters and to ensure that if they are spotted by the authorities, they do as instructed and pull the scuttle lever, sending the vessel and its cargo of Class-A narcotics to the bottom of the sea.

Aroldo has never seen Scotland before. He has captained three narco subs on trans-Atlantic runs. Each time he has put in at Spain and made his way home via cargo ship. This is the first test of the route that they will be taking from now on. There are few eyes on this stretch of abandoned, rugged coastline. Nobody watches for South American drug runners at Britain's most westerly point.

Aroldo glances at the flimsy console desk in front of him.

He is an experienced sailor and has coaxed this ramshackle vessel across the ocean in a way that makes him proud. He knows himself to be worth far more than the 50,000 US dollars he will receive upon his return to Guyana, but he also knows that the men he works for do not appreciate their workforce haggling over payment. He has lost a brother to the cartel. Saw what they did to him. He's heard that the video is available online but he has no wish to see for himself if the descriptions of what occurred are actually true. He does know that they took his brother to pieces. They kept cutting him up long after he was dead, and at the end, in a vindictive codetta, one of the balaclava'd narcos held up his head and stared into the sightless eyes, then dropped it like it had already begun to smell.

'We nearly there, boss-man?'

Aroldo ignores the question from the engineer. He has been asking it hourly for the past twelve days. Of the three men he is bringing to their deaths in this remote land, it is the engineer he will grieve for least.

None of the passengers know that they are so very much more than crew. They are as much a cargo as the heroin and cocaine in the hold.

'Take your medicine,' growls Aroldo, over his shoulder. He hears a rustling, as the trio of passengers do as they are bid. Aroldo doesn't know what they are taking. He told them it was seasickness medication. It's not. It's some form of preoperative blood oxidiser, guaranteed to ensure they are in as presentable a condition as their long passage across the sea will allow.

They hit another swell, and suddenly he can see the triangular outline of the vessel that they are here to meet.

He has been told not to talk. Not to offer handshakes or to press for information. He is to deposit the cargo. He is to tell the three men that they have done their jobs well. And then he is to turn the sub around and head for the prearranged rendezvous, where it will be scuttled, and he will be picked up. He knows he is opening himself to risks by taking on such a dangerous job, but as long as he keeps his mouth shut he will be useful to the cartel. If he were to talk, word would soon get around that the drug runners are diversifying. They have found a market for meat.

'That it, boss-man?'

He glares through the glass at the approaching vessel. He fancies he knows the name of the man at the tiller, but he will not offer it in greeting. It is an overheard name: a snatched utterance spoken as they loaded the cargo, two narcos at the helm of a pleasure craft near the mouth of the Essequibo River. They had said the name "Bishop". And Aroldo, a God-fearing Christian, had taken note.

He glances over his shoulder. Six white eyes in the darkness, staring back. He does not let himself think about what awaits these eyes. What they will see. Their corneas alone are worth 25,000 dollars each. But their hearts – they are what makes this journey so important, and so very lucrative.

Aroldo says a prayer as the craft comes near. He feels certain that God will understand. These three men are worth more dead than alive. He is just the ferryman – just the navigator. He is simply the captain of this ship of souls.

Outside, the sound of surf, the swirl of snow, and the distant outline of an unknown land.

PART ONE

I

Now...
January 23, 7.54am
Murt Gorm Croft, near Salen, Ardnamurchan peninsula

'Daddy!'
  'No, Lilly. *Mummy*. Say "Mummy". Mummy's here. Mummy's trying.'
  'No. Daddy. Daddy!'
  'Daddy's busy, Lilly. Busy... somewhere else. I'm doing my best, just push... wiggle your foot...'
  'Not Mummy. No. Not Mummy! Mummy hurts.'
  'Please, Lilly. It makes Mummy sad when you say that. I'm trying, I promise. It still fits – you just need to push...'
  'Mummy mean. Mummy hurt toes. Daddy nice...!'
  'He's not here, Lilly!'
  'Where Daddy gone?'
  'Away, Lilly!'
  'Where, Mummy!'
  'Fort William, Lilly! He's banging Kimmy, because she's

9

twenty-three and doesn't have stretch marks and because she eats up all his bullshit with a spoon!'

There's a pause, as Lilly considers this. 'What *banging*?'

'Something you do to a drum...'

A crease appears between her eyebrows: a coin-slot in a jukebox. 'Eat thit with thpoon?'

'Oh bloody hell.'

It's somewhere between breakfast and elevenses and already I'm looking forward to bedtime. Bedtime's the best moment of the day. Not at first, of course – that's a nightmare of crying and begging and emotional abuse: a general symphony of anguish that sees my nipples treated the same way a Rottweiler treats a rubber chicken. But I'm usually a little bit drunk by bedtime and when I've taken the sharp edges off life with a gin and tonic, the things that Lilly says make me giggle more than they make me cry.

Tonight there's a chance she'll be sleeping in her shoes, just so we don't have to go through this again tomorrow. It shouldn't piss me off but it does. Why do kids have to keep growing? She's had these new peach-coloured brogues for precisely one month and already they're squeezing her toes into points and Mummy is the *bitch-queen-from-Hell* for trying to get her money's worth out of the damn things. I'm starting to think that the practical benefits of foot-binding might outweigh the moral concerns. The damn things aren't going to go on unless I butter her socks.

'Please, baby.'

'Mummy eyes wet.'

'It's just dust. And the smell of your feet.'

'Mummy not funny.'

I'm trying to keep the exasperation out of my voice. My

hair's in my eyes, and I'm getting sweaty and prickly and it feels like there's salt and pepper underneath my top layer of skin. I'm not going to lose it – I've promised myself. Whatever happens today, I'm going to roll with it. Bowl smashed at breakfast time? Not a problem. PE kit shrunk in the wash? Okay, could be worse. Full nappy stuck to the glass doors like some sort of spatchcocked diarrhoeic albatross? Just keep it together. Count backwards from ten, then forwards from one. Draw a mandala with the pen of your mind's eye. Breathe. Just breathe. *Make fists with your toes.*

'One last push, baby girl. We've got things to do. You can't run around barefoot and I haven't time to hoover and I know your sister smashed a glass and hasn't told me…'

'Mummy sad?'

'No. Well, yeah. A bit.'

'Mummy sad. Mummy cross.'

Then she does it. Says it. Wins me back around as easily as her bloody father used to. Puts one clammy pink hand on my cheek and looks into my eyes, her blue mixing with my brunette. 'Love you, Mummy.'

I melt: a snowman in a sauna. 'You are the best,' I say, and I swear the knots in my back straighten themselves out. I'm three inches taller in moments. 'You're brilliant.'

'Mummy blirriant. Play Fairy Garden? Do painting?'

And I'm grinning again. Hugging her to me and pressing her forehead against mine. It's not easy, looking into eyes that are absolute replicas of the person I'd most like to punch. She's every inch her father's daughter. Twenty-six months old now, and taller than the other two were at her age. I tell her she's a chunky monkey whenever I'm sprinkling talc on her lovely pink puppy fat and I do have a habit of telling her she's a big lump when I'm trying to carry her and do the shopping at the same time, but it's meant with love. I should probably stop that before it starts causing emotional damage. I've certainly not got round to extricating my parents from my psyche. I don't know anybody who has.

'Fairy Garden?' she asks again, tactfully, as if querying whether I'd like a glass of wine. Then she wriggles her toes and her foot slips effortlessly into her left shoe. She gives me the cheekiest look I've ever seen. 'Yes, Mummy. Fairy Garden.'

'Oh you little rotter,' I say, laughing, and she giggles as I tickle her. She slips down from the chair and runs to the sliding doors, presses her face to the glass and leaves a perfect Rorschach of smudges.

Fairy Garden is her favourite game. There's a patch of rockery and wildflowers at the top end of the garden, covered by a parasol of interlinking trees and the sort of creepers that look as though they're waiting for a chance to grab you by the ankle. We've made it pretty. Her brother and sister like sitting there too but they only go outside when I cut the plugs off all the electrical gadgets, so by and large, it's Lilly's.

We've gathered some big rocks from the beach and managed to cobble together a little circular table and chairs. We take plastic cups and saucers down there when the weather allows for it and the two of us sit there pretending to be fairies, sipping imaginary tea and making "*mmmm*" noises as we chew on invisible scones and talk about the adventures we've had riding on the backs of squirrels or making children's dreams come true. I do a lot of the talking, but Lilly's very good at telling me when I'm going wrong. She shouts at me a lot. I shout back. She's my third, but she's the hardest to deal with. Cleverest, if I'm honest.

Atticus and Poppy, nine and seven, are pretty smart but I can't help thinking I've already lost them. They're screen junkies. If they're not watching Netflix they're playing Xbox or glaring at some godawful tripe on YouTube. I try to show an interest, because the parenting books say you should, but I'd honestly rather watch a baked potato rotate in a microwave than give my eyeballs to the kind of dross that makes them giggle like they're not quite right. At least Lilly still has a bit of imagination about her – even if she does look annoyingly like her bastard of a dad.

'It's a bit rainy to play Fairy Garden, Lilly,' I say, looking through the huge glass windows and wiping the snot and smudges off with the hem of my nightie. I see myself looking back in the darkened glass. No trace of Mum in my reflection yet. Not Dad either. I'm a bit of a cuckoo in my family, which means that at thirty-five I'm still okay to look at. Bit bigger around the middle than I'd want but not so big that exercise or restraint are starting to appeal. I'm still pretty strong and on the rare occasions I get to take the canoe out on the water I feel physically capable of keeping pace with the inquisitive seals and dolphins who raise their steaming heads above the cold water. I certainly don't look like anybody else on the peninsula. I'm dark, even in winter. Dark eyes, dark hair, eyebrows that look like moustaches if I don't keep the tweezers handy.

'Nor raining,' says Lilly, shaking her head. 'Me not inside. Fairy Garden. Nice.'

She's got that pouty look on her face again, spoiled a little by her runny nose. Her eyes are a bit glassy, like sucked humbugs. She didn't sleep well last night. We're still fighting about the sleeping arrangements. She's meant to fall asleep in her own bed, which sits at the foot of mine. I've never had a problem with her joining me before the morning, but when I booted Callum out I started letting her join me from the off. I needed somebody to cuddle, and so did she. A proper Daddy's girl, is our Lilly. Four months he's been gone now and still she expects him to be there at breakfast to butter her toast and kiss her head and tell her she's his princess.

I'm trying to get her back into her own bed but she's not having it, and I haven't got the strength for the fight. She seems to remember a different man from the one who has torn me to bits. She remembers the funny, kind, silly soul he used to be. I can only think of him this past year: cold, distant, forever on his phone or popping out late at night to pick up things we didn't need; coming back glassy-eyed and breathless.

'Lilly love Mummy.'

I can't take her outside. The weather's frightful. The air's the colour that wet wood chuffs out when you throw it on a fire. The wind is blowing in great lazy pirouettes, bending the trees and picking up the fallen leaves that carpet the soggy, overgrown garden. I'd be a terrible mother if I took her outside when she's not well. Too much to do, anyway. Things to plan, stuff to organise, errands to run...

'Daddy!'

'Lilly, please – you said. You said you'd be a good girl for Mummy today. You remember Grandma and Grandad are coming, yes? And my friend might be coming over tonight and it would be nice to make the place look at least a bit presentable...'

''Sentable? What 'sentable?'

I glance around. I live in a nice house. It's a converted croft, but there's not much about it to suggest its humble beginnings. It's two-storey, Scandinavian-looking and glass-panelled at the front and back: big Velux windows and sliding doors offering an extravagant view out across Loch Sunart: picture-postcard perfect whatever the weather. The barn out back has been converted into three little guest apartments and renting them out to hikers, bikers and ornithologists manages to keep a thin buffer between bankruptcy and me. It's a buffer that's been getting thinner since Callum went. He's trying to pay me maintenance and spousal support but I'd rather accept pieces of silver from Judas Iscariot than let Callum think we can't cope without him.

He earns okay money, taking on casual work on whichever oil rigs or wind farms need geological surveys carrying out, and when he's not there he takes people for canoe trips out on the loch. *Took* people. I'm having to work hard to put him in the past tense. It's over. Absolutely, totally over. The lying, cheating, conniving, back-stabbing bastard can rot in his love nest with Kimmy until he realises just what he's lost. And when he comes crawling back he'll find I've moved on, I don't care, and he's thrown away his only true chance at happiness.

I just wish I could get a job that brings in some decent cash. That way when he comes crawling back he'll see just what I can do without him. But Lilly's a handful, and running the guest lodges is a full-time job, and I really can't see how I can go back to doing what I used to do living in an isolated place like this. There's still a need for good probation officers, but on this saw-toothed peninsula, the demand is pretty much zero. There's barely any crime, the population could be relocated to a football pitch and still find space to mill around, and "being on probation" means watching your step for a bit so that Big Denis the Fisherman doesn't come and give you a hiding for stepping out of line.

So I run a guest house. I'm a landlady. I cook, and handle the bookings and the correspondence, and I order the supplies and make things pretty and deal with the website and the weird demands of my guests. I take it seriously. The lodges gleam. Every five-star review on TripAdvisor makes me strut like a Siamese cat. But I haven't the time to keep the family house to the same standard and the living room is a catastrophe of abandoned footwear, school uniforms, toys, books and food-smeared plates. They'd still be wearing crisps and crusts and pizza cheese if not for the attentions of Barrel, our fat cat. She's a big help with the housework, though she does leave a snowstorm of dandruff and white hair on every fabric surface she can find.

'Where Atticus?' asks Lilly, and my heart sinks as I realise we're about to go through the routine.

'At school, baby.'

'Poppy?'

'At school.'

'Daddy?'

'Away.'

She nods, satisfied. 'Nose 'sgusting.'

'Sorry, darling?'

She's pointing at her face, where the twin trails of snot are starting to inflate like bubbles of chewing gum. She goes cross-eyed for a moment, staring at them, and when she giggles, they pop like a frog on a hotplate. I use the hem of my nightie to wipe her up, telling her she's "gross", but laughing while I do it so she doesn't get a complex. I check her out, still in her onesie and wearing a sock as a mitten. She's got a crust all the way up one cheek to her eyebrow.

'Niclas.'

I give her a smile, pleased at any variation. I'm pretty good at speaking her language and cotton on quickly. 'Nicholas? You mean Mr Roe? He's probably out on the water.'

'He *'sgusting*.'

'No he's not,' I say, though she can tell I'm lying. Nicholas Roe has been with us for three weeks now. He's not exactly a looker, and while I keep telling the children that looks don't matter and that it's rude to stare, I'm every bit as guilty as they are. He looks like a vampire who seriously needs to feed. He's probably around sixty, though it's hard to tell with his yellowed skin and the mottling of moles and ruptured blood vessels that work their way up his neck towards a swoop of limp hair: the same shade of brandy brown as his fingernails and teeth. He's a good guest though. Keeps himself to himself, eats every scrap of his breakfast and doesn't complain when the older kids forget that Mummy runs a guest house and make enough noise to wake the dead.

I see him through the window, scowling out into the swirling rain. He always has his teeth bared, like a rat poked with a stick, but he's been nothing but polite since he arrived. He's trying to find a hobby, or so he says. He's come to Ardnamurchan to see if he can develop a love of wildlife photography, though the way he says it suggests that he has serious doubts about the whole affair. I get the impression he's not been well. I try not to pry. People invariably tell me things in their own time.

'Mummy phone. Phone, Mummy. Daddy? Daddy talk Lilly?'

It's buzzing away on the table, merrily vibrating between the dirty dishes and the debris from Atticus's sports bag. Letters, reports, requests for donations. Packed lunches, reduced to component parts. There's a thing that used to be a banana, slowly evolving into intelligent life. A sports sock, containing a handful of dead batteries: a weapon he fashioned having watched a YouTube video on self-defence. He's not doing PE today. He's got the same cold as his youngest sister and probably shouldn't have gone in, but I'm trying to keep his attendance up so that if Callum starts making a fuss and demanding better access or full custody, he hasn't got that to throw at me. That's why I'm keeping Bishop quiet too.

I'll admit it, I get a bit of a thrill thinking about him. I haven't had a boyfriend since I was seventeen. He's no Callum, and that has to be a good thing, even if he sometimes does seem as though he got through school without anybody giving him a dead leg and telling him to stop being so bloody big-headed. He's a bit fond of himself, though I can't help wondering if it's all an act. He does have a tendency to only tell stories that make him sound good, whereas I have no shortage of anecdotes in which I'm hopeless, hapless or helpless. I cringe if I have to tell a story in which I come across as a bit of a hero.

Still. I'll do my best.

2

'Hello, er… *you*,' I say, awkwardly. I feel fizzy inside, as if I've been shaken like a bottle of fizzy orange. I cringe instinctively, knowing I've misjudged it. I'm not sure we're at the *"hello you"* stage of the relationship. Not sure we're having a relationship. Not sure about any-bloody-thing.

'Hey yourself. I was just thinking about you.'

'Yeah? Ha! You'll go blind.'

A hiss of static: bacon sizzling in a pan. Then he's back. 'Sorry, Sweetheart, lost you there. What did you say?'

'Nothing. Doesn't matter. You good?'

'Best you'll ever have.'

We can talk like this for a while. He's one of those people who talks a lot without ever really saying anything. "Glib", that's the word. He's charming, in a *roll-your-eyes* kind of way. I don't think I'd have fancied him on looks alone but he's definitely got a confidence that makes him attractive as a package.

'Did you want something specific or were you just calling to flirt?'

'Bit of both,' he says, a smile in his voice. 'Checking you're home, actually.'

'Yep. Epic battle with Lilly over her shoes. Place is a pigsty. I'm sort of dressed. Still got the breakfast baskets to clear and dinners to chuck in the slow cooker and I've got parcels waiting at the Post Office. All in all, it's as rock and roll as ever.'

'Cool. I'll see you in ten.'

I feel a little twist of panic. I haven't shaved my legs. The place is a mess. Lilly's in a foul mood and I've got loads to do. God, I hope this isn't the big seduction. It's all been a bit teenage so far – nothing below the waist and lots of sweaty, tremulous promises about what it will be like when it happens. Truth be told, I'm not ready. He says he won't push, but he has a way of not pushing that makes it clear how hard he's trying not to push. I've only ever been with Callum. I'm pretty sure we've been doing it right, but I thought I was genuinely good at singing up until the point Dad took a hammer to the karaoke machine.

'Oh, okay then, you'll have to take us as you find us.'

He blows a kiss and hangs up. I look at Lilly, who's awaiting an update. 'Daddy?'

'No, baby. Bishop. You know Bishop. He's Mummy's friend.'

'Shibop?' she asks, looking distinctly unimpressed. 'No. Funny theech.'

I can't work that one out. 'Theech?'

She points at her mouth. 'Theech!'

'Oh right. Teeth. Don't be mean, Lilly. They're expensive.'

She looks at me as if I've let her down in some way. I must admit, the gold teeth are an acquired taste and I haven't completely acquired it yet. Three of them on the lower row, gleaming like Mr T's chest. He doesn't look like a gangsta rapper – more like somebody who runs the waltzers on Princes Street at Hogmanay.

'Can you help Mummy, darling? Tidy up a bit? Brush your hair...?'

She looks up at me with a face that says "Mum, I'm two" and we both start laughing. I swing her onto my hip and plunge into eight minutes of full-on whirling-dervish mode. By the time I'm done, the big open-plan living room looks cleaner but anybody opening a drawer or a cupboard or peering under the rag rug runs the risk of causing a small explosion of clutter. I look a bit more presentable too. Jeans, vest, a woolly jumper. It's only as Bishop's Mercedes crunches into the driveway that I realise I'm dressed almost exactly the same as Lilly.

He opens the back door like he owns the place. He looks like he always does. Fur-lined parka, a hoodie over a black shirt, and jeans that taper down to grubby white trainers. He's in his forties and would have an air of Liam Gallagher about him if not for the bald-head-and-beard combo. If he's ever wanted by the police, it will take the coppers an age to find enough people for an identity parade.

'Hey you,' he says, and he kisses me without preamble. He tastes of strong coffee and mouthwash. He looks around, pretending to search for Lilly, even though she's still sitting on my hip. 'And where's my girl?'

I don't know how I feel about that yet. She's not his girl. I don't like the idea of anybody belonging to anybody.

'Shibop,' says Lilly, somewhat joylessly. 'Funny cheeth.'

He looks to me for a translation. 'She's just being silly,' I say. 'Can I get you something?'

'Coffee would be good,' he says, taking his coat off and

slipping it over the back of the chair. We've got an open-plan kitchen, which means the rubbish from one room frequently overspills into another. The table and chairs are in what passes for the living room but we also have a breakfast bar with a sparkly granite top, and I've never worked out which area to usher people towards when they visit. He makes it easy for me by jumping up and perching himself on the breakfast bar, the way I would have done if I were still twelve. He rubs his hands together like he's got something on his mind.

I put Lilly down and she runs off to do something undoubtedly dangerous in the living room. There's a fire burning and she isn't daft enough to touch it, but she does seem to enjoy pulling the heavy books off the low shelves and creating a little tower that she can climb up and fall off. She puts a lot of effort into hurting herself.

'You look a bit stressed,' he says, watching me as I bang around in the kitchen, filling the kettle and trying to find the filters for the coffee machine.

'Stressed?' I ask, hoping it's not going to turn into one of those conversations. He likes me being "chill". Likes me to just slow down and forget all the pressures of life. It takes a great effort of will not to laugh. He's got no kids and only works around four months of the year – heading out to the Middle East to provide training in corporate cyber security, which is not at all what I'd expected him to be into. A roadie, perhaps. Part-time dealer, maybe. There's a scally look about him, and he tells me damn little about his life before he moved up from Nottingham. He lives in one of the little houses looking out towards Mull. It's decorated to the taste of the previous tenant and the only personal items I've seen have been a record player and a trunk full of vinyl, and a couple of fixed-screen computers set up in the kitchen.

'Anything I can do?' he asks. 'Shoulder rub? Foot rub? Anything-you-like rub…?'

'You fancy helping me make some soup for tomorrow's packed lunches?' I ask, answering the way I would if Callum had asked the question.

'No, not really,' he says, laughing, as if it had been a joke. 'Don't suppose the little terror needs a nap, does she? Would love a bit of time just you and me.'

I close my eyes. Here it comes. 'Sorry,' I say, keeping things light. 'Wide awake. She doesn't really get daytime naps now. I've tried to get her down to just getting booby feeds at night and first thing but she's not cooperating and can't self-soothe…'

'Booby feed?' he asks, cocking his head. 'Oh, breastfeeding? Not my area. Bit grim, isn't it? Bit weird too. I mean, you can make a drink with your body. That's way out there.'

'It's bloody painful, is what it is,' I grumble, and hand him a mug of rather crap coffee. He takes a slurp and grimaces but doesn't make a verbal complaint.

Awkwardly, feeling distracted, I lean against the sink and raise my eyebrows expectantly. 'So,' I ask. 'You just wanted to feast your eyes on me or was there something…?'

He purses his lips and puffs out a sigh. Takes another swig of coffee and puts it back down. Pulls a face. 'This isn't easy…' he begins.

'You don't want to see me anymore,' I say, finishing the sentence. I feel a mixture of disappointment and a weird kind of relief. It's all been a bit inconvenient anyways. I should concentrate on the kids. On the guest house. Just concentrate on being myself for a while…

'No,' he says, surprised. 'No, not at all. The opposite, in fact.'

I flinch as if I've suffered an electric shock. I know so little about him and here he is about to pop the bloody question!

'Mummy!'

'Not now, Lilly,' I shout, and there's a little bit of madness in my voice. If I'm not careful I'm going to start giggling.

'Lilly up high, Mummy. Lilly fly. Lilly jump!'

I dart through from the kitchen just as Lilly launches herself from a tower of hardbacks and comes down with a clatter in the basket of logs and pine cones by the fire. She smiles for a moment, pleased with herself, then takes an inventory of her injuries. Yes, she decides. That really hurt.

'Mummy!'

I'm back in the kitchen five minutes later, holding Lilly to my chest, rocking her the way I did when she was tiny. She lets out the occasional sob but she's okay.

Bishop doesn't ask about her. He looks a bit put out, as if I'd cut him off to go and do something unimportant.

'Can I get this out now?' he asks, cocking his head. 'It's important.'

'Bishop,' I say, and it still feels weird calling him that. But he says he hates his first name. He's never used my name. I've been Babe and Princess and Sweetheart from the off. 'Look, maybe this isn't the best time…'

He frowns. Closes his eyes tight and seems to be counting backwards in his head. I stand still, waiting for more, gazing past him to where one of the fishing boats is fighting a choppy tide, cutting through the silvery water to where the far side of the peninsula rises up out of the fog.

'Look, I want us to be more than we are,' he says, quickly. 'I'm not one for seriousness if I can help it but you mean a lot to me and I think I mean something to you too. So I want to be totally honest with you.'

'You're married?'

'What? No. Not for ages, anyways.'

'You're a serial killer,' I say, my voice too loud. 'An axe murderer. You're the Silesian nun killer and you're here to lay low until the heat's off...'

He doesn't laugh. 'Not as far off as you'd expect,' he says, quietly, and Lilly lifts her head as if she's been following the conversation. 'Seriously, Babe. It's important you listen to me.'

'Bishop, I don't know if it is,' I say, and suddenly all I want is what we had until half an hour ago. Flirty talk, mucky texts, a couple of drinks; some snogging on the sea wall. I don't want to be his confessor.

'I'm not quite what I said I am,' he says, quietly. 'I'm trying to be a better guy than I used to be. They've given me a fresh start and I'm trying to make the most of it.'

I don't really know what he's talking about. I suddenly realise how little he's told me of his past. I've given him chapter and verse on my own life. I chatter when I'm nervous. But other than his job and the fact he moved up from Nottingham, he's kept everything pretty frothy. I've told him so much more than he's ever told me. And here he is, in my house, thinking about baring his soul.

'People can change, can't they?' he asks, and he starts

rummaging around in his pocket. He pulls out his mobile and starts fiddling with it, nervously. I want to put a hand on his and tell him that whatever it is, will be okay. But that instinct is a lot less powerful than the other: an overwhelming surge of protectiveness for Lilly. 'Have I said anything to you since we met that makes you think I'm a bad guy?'

'What?' I ask, screwing up my face. 'Bishop, where are you going with this?'

'You know what I do, yeah? My skills.'

'Cyber stuff, yeah?' I look at him and the penny drops. He's seen something private. He's helped himself to some of my private correspondence. I can't think of anything I've said that might be offensive, but then, I'm not really concentrating anymore. I'm too busy trying not to lose my temper. I hate any invasion of privacy. When I was nine I broke my brother's eye socket with a telephone because he tried to unlock my diary with a twisted paper clip. This is way beyond what I'll tolerate.

'Cyber stuff, yeah,' he says, and looks down at the floor. 'I need to just come out and say this...'

There's a knock at the door. Three loud bangs, as if the person beyond the wood and glass is well practised in waking the dead.

I let out a great gasp of mixed feelings. 'Leave it...' begins Bishop.

I yank the door open, feeling all kinds of messed up. It's Mr Roe, the aspiring photographer from Cabin 3. He's got a pissed-off expression on his face, though I know from experience that this is his normal look. His hair's sticking up as if he's just had a balaclava yanked off his head, and up close I can see how unhealthy his skin seems. I find myself thinking of gone-off meat. His gums, too, are purplish and pulpy, and I get a distinct smell of dry-mouthed foulness as he licks his lip, pushing flecks of white crust into the corners of his lips.

'Sorry to trouble you,' he says, his accent English but no more identifiable than that. 'Could be using a map, if you had one. The gadget on my phone's gone haywire and I'm walking around in circles…' He stops talking as he looks past me. Bishop's still sitting on the counter, looking at my guest as if he's just let out a fart at a funeral. Mr Roe, to his credit, doesn't look intimidated. Just gives one of those chin jerks of greeting that men do when they're saying hello. 'Sorry, love,' he says, to me. 'Saw the car – didn't think…'

'You know what, let's do this later,' says Bishop, sliding down off the counter. He snatches up his jacket. Moves to push past me: a stroppy teenager storming out after a row. Lilly turns just as he does so and gets a face full of his shoulder as he barges past.

'Ow!' she shouts, and it becomes a cry immediately.

Bishop doesn't look back. Stomps past, yanking his hood up as the wind and rain howl in from the water.

'Oi, you knocked the little lass,' says Mr Roe, his face twisting. Now he doesn't look unattractive – he looks nasty. 'Here, dickhead – you knocked the little girl.'

'It's okay,' I say, cooing in Lilly's ear and checking her. 'An accident, an accident…'

Bishop turns back. 'What did you call me?'

'I called you a dickhead, lad. Say you're sorry.'

'I barely touched her.'

'I've heard that before. You want to watch where you're going.'

'And you want to watch your mouth. I'd snap you over my knee.'

'Would you?' Mr Roe opens his arms, inviting the attempt. 'When you're ready, son.'

I don't want Lilly near any of this. I play peacemaker. 'It's all good, Mr Roe – she's fine, no problems... a map, you said – of course, come in, no problem. The kettle's boiled. Have you had any luck with the photographs? Did you try peanut butter for the pine martens, like I suggested? Works a treat...'

Bishop turns away and jumps into his car. Reverses away in a screech of rubber that's far too theatrical for my taste. I catch a last glimpse of him as he goes. I'd expected temper. I'm appalled to see he has glassy eyes, as if this has all been terribly emotional. I feel guilty at once. He'd been trying to open up to me. To talk to me the way I'd hoped he would, and I'd shot him down. I'll give him an hour, I think. Let him calm down. Send him a text or a dirty joke or something...

Mr Roe follows me into the kitchen. There's not much meat on his bones. He's skinny to the point of cadaverous. He's got a whiff of cigars about him. A smell of the outdoors, but also that stink you used to get in the ashtray of a hired van.

'He's a dickhead,' says Mr Roe, as if stating a fact. He gives Lilly an appraising glance. She meets his gaze, and sniffs, dramatically. She whimpers against my chest.

'A ham actor, this one,' I say, smiling. 'She's okay. A map, you said?'

He looks at her for a touch longer than feels comfortable.

Looks at her hard. Intense. It's like he's trying to read something written in tiny letters on her skin.

'You know what? Bugger it for the day. Just point. Pub's that way, yes?'

'Well, the hotel isn't open today but the one at Acharacle should be by the time you get there…'

He nods. Sucks his teeth. I see pink in his spit before he swallows it.

'Cheers,' he says, and turns so fast I half expect him to screw a hole into the floor. 'Sorry for the unpleasantness. She's a pretty one. Treasure her.'

And then he's gone. And I'm left holding Lilly, and breathing in the lingering smell of damp earth, and tobacco; the air still cracking with the static of two men sizing each other up.

'Fairy Garden?' asks Lilly, brightly.

I lock the door, and hold her tight.

3

Eight months ago
Somewhere near Chelmsford, Essex

A green-and-pink canal boat, tied up at a shabby marina on the Chelmer and Blackwater Canal. Dirty lace curtains cover dirtier windows. Over the rail, black water holds a sickle of moon and gaudy puddles of coloured light.

Inside, three men. One handsome, one big, one not far off dead.

On the floor of the galley, the handsome man is making hard work of a simple task. He's playing with tools, and tanned skin. The screwdriver won't go in at first. He has to put his whole weight behind it. His palm pains him, like some lacklustre stigmata, as he channels his strength into one almighty shove. He gives a grunt of satisfaction as the point emerges on the far side of the leather. His hand shoots forward and he raps his knuckles, painfully, on the hard tiles of the kitchen floor.

He stands up, acting nonchalant, hoping that neither of his companions have seen his difficulties. He resists the urge to suck his bruised fingers and focuses instead on checking his handiwork. The hole he has punched in his leather belt is a little off-centre but it will suffice. He begins threading it through the loops in his black jeans and pulls it tight.

'Bleach.'

The handsome man curses under his breath. The big man has seen.

'Cupboard under the sink.'

The handsome man gives a polite nod. He replaces his gloves and fetches the bleach and dishcloth. His knees click as he bends down and he wipes the floor where his skin had made contact.

'Just be careful,' comes the voice. It is a gravelly, guttural sound, like stones rubbing together in a serpent's belly. 'Don't take the gloves off unless you have to.'

'I know,' says the handsome man. 'You've said. You've said quite a few times. To be honest.'

'And yet you're still taking them off. Is there another way I should say it? I have plenty of other ways to get the message across.'

'Is there any point?' asks the dying man. He sits at the kitchen table, broken, ill and old. 'He never listens.'

'He's young. He thinks he knows it all.'

'They all bloody do.'

The handsome man stares out of the window, refusing to rise to the bait. They're older than him. More set in their ways. Less adaptable. He does what they ask because they have sworn a bond of brotherhood, but he wishes that just once in a while they would relax a little. He wants to go and be among other people. Wants to feel fresh air on his skin. He likes it outside. There's a light rain, falling in soft serpentines into the murky green water of the marina.

He likes the way the colours bounce off the other canal boats. Likes the distance between themselves and the next one along. He would like to sit out on the deck and let the rain dampen his face and soak his clothes. He likes all such pure communion. He cherishes the unsullied touch of the wind and rain; adores every naked connection between himself and that which he holds to be untainted. It is the intercession of people that begins the process of defilement. He learned that in prison, and the knowledge was dearly bought.

The handsome man straightens up and considers his two companions. The big man is sitting in a rocking chair, blanket over his knees. He has a newspaper folded in his lap. He completed the crossword and Sudoku inside ten minutes and it took him another five to digest the news. He is now perusing the holiday cottages listed for rent in the classifieds. He likes them to keep moving. They have been here for the best part of a month and though it is the most comfortable place they have stayed, he will soon tell the others it is time to move on. There is an art to remaining undiscovered and his very existence is proof that he is a master.

'Top-up, please, lad.'

The man at the table looks as though he has recently been disinterred. His skin puts the handsome man in mind of mouldy bread. He too has shaved his head down to the skull and revealed a patchwork of scars and stains that make him look as though he has been picked up between a colossal finger and thumb; collected for inspection and discarded. He is a haphazard assemblage of bones and sagging tendons beneath loose flesh; a makeshift tent of splinters and poles. When he speaks, his remaining teeth seem to be slipping in his rancid gums, like stones pushed into rotten fruit.

The handsome man crosses to the fireplace and collects the bottle of discount whisky that stands on the mantelpiece. He pours a healthy measure into the dying man's glass and catches the putrid odour of a body that is decaying from the inside out. It makes him think of a bin wagon on a hot day and it is all he can do not to retch.

'Cheers, lad. Having one?'

The handsome man sits down in the chair opposite and takes a crystal tumbler from the tray in the centre of the table.

'Your health,' he says.

'It'll take more than a toast, but thank you anyways. Wish I could taste it.'

'Still no taste?'

'Just blood.'

The handsome man looks to his companion for guidance, but he is staring out through the window of the barge. They have both done their best by their rotting companion. When they retrieved him they hooked him to a saline drip and helped flush his system of toxins. The big man reset his arm, which had been broken and left to fester. They pulled the worst of his teeth and set about him with mouthwash and disinfectants. A powder killed the lice in his hair and the ticks that ate into his skin.

The handsome man sits and enjoys the quiet. The big man's rocking chair makes a soft creak each time it moves upon the threadbare carpet that covers the floor. There is a soft, barely audible gurgle each time the dying man breathes.

The old pipes give the occasional *ting*, causing an answering chirrup from the birds that nest in the thatch. There is the sound of a vibration and then the assorted noises of the big man putting down his newspaper, reaching into his pocket and reading the words on the phone screen. Then comes the sharp intake of breath that the handsome man has come to associate with unwanted developments.

'A print,' says the big man, with a low growl. 'She's got a print.'

'The screw?' asks the dying man, looking up. 'A prison warder, you mean?'

'No. The screw. In the ceiling joist.'

The handsome man closes his eyes. How had they managed that? He'd been so careful. He'd wiped it down. His gloves had only been off for a moment...

'They're waiting for results but I think we know what they'll find.'

The big man rubs a gloved hand across his upper lip and stares at nothing as if making calculations. 'She already has her suspicions. She'll tell them who to check against.'

The dying man gives a little nod. 'It won't take her long.'

The trio sit in silence. They are each thinking of the officer who runs the specialist unit at the National Crime Agency. To two of their number, she is just a name; a dangerous and unswerving officer who wants to know who is killing the gangsters that her unit is supposed to be trying to imprison. To the third man, she is something else entirely.

'We need to solve the problem...'

'Not like that. Not the way you mean.'

'What do I mean?'

'We can't hurt her. She's done nothing wrong.'

'I didn't say she had. I didn't say anything. But she's a problem.'

The dying man taps his whisky glass against his teeth. 'I don't know why we go to all this bloody bother. Hiding out. Covering our every trace. They're onto us. You know what we did.'

'We had to do it. They deserved what was coming to them.'

'But the chainsaw? The hammer? Jesus, I'll never sleep well again. It was murder – you know that. You murdered those people, clear as I'm sitting here.'

'We did. All of us. We did what had to be done and I don't feel any guilt for it. Nor should you…'

The dying man looks into the bottom of his whisky glass. He's sorry about what has to come next. He's enjoyed the past few weeks in the company of these vigilantes. They've taken out some very bad people. He doesn't want to have to do what he's about to do. But it's the price of what he wants.

'I want you to know, lads. There are no hard feelings.'

'What do you…?'

'Nightingale,' he says, sadly, into the microphone on his lapel. 'Go, go, go…'

The big man doesn't move. The handsome man thinks it's a joke. And then there are men and women in blue and yellow boarding the vessel and shouting for them to lie flat, to put their hands up, that they're under arrest for the murders of six different mid-level crime bosses; and their wrists are bound behind their backs and it's all rage and tears and *I'll-get-you-for-this*.

And the dying man is standing up. He's not dying

anymore. He's pulling out his yellow teeth and peeling off the yellowed fingernails and he's taking the whisky bottle from the table so he can swill out his mouth and spit out the past six weeks of his life into the dirty water.

Up on deck, the rain on his face, he listens to the commotion coming from below. He would feel guilty, if he had such a capacity anymore. The two men had trusted him with their lives. They'd believed him to be third of their number: somebody willing to take revenge in whatever fashion was required. They'd thought him broken. Weak. They'd embraced him as one of their own and given him friendship and brotherhood. Committed murder and let him watch. And he has betrayed them.

He doesn't feel bad. Just wishes, as he so often does, that things were different.

'Perfect recording,' says a polished female voice, behind him. She stands on the bank: exquisite blonde hair and sumptuous black coat, casting a long, elegant shadow onto the water. 'You've got some nerve. How did you even know we were here?'

'Saw you,' he says, in an accent that is unrecognisable from the one he spoke to the two men below deck. 'The ash-blonde. Catches the light. You look like a fucking iceberg.'

'And you look like Count Fucking Nosferatu.'

They stand in silence for a time. They have known each other many years, this attractive woman and repugnant man. Have fought on the same side. Fought one another. They no longer know who the enemy is, but both are very good at what they do.

'I wasn't sure how much was fake,' she says, and he hears the rustle of silk as she fishes out her cigarettes from their silver case and lights them with the Zippo she keeps in the elastic of her suspenders. 'Cold bitch. Evil bitch. Worse than the people she locks up... I wasn't sure how much of what you told them about me you really meant.'

He turns to her. Pulls a cigar from the pocket of his coat and lights it with a match held beneath his thumbnail. He puffs out a greasy ring of smoke. Shrugs. 'Neither was I.'

They leave together, stopping at an after-hours pub and talking, quietly, in a corner booth until neither of them can stand, or speak or keep up the lies without fear.

Later, the detective chief inspector and her number-one covert operative will receive commendations for their part in bringing the two vigilante killers to justice. Neither will attend the ceremony. By then, the dying man will have all but forgotten who he briefly invented. He will already be pretending to be somebody else.

4

The new couple arrive mid-afternoon. They're staying in the second cabin, sandwiched between Mr Roe and an American college professor enjoying some tedious *find-your-ancestors* genealogy trek. Mr Paretsky's his name, which sounds about as Scottish as vegan cuisine. He's been telling me that he's a "true Celt" ever since he arrived, which sounds weird when said in a Texas accent. Apparently his family came from Strontian, just down the road from here, and left for the New World in the 1880s. I've told him not to get his hopes up about finding anybody who remembers them. He'd nodded solemnly at that, as if I was offering some sincere pearl of wisdom, and I'd been too embarrassed to tell him I'd been taking the piss. I've met his sort before. I guarantee by the time he goes home he'll have ordered a kilt in the clan tartan and commissioned a family tree on yellowed parchment, tracing his lineage back to a Gaelic king.

Theresa finishes cleaning the room about half an hour before they turn up. She's a help and hindrance in one. She only comes and cleans three days a week, and they're three more than I've asked her to. I've told her half a dozen times now that I can't afford her and that there's no job for her here anymore, but she just keeps turning up anyway and I find myself paying her wages just to avoid having another awkward conversation. We're not exactly friends, but we do have enough in common to be able to have a gossip. It's weird the way we switch roles once she's finished doing the lodges. One moment she's the cleaning lady and I'm asking her if there's any way she can scrape the grime from under the taps in the bath, and the next we're putting the world to rights over tea and home-made biscuits and she's making fun of me for not remembering anybody's names or have heard about what such-and-such is getting up to with you-know-who. She's better than a newspaper, is Theresa.

She's lived here the best part of twenty years, which doesn't make her local but makes her a damn sight more in tune with the peninsula than me. My two years is nothing, even if I did provide plenty of material for the gossips when I threw Callum's stuff out the Velux window and burned it on the front lawn.

'Nice couple?' asks Theresa, sitting down on the windowsill and leaning against the glass.

'The new arrivals? Seemed fine from their emails.'

'No, I'm saying. The ones who've gone. Place was clean as a whistle. Needn't have changed the sheets.'

'You did though, yes?' I ask, worrying.

'Yes,' she grumbles, tutting at me. 'If it hasn't been shagged in, a bed's clean, if you ask me.'

'That's inspirational.'

'Cleaner than the Birmingham lot…' she begins, dunking a piece of flapjack in her mug. 'Oh, I still have nightmares. I still can't work it out. I mean, how did she…?'

We have a laugh, and I feel better. I enjoy these moments.

Theresa has got more children than she knows what to do with and she brings an air of experience and calm to my manic household. Lilly is watching TV in front of the fire, lip-syncing along with Peppa Pig. I only let her watch two episodes a day; I can't stand the programme myself. There's no dressing it up: Daddy Pig looks like a cock and balls. That can't be good for young minds.

'Nice to see you smiling,' says Theresa, wiping her mouth with the cuff of her jumper. 'Look like yourself again.'

I take her in, sitting there on the windowsill like a rare bird on a perch. She wears a pink-and-white gingham top. Blue leggings and neon pink Crocs. She's a meaty creature: big ham-hock arms and ram-bollock jowls, but she's got a sparkle about her that's got as much to do with her zest for life as it does her glitter body spray and big pearlescent grey hair. She's probably the person I find easiest to talk to.

'Bit of a row with Bishop,' I say, trying to sound nonchalant.

Theresa gives me an *I-told-you-so* look. She's not a fan. 'Man's a gobshite. And you, all those years with your childhood sweetheart and the next minute this stranger's swooping in and bringing flowers and chocolates and telling you you're a stunner. Sounds fishy to me.'

'Oh thanks.'

'You know what I mean. You are all those things and I know many men can be opportunists but it just seems a bit bloody convenient. I mean, who is he?'

I turn away, glaring through my own reflection to the shifting quicksilver of the lake. The sun's sinking back below the waterline. The kids will be home soon. They'll want feeding. There'll be homework. Lilly will want more than I can provide. It's all too much sometimes. Too much for one person, and it was hard enough with two.

'He was asking about you long before he came and charmed you,' says Theresa, watching the sunset. 'Otter, look,' she says, quickly, pointing past me. 'Rolling about in the bladderwrack, down by Wilkie's boat...'

I turn, trying to see what she's pointing out. I can just make out a small, sleek outline: a greasy silhouette slipping nimbly over the green-coated rocks towards the water's edge.

'He wanted to tell me something today,' I say, sheepishly. 'It wasn't a good time. Lilly was acting up, and then Mr Roe arrived and there was a bit of argy-bargy...'

'Oh yes?' She sits up like a meerkat, scanning the horizon for gossip. 'He's a funny fish as well. I've seen him walking up and down the treeline with his camera but I don't think he's sat still long enough to get an actual picture. Not well, is he? More pills in his bathroom cabinet than they've got on special offer in Boots.'

'You shouldn't be looking!'

'I wasn't. I have eyes, and this stuff just sort of passed into their range.'

I try to look unimpressed. Can't keep it up. 'What's he on?'

'Haven't heard of most of it and some's in a foreign language.' She squints, trying to tweeze out a memory. 'Dia-something. Not the one that chills you out. Anyway, high dosage. And you can see he doesn't look well. He cleans the toilet after he's sick but it's not a professional job. Splatter-spray on the bathroom mirror too, like he's been coughing his guts up. Looks like he's three days dead, that one.'

'He didn't take to Bishop,' I say, thinking back to the unpleasantness of earlier. I've tried to call him but he's not answering. Sent a silly photo and lots of question marks. There's not much more I can do. I can't help but wonder what he wanted to say, but I also know that whatever it was, the moment was definitely wrong.

'You should be a copper,' I say, swivelling around to face the door just as the headlights gleam through the glass. I can see the outline of a man, one hand to his forehead, salute-style, as he peers through the glass at where we're sitting.

'Are you serious about him?' asks Theresa. 'I know Callum's done wrong but if you wanted him back you could get him back. He wanted attention, that's all.'

'He's got plenty,' I say, snarling. I take a breath, composing myself before answering the door. Apparently I have a tendency to look through people. I don't have a welcoming visage. I'm not sure what to do about that, really, other than have *Welcome* tattooed on my forehead.

'Oh thank goodness!' says my new guest as he stands on the doorstep, damp and shivering, looking for all the world like the sole survivor of an expedition plagued by sub-zero temperatures, cannibalism and thrush. I know the roads aren't great and the forest can look plenty scary when the light starts to sink, but he still seems to be unnecessarily stressed.

'Hello there!' I say, brightly. 'I'm Ronni. Ronni Ashcroft. How was the journey? If you give me a moment I'll show you where to park…'

I stop. There's something not right. He's a tall man, with a big grey moustache and a hairline that has receded to a perfect horseshoe shape on his crown. He's dressed in his best touristy travelling clothes: striped jumper over long-sleeved shirt, with multi-pocketed combat trousers and hiking trainers.

'I thought I hit somebody,' he says, and his breath catches in his throat. 'I've been driving since this morning. I've had my coffee breaks and had the window down but I think I almost dozed off as I passed the last village and then there was this shape in front of me and I swerved...' He closes his eyes. 'I didn't hear a bang. But there's a smudge on the headlight.' He stops talking. Lets out a long slow breath and composes himself. 'Sorry. Sorry. All good. Just a long drive. When you said you were out of the way you really meant it, didn't you?'

I take a moment to process this. I'm no stranger to driving tired. The light here can play tricks on you. The way the trees cast their shadows on the road; the way the water seems to reflect a hundred different skies all at once; haphazard likenesses moving like a strobe light. I feel for him. It's no way to start your holiday.

'Is your wife with you?' I ask, peering past him. In the passenger seat of a big sensible Volvo, a small woman with an iron-grey bob sits glaring grimly at the twin circles of illumination being cast by the headlamps. Two big yellow orbs, each full of swirling rain, and beyond, the impenetrable mass of forest and rock and river that form the boundary at the rear of the house. After that it's all wild land. Miles and miles of bleak, black nothing. It's bliss.

'Want me to come check your car?' asks Theresa, behind me. 'Sorry, what was the name?'

'Trulove. Branwell. Other way around, actually. Branwell Trulove.'

'Christ, you must have got bullied at school. You sure you're okay?'

'I'm fine,' he decides. 'Could I perhaps have a small sip of water?'

'You can have a big old gulp of the stuff for me, pal,' says Theresa, and her accent slips back into Glaswegian. She sticks a glass under the tap and hands it to him. 'You don't think it might have been a deer, do you? They enchant you lot but they're a menace.'

'Us lot?' he asks, sipping from the glass.

'Tourists. Stopping on the only bloody road around the peninsula to ooh and aah at the mighty stag, while some of us are trying to get home in time for *Countdown*.'

He seems much better now. I take the glass and leave Theresa to entertain him while I grab my coat, boots and key ring and let myself out the sliding doors at the back. It's bitterly cold and the rain seems to come from every direction at once but it's only a couple of hundred metres to the old barn. I can see the light on in number one but I know there's nobody home because the occupant is out doing his family research. It's all black at Mr Roe's place. He's obviously found a pleasant way to pass the day.

I fumble with the keys and push at the door to number two. Theresa's done a good job. It's as welcoming and cosy a space as we could come up with. Tartan wallpaper on two facing walls and a low, heather-coloured paint to the other. Photographs of local landmarks and a great old Ordnance Survey map in a big frame on one wall. A tin of shortbread, home-made flapjack and two miniatures of Highland whisky are laid out in a wicker gift basket on the bed. The lights are set in a frame of interweaving antlers and the bedspread is all thistles. It couldn't be more Bonnie Scotland if it offered a bunk-up with the Loch Ness Monster.

From behind I hear footsteps. Quick, sudden: moving rapidly over wet grass. I turn around, expecting to see the new visitors, hurrying through the rain. Instead, I catch a glimpse of a disappearing shape: a blob of spilled ink, tadpole-black, disappearing around the gable end of the house, head down.

'Gee, he was moving some!'

I give a little yelp at the sudden booming voice in my ear. Mr Paretsky: a bear of a man, with a beard you could lose a cat in and so much rain on his glasses it's like talking to a huge, hairy fly.

'Oh you nearly did me in,' I say, clasping my hand to my chest like a maiden aunt in an old movie. 'New arrivals,' I explain. I turn into the wind, glaring at the spot where I'd felt sure I'd seen somebody running. 'Did you say you saw somebody? Have you been there long?'

'Just back,' he says, taking off his glasses. I get a whiff of seafood and beer. 'I thought it was your gentleman. The man with the gold teeth? Is it Bishop?'

I chew my cheek, but am spared having to think about it further by the arrival around the far side of the property of Mr Trulove's car. The headlamps throw big spotlights onto the trees, clinging to the slope of the rocky hill. There's a little waterfall halfway up, before the water disappears underground and re-emerges near the house, surging, white-tipped beneath an old bridge and on into the loch.

'I saw your other guest as well,' says Mr Paretsky, lowering his voice. 'I popped in for a pint of conviviality and saw Mr Roe there looking considerably the worse for wear. The man certainly knows how to drink, but I don't think red wine with whisky chasers is anybody's idea of healthy. He's spending, so they're tolerating him, but a wise landlady might see if they could head off a tricky situation.'

I thank him, meaning it. I'm not unpopular here, but nor do I have any currency with the locals. I'm an outsider, and if my holidaymakers cause a problem, it reflects on me.

'This the one?' yells Mr Trulove, parking in the little paved area. He gives a nod of thanks, seemingly recovered from his ordeal. As she gets out the passenger side I hear his wife complaining that it's a long way to walk with the bags, and that the accommodation seems a lot smaller than it did online.

I drop a set of keys on the mat, and hurry back to the house. Theresa is waiting inside, coat on, bouncing Lilly on her lap. Through the dark glass behind her I see the school bus pulling up. Atticus and Poppy tumble out, their coats held on their heads by the hood, flapping loosely like capes. They run over the damp front lawn and bang their way into the kitchen, bringing the smell of the outdoors and whatever spicy snacks they devoured on the way home.

I put my arms out, hoping for a cuddle. They manage a smile, then go straight to Lilly. I can't complain – she's much cuter than me.

'Missed call,' says Theresa, apologetically, nodding at my phone. 'Bishop, five minutes ago. And I remembered that brand. Dihydrocodeine. You don't want to be mixing that with alcohol.'

I can feel my stress levels building. I want to talk to Bishop. I'm getting all sorts of bad vibes today. I'm worried about him. He seemed so strung out this morning and the more I think about it, the more I realise that I didn't do anything to make a difficult situation easier on him. I have an overwhelming urge to apologise, or make it up to him somehow, but I know so little about him that I don't even know what would be appropriate. I know he likes records, but what would be a good present? I feel out of my depth. I snatch up my phone and read the text that Bishop had angrily typed out when I failed to answer his call.

> Forget it, then. Wanted to tell you the truth about me. Maybe you'll never hear it now. But if you hear bad things about me or I don't turn up one day, just know this – I really tried my best.

As I head out the door, there's a feeling in my heart a lot like fear.

5

My house is called *Murt Gorm Croft* and sits at the foot of a hill, midway between Salen and Kilchoan. It's almost a mile to my nearest neighbour, and their house is only ever occupied during the summer months. The owners can afford to close during the winter. I can't. I have to chop my prices down to virtually nothing if I want to guarantee at least partial occupancy during the bleak spell between November and January – only briefly enlivened by Christmas and Hogmanay.

Now, in the fourth week of January, the peninsula is barely inhabited. As such, the locals feel free to put their foot down when driving on the slick, winding road that hugs the outline of the land. I've never found the time or the money to buy a car that's suitable for the local terrain, but the old Peugeot hasn't let me down yet and I've hit two stags, a motorcyclist and a Scotch pine since moving here. I can never decide if that makes me lucky or unlucky, or both.

It takes twenty minutes to reach the cosy, white-painted pub that serves as an entry point to the tiny village of Kilchoan. It's quiet to the point of deathly, but it's a bleakly beautiful spot. The gale whips in off the loch like the lash from a whip but it carries with it an uncanny ability to strip away all the tangled baggage of the day. To take a walk to the water's edge is to invite a bombardment from the elements. I've never come back from Kilchoan without pink cheeks, tired calves and considerably fewer woes.

I park up between a flat-bed pick-up and a VW Campervan and have to hold the door handle tight to stop the wind folding the door flat against the front panel of the car. Then I'm running through the swirling rain and the gathering dark and banging through the big wooden door and into the bar.

The warmth hits me as surely as if I'd opened an oven door. It's almost tropically hot inside the snug. At the bar stands Joy, a bottle-blonde barmaid with all the customer service skills of a school dinner lady. She's got a face on, all screwed up, as if she's got a sour sweet in her mouth and isn't allowed to spit it out. She's serving Denis, one of the local fishermen. He's a big guy with a bigger personality and he drinks his pints of IPA with such gusto that it sometimes seems he's eating the glass. Both give me the traditional raised eyebrows and half-smile of greeting, then jerk their heads to point out Mr Roe.

He's sitting in a high-backed green chair in front of a fire that is only another log or two away from melting the horse brasses that hang from the mantelpiece. He's got his head hanging over the back of the chair, mouth open, false teeth halfway out of his parted lips so that he gives off an air of alien. If it were a different time of year he would pass for a Halloween mannequin – a skeleton dressed in charity shop rags and laid out to scare the children. On the table in front of him, an empty glass, a smear of blood-red in the bottom.

'Has he paid up?' I ask, hurrying over to the bar. I don't

want to embarrass him. Nor do I want to wake him up and offer him a lift back to the house.

'Oh he's spent plenty,' says Joy. 'An impressive constitution, for an Englishman. He's got another couple paid for, actually, if you want to give him a nudge.'

I look at Denis in surprise. Judging by the state of him and the reports from Mr Paretsky, I'd have expected Joy to be about ready to sling him out on his ear.

'Maybe he's just allowing the equilibrium to settle a little,' suggests Denis, looking at him. 'Get his balance, then back on it.'

'What's he had?'

'Everything,' says Joy, with a touch of wonder. 'Likes the red wines though. Bought a nice packet of slims off Budgie when he was in. Smokes them like cigarettes. Cloud coming off him like compost.'

I give him a quick once-over. He's dead to the world. No trouble to anybody. I'm here now. The kids are home and safe and I've got a small window of opportunity: a chance to just be me. Hell, this was where I was going to be meeting Bishop anyway, so I'm not taking more than my allotted amount of "me" time.

Bishop, I think, and my heart sinks. I've messed it up – I know it. I haven't even worked out how I feel about him and already I've managed to cause him emotional harm. Then again, was there any need for the drama? He'd been such a diva the way he spoke on the phone, as if he was holding on to a secret of international importance. I've got no time for that – not with three kids and not having spent a lifetime listening to the bullshit stories of a serial liar. I would like to know he's okay, that's all. We could be friends, maybe. Friends, or something like it...

'Checking up, are you?'

I swear I never heard him move. One moment he was across the wooden floor, half-dead in the leather chair: the next he was right by my ear, whispering – so close to me I could feel his lower lip brush the tiny, delicate peach-fuzz on my earlobe. Mr Roe.

'Bloody hell, you scared the shite out of me!' I say, unable to help it. I put my hand on my chest like an old lady having an attack of the vapours. He gives me that smile: the one that doesn't make any attempt to reach the eyes. He smells of the log fire, of crushed fruit and damp clothes. I can see down the neck of his shirt and the tracery of purple veins on his chest makes me think of old maps.

'I'll have you down as a half-of-lager kind of girl,' he says, without apology. 'Maybe a splash of lime.'

I can't help but be impressed. 'Party trick, is it?'

'Some people can do star signs – I can guess alcoholic beverage of preference. Served me well. Nobody ever gets me right in return.'

'Anybody guess methylated spirit and grapefruit juice?' asks Denis, grinning. He's big enough not to have to watch his mouth.

'Eeh, you're a funny fucker,' says Mr Roe. 'Soon as I saw you I started laughing.

'Glass of the nice port for me please, Joy. Half of lager with a dash of lime for my hostess. Something with spit in for Denis here. And one for yourself.'

Joy starts pulling drinks and I feel Mr Roe's eyes on me.

He's not lecherous, not that. I don't know if he'd respond with some romantic overture if I was stood there stark naked. But there's such an intensity to him. Some people undress you with their eyes. Well he's peeling my skin off. I'm almost grateful to look up and see Denis being predictably pervy, trying to see down my top and giving the pursed-lip nod of appreciation.

'You still seeing that gobshite?' asks Denis, draining one pint and tapping the glass to show it's ready for replenishment. 'Gold teeth. Living down by the ferry port…'

I don't know how to answer so I try to say nothing that can be misconstrued. 'Taking it slowly. We're both busy people.'

'That fella of yours,' says Joy, putting the drinks down on the bar and shaking her head at the madness of it all. 'Prize prat if you ask me. Doesn't matter what he's got now, he'll regret it. The blow jobs and breakfasts-in-bed don't last forever. Something wrong with men, isn't there? Just dogs, really. A blast of pheromone or a flash of lifted tail and they're off. I swear, the only difference between a thirteen-year-old boy and a fifty-year-old man is that the lad doesn't need Viagra to be a wanker.'

I sip from my glass, cheeks turning crimson. I press them to the cold surface of the glass and have to resist giving a great orgasmic sigh of pleasure.

'That the chap who barged your daughter?' asks Mr Roe. He wrinkles his nose, thoroughly unimpressed. 'Looks like somebody from the fair? You been seeing him, have you?'

'Sort of,' I say, and suddenly wonder what I'm doing here, drinking with a relative stranger and having my private life dissected.

'You could do better,' he says, and downs his port in one go.

'That's sweet,' I say, hoping that's the end of it, and that there won't be some sort of elaborate come-on routine to follow.

'No it's not. It's the truth. You're a seven, he's a five, at best.'

I look at him wondering whether to be pleased or offended. My instinct is offence, but I can't help thinking that a seven is way above average. 'What are you then?' I ask.

'Me? I'm in minus numbers, love. I didn't always look quite so chewed but if you're judging me on how I look at this juncture in my life, then put it this way – I wouldn't even win any beauty contests on Leper Island.'

'That's a bit harsh on yourself,' says Denis, looking a bit taken aback by the level of self-loathing. 'You're all right. A bit knackered-looking but you're no spring chicken and you might have been ill.'

'Barrel of laughs this one,' says Roe, nodding at Denis. He taps his glass. Waits for Joy to refill it. 'Come back, has he? Your Bishop?'

'No,' I say, and the realisation makes me unexpectedly sombre in tone. 'I think it's probably over with. He wanted to talk to me and I kept cutting him off, but we were a bit of a non-starter to begin with. I mean, I don't know if I'm ready, and the kids are confused enough without having to work out what to call this strange man who could be sleeping in Mummy's bed, and then there's Lilly…'

'Can I stop you there?' asks Roe, putting his hand up. I stop talking, waiting for him to interject with some valuable point. Instead, he starts scrutinising the grime pressed into the welts and whirls across the back of his hand.

'Yes?' I ask, impatiently.

He looks confused. 'Oh right,' he says, as something hits him. 'No, no, I just wanted to stop you. It's very dull.'

Beside him, Denis sniggers, in a rather immature but largely harmless way. Joy elongates a vowel that implies Roe is a very cheeky monkey. And I find myself smiling and giving him a shove in the arm. He doesn't go over as easily as I would have thought. For all that he doesn't weigh very much, the framework he's built around is hard as iron. He's made of hammers and wire: a skin of disintegrating flesh stretched taut over the scaffold.

'Can I take it that you've knocked the wildlife photography on the head?' I ask, and notice with some sadness that I'm almost at the bottom of my glass.

'Found a much more fitting pastime,' he says, and I can see him scanning the spirits behind the bar. He selects a local whisky and requests a double, with one piece of ice. He pays for it with a Scottish note, which serves as a currency in more way than one. Any Englishman willing to go to the trouble of filling their wallet with Scottish notes is guaranteed a warmer welcome at the till than those who don't.

'So will you be heading home soon?' I ask, and I rather hope he won't be. There's something vital about Mr Roe, an air of anxiety and controlled aggression, as if every molecule in his body were a single angry wasp. I find myself keen to know more about him.

'You can give him a bell, if you like,' says Roe, nonchalantly, sliding his phone across the bar-top to where

I'm standing, trying to make my last sip of lager-and-lime last.

'No, it's fine – I've got my own phone anyway...'

'No you haven't,' he says, flatly, and I instinctively pat the back pocket of my jeans. It's there, safe and sound, and he allows himself a little smile as if he's been very clever. He stretches, his shirt riding up to reveal a jaundiced, surgery-scarred gut, yellowed and bloated like a dead fish. 'Put your eyes back in your head. I'm not a piece of meat,' he says, and downs his whisky in one go. 'There's a length of intestine that used to live in there,' he says, jabbing at his stomach. 'Wasn't pulling its weight. Had to go.'

I give him the look I give the kids when they tell me they've been left out by the other kids in some playground game. I check his eyes for signs of sadness or self-pity. I see none. He doesn't look like he's been drinking all afternoon either. If anything, he looks more clear-eyed and focused now than he did when he was trying to snatch a picture of an otter basking on a rock.

'What job is it that you're retired from?' I ask, trying to show an interest. In my experience, no man is capable of resisting the urge to talk about himself at length.

'Copper, are you?' he asks, closing one eye. 'Very boring, me, love. Shipping clerk. Took redundancy when my health took a turn. Not a bad payout, and the insurance was better than I thought as well. Could live for years on it. Trouble is, I've got nowt to do with myself except for this.' He waves his empty glass at the bakingly hot bar. 'Maybe I'll write my memoirs, eh?'

'You should. I sense you've had an interesting life.'

'Too kind,' he says, and as I watch, something seems to

change in the way he holds himself. The blood seems to fall out of him in one great rush. One moment he's an unhealthy yellowish pallor, and the next he's an ugly pearlescent grey, like the belly of a dead fish. I see him reach out for the bar, his knuckles turning white as they curl, claw-like, around the brass handrail. Beads of sweat break out on his face. He looks as though he's using every ounce of emotion to not cry out in pain.

'Pocket,' he whispers, teeth locked: Popeye without his pipe. 'Top pocket.'

I rummage in the pocket of his shirt. There's a cigar butt and a small twist of foil. I pull out both and he hisses at me to open the wrap. Inside are two small white pills. He nods, quickly, and I push them both over his fleshy, fishy lips. He swallows, drily, and in moments the colour comes back to his skin. It's still the wrong colour for a human, but it's better than the godawful grey. He gives a nod of thanks. Behind him, Denis and Joy don't appear to have noticed.

'What was that?' I ask, leaning in.

'Punishment from on High,' he says, and there's a little snarl to the way he holds his mouth, as if daring the Almighty to hit him again. 'He likes to test out his ideas on me – see how far He can push me. He's getting pissed off. I'm not bending.' He looks up, winking at the ceiling. 'That all you got?'

I realise that I've been gone longer than I intended and that I left Theresa literally holding the baby. The new guests need to be properly welcomed and Mr Paretsky ordered an evening meal. Despite it all, I want to stay here, in the bar, with Mr Roe.

'Where did you meet, then?' he asks, tapping the lager

pump and nodding at me. Joy does as asked before I have a chance to object. He orders a Talisker for himself. Two pieces of ice this time.

I feign indignation. '"I'll stop you there," you said. Moments ago!'

'I'm being polite now, because you fed me my pills,' he says, and I notice that as he speaks, the hinge of his jawbone seems to click. I've seen such injuries before. He's had the jaw dislocated and then improperly set.

I shrug, wishing it was a better story. 'Kids and me were at the beach. Ardtoe. Lovely little bay once you get past the mountain. He was new to the peninsula and was exploring. We got chatting. Just friendly, because Callum had only just gone…'

His face wrinkles at that. 'Sorry love,' he says, and seems to mean it. 'You don't have to talk about it…'

'No, I'm okay. Too angry about it all to be upset. Gone off with another woman, hasn't he? Well, I say "woman". She's one of those bright-eyed, empty-headed girls with the sparkly eyes and false eyelashes that men of thirty-nine go weak at the knees over. Turns out the chance to bang her twice daily for the next year or so is a better lifestyle than staying with me and his children. It'll hurt eventually, but for now I'm just going to seethe.'

He doesn't reply. Looks into his glass as if it has the answers. Drinks it, just to be doubly sure.

'Made mistakes myself,' he says, quietly. 'Got things wrong with a lot of lasses. Got things wrong with my kids. Just one long line of wrongness. Maybe that's why I'm hard to kill, eh? Far more penance to do on Earth than there is waiting for me in Hell.'

His words slip into me like ice water. I suddenly feel the waves of sadness and regret coming off him like malarial heat. I want to go home.

'Maybe give that Bishop one more try, eh?' he says, unexpectedly. 'Men are pricks – you know that. Women are bitches, of course, but you're prettier than us so it's allowed. Maybe he let himself down today. If you like him, give it your all. I've only ever seen real love a couple of times but it seems worth striving for.'

He stands up, quickly, almost knocking his chair over. Denis gives a little yelp of protest at having had his arm jostled, and Mr Roe turns on him, his whole being tensed to do violence. He's all but vibrating with a wish to do harm. I don't know if I want him to come back to the guest house. His words may have affected me but I think he might be genuinely unhinged.

'No worries, boss,' says Denis, smiling down into the deranged eyes of the small, much-older man. 'Repay you for the drink, can I?'

Mr Roe turns back to me, and the mania has entirely left his features. It's eerie, as if he has taken off a mask. I feel a sudden urge to be with the people I love. Out of nowhere I find myself thinking of Callum. I see him curled up on the sofa in his little flat in Fort William, his arms around Kimmy, a bowl of popcorn on her lap, watching a black-and-white movie. I feel tears prick my eyes as I realise that what I miss most is the soft, unspoken intimacies of marriage. I miss having somebody to complain at; somebody I can tell about my curious aches and pains or who would listen, genuinely listen, as I outlined the pros and cons of the different colour choices for the downstairs bathroom. I suddenly miss him. I wish I didn't, but I do.

I do the sensible thing. Nod my thanks to Mr Roe, pull out my phone, and send a message.

> Bishop. I'm so sorry it all went to crap today. Been thinking about you. Please call me. I think I might be ready – if you are… xx

I've barely had time to push open the door and step into the swirling rain when the reply pings through.

> I'm sorry too. Meet me tonight at nine – where we had our first kiss. I'll bring a blanket. I promise I'll treat you right. xx

6

He's twenty minutes late and I'm getting pissed off and cold and wishing I hadn't gone to the bother of painting my toenails or shaving anything sensitive. It's so dark outside that I can barely tell if I've got my eyes open or closed. I've dressed in a way that will be fine in company but which is bloody awkward when I'm sat shivering in the driving seat and tugging my skirt down far enough to try and at least keep the backs of my knees warm.

I glance at the clock on the dashboard: 9.20pm; no, 9.21. I'm getting a bit miffed now. It's a little scary too. I'm parked up in a little copse of woodland just off the main road, squished between the entrance to the big castle, and a little horseshoe bay. The mass of Glenborrodale is huddling in behind me; a big tidal wave of huge trunks and charcoal-coloured branches. If I switch the headlights on I can just about see the shimmering surface of the loch, but mostly I get to see my own reflection turned into a magic mirror by the wind and the rain. I can't believe I booked a babysitter for this!

Instantly I feel bad. What kind of mother am I? My "babysitter" is only just eighteen and her experience of looking after children involves keeping her own younger siblings from hurting themselves too badly while her mum and dad go for their biweekly night out. She's heading off to university in the summer and is saving up. She's getting thirty quid for tonight. All she has to do is keep an ear out for Lilly's cries, and she isn't likely to wake up after eating a massive plate of pasta bolognese for tea and then taking a double-dose of Junior Paracetamol. I don't normally hold with drugging the children but apparently it's still within recommended limits.

And now I'm feeling like a fool. A silly girl. God how I hate that word. I'm thirty-seven and it still makes me feel like I'm about to get the backs of my legs slapped. It's one of Callum's favourites. He says it in a complimentary way a lot of the time: a rhapsody of "good girls" and "that's my girls": a certificate of achievement for every act that met with approval. I wonder if he says that to her. To Kimmy. I feel my mouth filling with spit at the very thought of her. I think back to the messages I saw on his phone. Scowl, in the darkness, as I remember the way he'd talked to her. I'd barely recognised him. He'd been bold; a proper take-charge guy, telling her what he wanted from her and how she had to act for him in return. *You don't argue with me*, he'd said. *You stay meek, or you'll pay for it. You look at me like a dog looks at their master or it's over, you understand...*

She'd lapped it up. I'd called her as soon as I found the phone, tucked at the bottom of his overnight bag, in among the forgotten socks and the stolen hotel soap. She'd answered breathlessly, and my mind had filled with horrible images. He was underneath her. Behind her. He was sitting in a skanky chair in her skanky flat and she was making him happy in a way I'd never been particularly fond of: adding new bruises to her skanky knees.

'You're fucking my husband,' I'd said, through gritted teeth. 'Callum Ashcroft. The father of my children. The youngest isn't even two. I always told him he'd get one chance and he wasted that the first year we were together. So he's yours. Keep the prick. But don't ever think you're getting the kids.'

I'd been shaking when I hung up. I don't think I even let her speak. Callum phoned ten minutes later. He was out on the loch, escorting a father and son from County Durham who'd signed up for a last-minute canoe trip out to the bay at Sanna. He'd abandoned them. Paddled for home as if he was trying to whip the water into meringue. I'd already piled his stuff in the garden by the time he got back. Dropped the match just as he screeched into the driveway, still dressed in his waterproofs and life vest.

He left the same night. I didn't let him in the house. Didn't listen to a word. He'd begged, as I'd known he would. Literally kneeled on the front lawn, the flames from his burning clothes casting flickering shadows on his beseeching face. *Let me talk*, he'd begged. *It's not what you think. I swear, you have to trust me, it's not what you think...*

He only left when I stood at the front door with the phone in my hand and told him that the local police were on their way. He got in the car and drove away. That was the last week of September. Good riddance.

I glance down at the phone on the passenger seat. I'm not waiting much longer. I'll give Bishop until half past and that's that. I'm sorry about the way things went but I'm too old and cynical to be playing silly beggars. If he wants to meet me, I'm here and waiting. I've shaved my legs and put on a half-decent dress and I've even put on some lipstick and a hefty squirt of expensive Ariana Grande. I'm here and waiting. I can't say I felt much in the way of sexual excitement at the thought of an assignation in a car park with a man I'm not sure I fancy, but I know I need to do something that makes me feel at least as though I'm partway getting my own back on Callum.

Maybe that's why I agreed to meet up with Bishop in the first place. I didn't even really like his kisses. He'd tasted strange. I've only kissed Callum in my whole adult life, which I used to think was sweet and romantic and which now makes me feel as though I'm hurtling towards middle age without ever having really lived.

Another glance at the clock: 9.31. I suppose that's it. He's not showing. I've messaged him three times and called twice and although I'm not exactly up to date on the rules, I think I'm probably coming across as a bit desperate. He must be more pissed off with me than he let on. But why? I mean, what was he going to say to me that was so important? I've been through a dozen different hypotheticals and keep coming back to the same thing – he wanted to share a secret that was difficult to get out, and when he kept being interrupted he'd taken it as a sign not to open up. I wonder if I've messed up with some aspect of his therapy, or something…

Headlights, through the trees. A war of different sensations inside me. Relief, fear, anxiety. Somewhere in there, a thrill of satisfaction; a delight at knowing that I'm still an attractive proposition.

The lights carry on right by, following the outline of the road. A moment later, three more vehicles, all big and square: their lights full and bright and expensive. I glimpse what might be a Range Rover, another, sleeker, that looks like Callum's dream vehicle, a Porsche Cayenne.

I deflate. That's it, then. Most exciting part of my evening was spotting a fleet of fancy cars heading to the castle. My mind fills with all sorts of images of opulence and splendour. Perhaps the new owner is throwing a masked ball: a decadent evening of gold masks and cashmere capes; guttering candles and unbridled lust. It's what I'd do if I owned the big house that looks out through the woods towards the loch. It was on the market for nearly three years before the new owners snapped it up in the spring. Five storeys of red sandstone: a true Disney castle of a place; 130 acres of land, and ownership of three uninhabited islands.

The papers in London almost lost their minds when it came on the market with an asking price of just under four million. It was a posh hotel in its previous life. Sixteen big suite bedrooms, staff accommodation, a games room, a billiards room and no end of outbuildings and little hidden lodges, it was only a little more expensive than a three-bed semi in Bayswater. I've tried to keep my ears open for gossip about who finally did put in a bid but so far, the jungle drums have been quiet. All we know is that whoever bought it hasn't moved in yet, and that they made the purchase through an international broker. I feel quite pleased at having seen the fleet of fancy vehicles. I'll have something to tell Theresa in the morning.

On the passenger seat, a vibration and flash of light. I click my tongue against the roof of my mouth, the way

Callum says I always do when I'm getting exasperated. If it's Bishop he can bugger off. I've had enough. I want my dressing gown, a hot chocolate with a healthy measure of Tia Maria, and then I want to fall asleep with my head against Lilly's, her lovely garlic breath creating a warm, safe cloud around my face.

I look at the screen. It's Callum. As if things couldn't get any worse.

7

Four months ago
A park in Vauxhall, South London

His name is Oscar Parkin. He's a solid specimen. Stocky. Five foot eight, with a big bald head, neat beard and chunky Harry Palmer glasses. He's got nice eyes and big arms and has done quite well for himself, all things considered. He's a Deputy Director (Logistics and Synchronisation) with the National Crime Agency: boss of a department that owes explanations to nobody but the Home Secretary and the handful of puppeteers who tweak her strings. He's been in law enforcement for more than twenty years and his CV, should he ever need to fill one in, would deplete a rainforest in order to list the qualifications he holds, professional bodies he is affiliated with, and successful operations that he has led.

He's received the Queen's Police Medal twice, and has it on good authority that he will be on the shortlist for the Directorship of Organised Crime Command when the current incumbent makes a mess of things, which can surely be only a matter of time. He's popular with the troops. He's served his time on the front lines. Seen it all, done it all, and efficiently removed the stains from the T-shirt. The bosses appreciate his results perhaps more than they are comfortable with the individual, but he's at ease with that, having never been the sort of obsequious boot-polisher that the powers-that-be traditionally prefer for high office.

On balance, Oscar Parkin has quite a lot of reasons to be cheery. Today especially. The morning's inter-agency symposium has gone moderately well. He's made his case, told them why the top-secret operation should come to his specialised unit and not to any of the other slavering dogs who want it, and if they make the wrong decision, it's on them. His team leader will just have to live with that. He shouldn't be worrying about her reaction. Shouldn't care what she will say. Shouldn't spend so much time thinking about her that it sometimes seems as though he loses whole chunks of his day and night to nothing but fantasy.

'Focus, Oscar,' he mutters, in an accent that Southerners think of as Geordie, but which actually has its roots in West Cumbria. 'Breathe. Look at the trees. Feel the tree. Imagine the nutrients slurping up through your roots and into your branches. Feel it in your leaves. Stretch, and know you are at one with everything. Breathe. Be the tree. Be a part of the cosmos. Empty your head and know you are a part of something greater than yourself...'

It's a crisply blue June day. Ramona, his soon-to-be second wife, is returning from Cadiz this evening. The children will be home this weekend: no doubt full of delightful stories about how tedious it has been at Mum's place in Maida Vale, and quietly hinting that, if he's cool with it, they wouldn't object to splitting custody right down the middle and maybe spending more time with him. He knows that given time they'll like Ramona again. They were always very fond of her when she was their nanny.

Parkin considers this, and so much more, as he sits on his favourite green metal bench, tucked away down a secluded path in a quiet little communal garden in Vauxhall, and makes a piss-poor attempt at transcendental meditation. In essence, he thinks about nothing and everything and the bits in between, and occasionally pretends he's a sycamore. He's fifteen minutes from the office, but they're fifteen minutes that count. His is a job that takes a heavy toll. He's not a particularly New-Age chap, but these little moments of communion with grass and trees and sky are important to him.

He has colleagues who deal with the stresses of their working lives with all manner of less wholesome pursuits. Even those who find time for yoga and Pilates or who sit at their desks colouring in mandalas on smartphone Mindfulness Apps seem no less tightly wound once they return to their realities.

He seems to recall that drinking always helped him unwind, but he spoiled that for himself a decade back when he underwent an aloe vera detox regime and reset his pH level to neutral. After that, the hangovers were so horrific that it took the pleasure out of the drinking, and he's been largely teetotal since. He's stopped smoking too. Tried vaping, and the experience was so far removed from the joy of a cigarette that he'd quit after a week. He still likes his food, but acid reflux means that he can't eat anything if he's planning on lying down within the next four hours, and the spicy curries and creamy soups that initially contributed to his waistline, are now pleasures he foregoes.

'Got any change, please? Anything really. I see you're busy, like, but owt would be a help, owt at all...'

Parkin looks up. A homeless man in a tatty wool coat is holding out a palm. He's wearing fingerless gloves, exposing long, yellowed nails, and has his other arm wrapped across his gut like a belt. He's suffering. Stomach cramps and shakes. He's positioned himself so that the glare of the sun obscures his features but there's no masking the smell. Parkin tries not to let his distaste show as it assaults him. Mould and bacon fat, piss and unwashed laundry.

Parkin nods. Slips a hand into his trouser pocket and his fingers sift his coins for something with angled edges. He's heard people refer to the homeless as an extra tax for Londoners, and apparently the going rate for donations is a pound a time. Parkin isn't mean, but he'd rather spread the goodness a little more evenly. He'd rather give a donation of 50p to ten different homeless people than give a quid to just five and then plead poverty when next approached. It's his own little contribution to the socialist utopia he used to hope for when he was young.

'There you go, mate,' he says, putting the coin on the man's palm. 'On you go.'

The man doesn't move. Doesn't withdraw the hand. 'There's a hostel,' he says, slurring his words. 'I'm still four quid short.'

Parkin doesn't let himself sigh. He's a well-paid man. He became a police officer because he wants to do good. He takes the rest of the coins from his pocket and deposits them on the grimy woollen glove. 'All I've got, mate. Now I'm just having a quiet moment. On you go, eh?'

The homeless man looks at the coins in his palm. Counts quickly. 'I'm 40p short.'

'You'll sort that,' says Parkin, brightly. 'Man of your talents. You'll sort that in no time. I've nothing left.'

'No notes?'

Parkin laughs. Shakes his head. 'Fair's fair, mate.'

'There's a shelter,' he says, tottering backwards and squeezing his stomach as he fights for balance. 'I need 6.90.'

Parkin smiles, shaking his head. 'You're making this up on the spot. Can't blame you, and you've done okay here, so on you go, eh? I'm just soaking up the sunshine.'

'Come on, it's just 4.95…'

'Look, if you're going to have a story, at least try and keep it consistent, eh? You'll be telling me you need it for your bus fare next.'

'I've got kids. I don't see them. One of them, the middle girl – she needs an operation. I'm doing posters. I need another tenner to pay for the print run…'

'That's much better.' Parkin smiles, wishing he had a tenner in his wallet to give the man as a reward for improvisation. 'But unless you've got somewhere I can swipe my card, you're still out of luck.'

'Prick!' spits the man, and the word comes out with such force that it's as if he has hurled a rock. 'Fucking rich prick! Bald prick! Tight prick!'

'That's a lot of pricks,' says Parkin, feeling a bit hard done by. 'Have you got a case worker? Somebody I can call? You don't look well.'

'Prick!'

'Yeah, you said.'

Parkin becomes aware of another figure, watching the dialogue with an air of amusement. His heart clenches as he looks at her. She's not somebody a person ever feels truly comfortable around. He's never been able to look at her for more than a moment without feeling embarrassed and self-conscious. She always makes him feel as though his flies are undone. It's a curious balance of power. On paper, he's her boss. Her department answers to him. And yet she's never once managed to call him "*sir*" without it sounding like a synonym for "*arsehole*" and she looks at him as if trying to decide what colour she should paint the wooden stake upon which she will mount his severed head.

He's never got the hang of being a disciplinarian. He's got a matey approach with the troops and when somebody needs a bollocking he tends to blame "those upstairs" who have forced him to "have a word". When he does lose his temper, he veers towards sarcasm. If he finds his team looking idle he'll tell them it's good to see them working so hard. If somebody's turned up for a shift hungover to the point of lockjaw, he'll make little jokes about how much they'll be missed "after they've gone", in the hope they'll turn his snippy comments into a more obvious threat within the sanctity of their own thoughts.

The homeless man follows his gaze. Sees the extra-ordinarily attractive blonde leaning against the trunk of the nearest tree: all Parisian cool and big sunglasses: a Silk Cut between her full, made-up lip.

'You a Kardashian? You a fucking Kardashian? Put me on the programme! Put me! I've got an arse – I can do what you do... I've got an arse!'

Parkin stands up abruptly, and the homeless man teeters away, trying to pull up his coat to reveal his posterior. 'Best of luck to you,' mutters Parkin, and as he walks towards his covert team leader he takes a twenty-quid note from his wallet and prepares to hand it over. He hears a "tut", and finds himself tucking the note away before the homeless man has even seen it. He doesn't really know why. She just has that air about her: an almighty confidence that says her suggestions should be thought of as instructions, and her instructions taken as a message from God.

'We said 1pm, didn't we?' asks Parkin.

'I always add an "ish" to the end of appointments,' she says, coolly. 'Anyway, I was here, but you seemed to be enjoying the sunshine. And the tramp.'

'We don't say "tramp" anymore,' says Parkin, with a silly schoolboy smile.

'No? Shall we say "irritating twat" instead?'

She pushes off from the tree and heads back down the path from the direction she's come. She's wearing a yellow dress with black boots and a sleek black trench coat. With her big designer sunglasses she'd only need a beret to pass for a member of the French Resistance. Despite being in charge of undercover operations within the National Crime Agency, she's the least anonymous person he has ever met. Parkin follows. If he were trailing water he could pass for a duckling following Mummy.

'How did it go?' she asks him, as they meander through the park. It's not warm, but the blue sky has tempted a few optimists into coming to their local park for a picnic or a lie-down in the sunshine. He fancies he can hear teeth chattering.

'Straight down to business, eh?' asks Parkin, and feels a sudden urge to slap himself in the forehead. He's pretty good at talking to people. He's personable. Occasionally charming. In her presence he feels like an ardent Royalist suddenly given a private hot-tub session with the Queen. He has a tendency to gabble. He's not one given to blushing, but his Operational Lead could cause a Greek statue to displace its fig leaf. He doesn't fancy her, it's not that. She's too cold, too mannequin-perfect to be an active figure of fantasy, but there is something about her that, in a different age, would have led to wars between neighbouring kingdoms and fights to the death between rival suitors.

'I've places to be. If we're doing this, it needs to begin now.'

'They're considering,' says Parkin, wincing in advance. 'No hard-and-fast answer.'

Beside him, the woman stops and moves her sunglasses down her nose. 'That's not an answer. That's a continuation of an unknown. I've walked from Lambeth for this, Parkin. How did you pitch it?'

He feels an urge to explain himself. To tell her he's done his best. Then he reminds himself that he's in charge, he's her superior, and tries to cough some assertiveness into his voice.

'I pitched it exactly as it needed to be pitched. We are the only department with the skills, the experience and the contacts to run the operation within the timeframe required and in a manner that leaves no department embarrassed or under-represented.'

She drops her cigarette. Grinds it out. Takes a silver case from a pocket and slides out another cigarette. She turns the case. Pushes a button on the hinge and a flame shoots out. Paper crackles. She inhales, exhales, eyes never leaving his.

'It's my operative, isn't it? There are still doubts.'

Parkin looks away. He's not permitted to reveal what went on within the confines of the meeting room on the third floor of the big rectangular building in Lambeth this morning. All the big players were represented. Border Force, Police Scotland, Europol, two faceless bureaucrats from the Home Office, and a tall sergeant-major sort from Scotland Yard. They'd each guarded their intelligence and information reports like children hoarding sweets. What happens next isn't up to him. He knows he's done his best. And yet, he wants her to know it too. Wants her to be pleased with him. To treat him like a good doggy, and perhaps, throw him a bone.

'Of course there are doubts. You must understand that. I trust you implicitly and would go to the gallows to protect your reputation but while the rumours persist, people will be wary. There must be other people.'

'There are. But he's who I want to use. You've seen the results. You've done well out of the results.'

'We both have,' points out Parkin, diplomatically, as they continue to mooch along the path. 'Quite a turnaround. You were facing charges two years ago. Now you're next in line for my job.'

'I don't want your job.'

'Well, that's reassuring to...'

'I want your boss's job.'

Beside him, the woman says nothing more. He finds the silence uncomfortable. Finds everything about her company uncomfortable. In such moments he can't help wonder which of the many rumours surrounding her and her favoured operative might actually hold some weight.

'If I could at least spend some time with him...' begins Parkin.

'No,' she says, shaking her head. 'That's not how he works. He's got his own methods. Unorthodox. Eccentric, even. But effective.'

'We're not spies,' he says, with some degree of regret. 'It's not *Mission Impossible*. We're a law enforcement agency. We have to stand up to scrutiny. We don't have the luxury of saying "trust me", because people simply don't. All those weeks and months he was playing a vigilante, worming his way into the confidence of those two killers – you're saying it's all just an act, eh? That he knows where to draw the line? Are you saying he obeyed operational protocols at all times? Stayed in contact, filed the necessary reports, met his handler?'

'I'll say whatever you want to hear,' she replies, without rancour. 'I'm saying he'll get it done. Minimum fuss, minimum spend, maximum results. That's what I've done my whole career, Oscar. I don't leave people disappointed.'

He finds himself smiling. She's never used his first name before. He manages to look at her properly, despite the burning sense of embarrassment and awkwardness. Not for the first time, he considers the rumours. He has no option but to think of them as tittle-tattle, because all of the files in relation to Operation Artemis have been classified. All he knows is that she posed in deep, deep cover and got caught up in something that she couldn't get out of without blood. The gossips would have it that her months spent posing as a corrupt detective were not much of a stretch. She's not short of enemies and they would have it said that she turned native without much in the way of encouragement from the group she was infiltrating. The organisation had made a fortune taking over crime syndicates and gaining leverage on bent authority figures, and they left a trail of burned, bloodied bodies across the country.

When the police began to get some decent results, the gang suspected an insider had turned. She made a decision. The result was more important than anything else. To maintain her cover she sacrificed another officer to the group. Gave him up, with every intention of getting him back as soon as she could. Opportunity never arose. He suffered the agonies of Job during a year in their clutches, before freeing himself and assisting in the operation that left the leader of the group dead and his network on the run. In the investigation that followed, she was cleared of any wrongdoing, thanks almost entirely to the testimony of the undercover operative she had given up to maintain her own cover. Instead of being charged she was given a commendation and a posting to the National Crime Agency. And she brought her faithful, near-dead operative with her.

It was all presented to Parkin as a done deal. None of it has ever sat right with him, but he cannot argue with her efficiency. The people who work under her have never worked out whether she has their best interests at heart, and most secretly believe she would sacrifice them in a moment if it offered personal advantage, but most are willing to take that chance in order to be part of a team that has become near legendary since she took over.

'There were raised eyebrows in the room, let's put it that

way,' mutters Parkin. 'The Deputy Chief nearly swallowed his coffee cup when he worked out who I was suggesting.'

'Me, or my operative?' she asks, with the merest hint of a smile.

'Both.' He grins, and glances discreetly at his watch. 'I should have an answer by close of play. I'll push. I know this is the right way to do it; I just think they'd be more comfortable if there weren't so many unknowns.'

'Then take their fears away, Oscar. Tell them that you can personally vouch for the operation. Put your name to it. When it works, the glory's yours.'

He takes a breath before speaking. 'I want to,' he says, as if discussing the possibilities of a clandestine and ill-advised romance. 'I really do, but I've a lot to consider, and if it goes wrong, or if he's not as ready for this as the psychological evaluation would suggest, then...'

She stops still. Shakes her head at him. 'Don't trust him, then. Trust me.'

'But I don't know you,' he says, and the words are out of his mouth before he can stop himself.

She steps back. Looks him up and down. Then she steps forward. Close. She's all warmth and cigarettes and expensive perfume and she's got her head angled like a vulture looking at a dying wildebeest. 'You're the boss,' she says, quietly. 'You're in charge. I work under you, Oscar. I'll keep you informed all the way. I know you're an experienced officer. I know how frustrated you must be not getting all the recognition you deserve, and how hard it must be having somebody with a bit of dirt in their record on the team. I want to reassure you.' She reaches out, about to put her hand on his arm, then stops herself, making a fist, as if fighting an urge. 'What can I do to reassure you?'

He doesn't know how to respond. Just knows that whatever happens, he will go back to the symposium and do whatever is in his power to persuade the other agencies that his team is the only one that can mount this operation, and that he can personally vouch for the officer in charge. All he needs is their blessing, and they will each come out of it looking good. And if things go according to the plan that has just presented itself to him, Oscar Parkin might come out of it smelling of her.

'Can I take it you're on board?' she asks, sucking the last of the cigarette down to the filter.

'If only I could meet him,' says Parkin, distantly, dry-mouthed, his last doubts stirring like ashes in a hearth.

She cocks her head. Smiles: a slash of crimson, curving to show perfect teeth. 'You did. You just gave him what he needs for tonight's hostel.'

Parkin's eyes widen. He spins back to where he left the homeless man. He's nowhere to be seen.

'He's good,' says Parkin, half embarrassed, half impressed.

For a moment she looks serious. 'No,' she says, quietly, looking away.

Then to herself: 'Not deep down.'

8

'What do you want?'
        'I called the house phone. That daft lass from
Acharacle answered. She said you were on a date.'

I sit back in my seat, feeling rather satisfied with the
evening's turn of events. He doesn't sound angry, but there's
a note of incredulity in his voice, as if he's been told I'm out
crocodile wrestling and needs to check he hasn't misheard.

'Yes,' I say, quite pleased with my tone. 'And?'

He's quiet for a moment. I feel a lovely warm tingle in
my fingertips and toes, as if the blood is starting to flow
again after a wee nip of frostbite. I don't get many chances
to be nasty and I save them all up for those who deserve to
see that side of me. Callum's never really seen it. He's heard
me whine and sometimes get a little snappy when I'm tired
or things aren't going my way, but the person I've been
since I found out about his lies must have boggled his mind.

'You're on a date,' he says again, as if trying a foreign
language for size. 'And you've left Lilly at home with that
girl?'

I feel as if I'm a bottle of Irn-Bru and every word he says
is giving me a good old shake. I'm going to go off soon.

'It's none of your business, Callum. You made your

choice. You turned your back on us. You don't ever get to judge how I raise my children.'

'Our children, Ronni,' he says, and I hear how hard he's trying to keep the temper out of his voice. 'They're my children too. We need to talk things through properly. We need to discuss proper access.'

'We can discuss maintenance,' I say, feeling hateful. 'Do you know what it was like paying for Christmas?'

'I tried to put money in your account,' he says. 'You wouldn't take it.'

'We need nothing from you,' I hiss, and I can picture his face, all smug, as he processes my contradictions. I dare him to mention it. To say anything at all.

'Who is he?' he asks, quietly. Something stirs within me, as if a faint gust of wind has illumined a near-dead ember in a cold hearth. I feel a tiny spark of compassion. He sounds so broken. So far away.

'You don't get to ask,' I say, and I hear my breath catch in my throat. I cough, trying to cover it. To stay resolute in my hatred of this lying, cheating, two-timing bastard. 'You won't know him anyway.'

'I can find out,' he says, simply. 'Would be easier if you told me.'

'Threatening me now, are you?' I snap, and in my head he's lying in bed with Kimmy and she's kneading his temples to keep him calm.

'I want us to talk properly, Ronni,' he says. 'I've tried so many different ways but you won't hear me. What you found – what you think: it's not like that. It never was.'

'Friend, is she?' I snap, and a sharp pain in my palms tells me I'm making fists. 'I can't believe your bullshit, Callum.

There's no way you're going to talk your way out of this. I saw the messages. You had a secret phone for God's sake! The only thing that will happen if I let you talk is you'll convince me I'm insane and that I've imagined all this, and I can't allow you to do that, even if I want you to. I don't think you understand how much you've hurt me.'

He doesn't speak. I realise my eyes are wet and it pisses me off even more. He doesn't get to upset me anymore. I have to cling on to my absolute hatred if I'm going to keep myself together.

'He's called Bishop,' I snap, sounding very pleased with myself. 'He's single. Bit of a lad. Got a sort of Liam Gallagher look, if you need to picture him. Works in cyber security. Makes me laugh. Makes the kids laugh…'

'He's met the kids?'

'Oh yeah,' I say, enjoying myself now. 'Had Atticus in bits. Lilly's a bit stand-offish but give it time…'

He doesn't speak. I hear him breathing. Feel the fire go out within me. None of this feels as it should.

'Bishop,' he says, at last, and for the first time since Poppy was a baby and we had to rush in to hospital with suspected meningitis, I hear tears in his voice. 'He's okay with you, is he? Treats you right?'

'We're in the car park at Glenborrodale, actually,' I say, and I slap away the tear that runs through my make-up. 'Having a lovely time.'

He doesn't reply. I start to think he's hung up. Then, just as I'm about to drop the phone, he speaks again, in a rush. 'Gold teeth, Ronni? Scruffy. Beard. Rents the place overlooking the ferry harbour. No, Ronni, I know you don't want to hear it but you have to listen to me – all the stuff with the phone and the messages, and him wandering into your life, it's all part of the same...'

I see my face reflected in the darkened glass. I'm pale, with red spots high on my cheeks, and the face I'm pulling is one of absolute rage and disgust. How dare he! How dare he try and use any of this to gaslight me into forgiving him.

I end the call. Switch the damn thing off. Scream, desperately, into the crook of my arm. Then I drive home, slowly: every bend in the road made perilous by a veil of tears.

9

There are four voicemails from Callum when I switch my phone back on. It's a little after 5am and Lilly has already begun grizzling. She can start to complain even before she wakes up. She roots for my nipple like a pig snuffling for acorns. Latches on. Burps, milkily, and starts to play with my other nipple as if searching for a favoured station on a transistor radio. I try to pretend I'm still asleep but I can't keep up the fiction for long – not when my phone is blinking and beeping and calling out to me like an ice cream van.

I ignore the messages. I don't want to hear anything else he has to say. I check every app on my phone for something from Bishop. Nothing. Absolute bloody silence. The last I heard he was telling me to meet him where we had our first kiss. He'd bring the blanket. Yeah, okay, Bishop. Whatever. Would have been good if you'd brought yourself, too.

I lie and stare at the ceiling for a while, emotions coming in waves. One moment I'm relieved to have extricated myself from what felt like a relationship without much in the way of a future. Then I'm missing him. He makes me laugh. And he's got that confidence about him, as if he's never met a problem he couldn't sort out. But he hadn't really warmed to the kids, had he? And there was a petulance about him – a self-importance that shaved the attractiveness off his self-belief.

But to be dumped? To be stood up? Am I somebody who should get used to this? Am I the sort of person who can look forward to driving home sober and depressed after a no-show? I didn't think I was. There are bits about myself that I'd have tightened and twanged if I had the money and I'll admit that in temper I have a face that could sour milk, but I'm pretty switched on, and I'm funny and can do a crossword without really thinking about it and can do the kids' homework with my left hand while making dinner with my right. And I look okay. He'd seemed to like it, anyway.

I find myself growing more and more agitated. He just doesn't seem the type to stand somebody up; that's the problem. Maybe something happened, I think, chewing my lip. Maybe there'll be flowers and chocolates before lunchtime and a lengthy message explaining that his car broke down and his phone fell in the loch...

I'm so deeply involved in conversation with myself that when I hear the crash, it takes me a moment to realise that it's coming from the real world and isn't a projection from the deep, deep place in which I have my most private chats. Lilly sits up as if yanked by a string, the shock sparking immediate tears. I have to shake myself to reconnect with reality, and then I'm half running, half stumbling out the door and down the stairs, Lilly bouncing on my hip. Both kids are in the living room, faces pressed against the dark glass, staring through their reflections at the silvery black surface of the loch.

'Mum, you've got a boob out...'

I grab my coat from the peg, plonk Lilly down on the floor, pull my walking boots over my bare feet and barrel through the kitchen to the back door. I spill out into the pitch dark of early morning as a fine rain is swirled by a hard wind. A large white van is noisily trying to extricate itself from the stone wall that marks the boundary of my property; its sidings wedged into the branches of a high, thick-trunked tree.

'Hey!' I begin, running down the drive, pulling my coat around myself and trying not to appear unnecessarily demented. 'Hey, did you do this? Don't be thinking you're just going to up and leave. You woke my baby... How the hell did you hit it?'

I can feel my temper bubbling like lava. I skid across the wet shingle of the driveway and bang on the glass of the driver's window. It's tinted, so I can only see myself. The van gives a roar and I realise I'm being ignored – the driver is still trying to get away without facing up to what he's done.

'Oi!' I yell, and decide to let some Glasgow bleed into my voice. 'Oi, pal, I'm talking tae ye! Buzz it down noo or ah'll tek a rock tae it, understan'...?'

The revving stops. The window slides down. A big round face looks out from the driver's seat. Red hair peeking out from under a baseball cap, a camouflage jacket. A three-day stubble smear on his fleshy chin.

'Sorry love,' he says, wincing. 'Bad bend, that, innit? Did I catch the wall? Thought I felt something go under the wheel. Thank Christ it's just bricks and mortar, eh?'

I give him some serious eyebrow work in response. They almost reach my hairline. 'Thought you felt something?

You've taken half the wall. And you were about to drive off!'

'I wasn't. I was just trying to back out; see the damage. I'm not that sort of chap, I swear.'

He gives me a look – the sort that says "butter wouldn't melt in my mouth". I look past him. There's another guy in the passenger seat. He's a colossal specimen: tall, broad, heavily bearded. He'd only need some furry trousers and a dab of face paint and he'd pass for a Viking. He's staring ahead, saying nothing.

'You must have been going far too fast,' I say, trying to maintain my anger. 'I've lived here long enough and nobody's ever wiped out the wall.'

'Bloody satnav,' says the driver, looking apologetic. 'Trying to follow it and watch the road at the same time. Recipe for disaster. The boss'll pay for any damage, I promise you.'

'You're damn right,' I say, and suddenly all I want to do is go back inside and make a cup of tea. I want to invite these lads inside and be all hospitable and welcoming. I feel bad for my outburst. I hate this aspect of myself – this inability to stay cross for long.

'We'll be here for a while,' says the driver, and he sucks on a vaping machine as if he's a diabetic and it contains insulin. 'What's your name? I'll ask the boss to pop by, sort all this out…'

I take a breath, not sure if I want to give any more information to this total stranger. I step back, looking at the damage to the wall. It's come apart in places and the rest will fall down when he backs out, but the masonry has been crumbling for an age. And now he's been caught, he seems quite happy to sort out the cost of repairs. Maybe I should be thanking him.

'You should be able to pull out okay, I reckon,' I say, casting a critical eye at the tyre. 'Your van's okay too. Dent or two and the headlight's gone but it could have been worse.'

'Boss's van, not mine,' says the driver. 'You okay to step back a bit? We'll back up and be out of your hair.'

I do as asked, squinting into the wind and rain as he crunches the gears. There is a moment's resistance and then the spinning wheels find the driveway and the vehicle lurches free in a small avalanche of bricks and dust. I look at the ruined wall and find my energy draining away. I don't need this. Even if somebody else foots the bill, I can't face all this on top of everything else. I turn to the driver, who's giving me a thumbs-up out the window. I walk over to him before he can put it into first gear and roar away.

'How do we do this then?' I ask, tiredly. 'Do you have a card or something? Or do you want to come in and leave your details?'

He glances across at his companion before answering. When he does look back at me I can tell at once that he's been given instructions. 'We've actually got a stupidly early start today, love – we're already running late. I'll pop back after we've finished for the day, or the boss will. We're just working up the road.'

I shake my head, unimpressed with the offer. 'No, I think we need to get this sorted – it's quite a lot of damage...'

'We're working here for a few days, love, we're not doing a runner. We just need to get moving.'

I look at the side panel of the van. There's no livery or advertising on the bodywork. 'Where are you working?'

'Big old place,' he says, waving his hand, vaguely. 'Castle. Old folks' home, isn't it?'

I give him a look. 'Is that what they're doing with it? I saw some cars heading up there last night – very expensive-looking.'

The driver shrugs again, and I sense that he's already wishing he hadn't started this conversation. 'Aye, well, we're just doing the wiring, love, but it's an early start and like I say...'

I'm about to ask more questions when he suddenly begins to roll the vehicle forward, crunching over the fallen bricks and moving back towards the road.

'Hey! Excuse me, we're still talking...'

'Bishop'll be by, I'm sure. Don't fret, love...'

And then I'm standing on the driveway watching the van disappear into the distance; red lights flicking on as he slows down at the last possible moment before vanishing around the bend and the view is obscured by a thick black band of trees.

I throw up my hands, pissed off beyond description. Had he said Bishop? I scowl out at nothing, wondering what the hell I've done to deserve any of this, and then the silence makes way for the unhappy screech of a toddler who's been without her mum for longer than she considers acceptable.

I turn and start to trudge up towards the house. And I see Nicholas Roe, standing by the garage: a raincoat over his pyjamas and dressing gown and a soggy cigar protruding from his closed mouth. He's watching me. Must have watched the whole exchange.

'Morning,' I say, flustered. 'Did it wake you? The bang? He must have been going at a hell of a speed. Says he'll sort out paying for it, but the cheeky sod shot off before leaving his contact details…'

He looks at me for a moment too long before speaking. Then he nods at the floor. In the dirt on the paving slabs in front of the garage, he's scrawled down the registration number with the toe of his boot. 'Doubt it'll do you any good,' he says, and there's a horrible rattle in his voice, as if his lungs are full of marbles. 'That registration doesn't match that van. They didn't make that style of transit in '06.'

I let out a deep sigh of disappointment. Something about his manner tells me he's totally correct in his information and it doesn't occur to me to ask how he knows.

'They said they were working at the castle. Doing it up as an old folks' home, he said…'

Mr Roe shakes his head. 'No, it's going to be a private hospital. I spoke with my neighbour last night. Mr Paretsky. Surprised you didn't hear him talking – not a man with a gift for Chinese whispers, that one. He's got all the gossip. New owners are turning it into a rejuvenation centre, whatever the hell that is. Facelifts, tummy tucks, designer vaginas, that sort of thing.'

I start smiling at once. He's got a way with words, has Mr Roe. I feel a wave of warmth towards him.

'I'll be starting breakfasts soon but you're welcome to come in for a coffee and a croissant if you can handle the wailing baby…'

I expect him to say no to the offer. He seems the sort more comfortable in his own company. But he gives a nod of what seems to be genuine thanks, shoving himself off from the garage door. Before he moves any further he stops and takes a phone from his pocket and photographs the digits scrawled on the floor. I give him a curious look. Why hadn't he just photographed the van?

'No good without a flash, and I didn't want to tell your friends they were being watched. Some people react badly.'

I size him up. Today he looks worse than yesterday: a greenish tinge to his skin, as if he's been hewn from rotten wood. I watch as he extinguishes his cigar on his tongue, and pops the butt in the pocket of his coat. As he steps past me into the kitchen I get a whiff of him. Nicotine. Ethanol. Some kind of medicated ointment. And something else: that meat-gone-bad aroma, as if one of his organs has begun to putrefy within the frail shell of his body.

'Welcome to the madhouse,' I say, trying to sound glib, as the mixed sounds of my warring children spill out of the house.

'No,' he says, cocking his ear. 'Madhouse doesn't sound like this.'

'No?' I ask, unsure what to say.

He catches my eye, and I see something in his face that makes me want to hold him tight and run away all at the same time. He has seen terrible things, has Mr Roe. Has witnessed them, experienced them, and dished them out.

And then he's bending down to pick up Lilly. Hoisting her up without any obvious effort. And she's smiling at him like he's some favourite uncle.

He turns to me, this monstrous thing, and his whole being is transformed by his proximity to this vibrant young life. She revitalises him as surely as if he were a vampire sucking her blood.

'I like the little ones,' he says, and as he smiles I see the blood where his dentures hurt his gums. He swallows, and puts Lilly down. Whatever I showed in my face, it spoiled the moment for him.

'On second thoughts, I'll leave it,' he says, shrugging, and before I can tell him to stay he has pushed past me and is crossing the garden towards the guest house. I wait for the security light to come on: to illuminate him as he stalks, darkly, towards the woods.

The garden stays dark. He passes through the sensors like a ghost.

10

Four months ago
A black-painted, candlelit restaurant down a side street in Soho

He's brought flowers. Half a dozen red roses and half a dozen white. They lie on the table, wrapped in shiny plastic. There are tiny bugs climbing in and out of the folds. They smell more of funerals than marriage.

'Bit feeble, aren't they?' says the man seated across the table. 'Got that bottom-of-a-fish-tank smell, though I've had similar accusations thrown my way. I'd have got something more expensive, but you know petrol stations.'

The NCA Lead in Covert Operations looks at him from across the table. She rolls her eyes, indulgently, and smiles. If Oscar Parkin were to see the gesture he would no longer recognise the cool, glacial beauty who so terrifies and mystifies him. Smiling, she is a different person entirely. In tonight's company, she feels free to be herself. Her companion knows all there is to know about her. They have been friends a long time and their dalliance as enemies was brief and hurtful. She's accepted that he has every right to kill her for what she did to him. Instead he found a way to turn a grotesque situation to their advantage. Forgave her trespasses, in exchange for a chance to be a police officer one last time. To do some good, even as everything about him suggests he is rotten to the core.

'At least they're not carnations. I hate carnations.'

'Strange thing to hate.'

'Not really. I hate a lot of things.'

'Example?'

'A random?'

'Yeah, first hatred that pops into your head…'

'Pistachios that don't open. I fucking hate that.'

'Not a fan myself. No snack should contain the word "pis".'

'And geese. With their green shit and that honking noise they make. I'd snap a goose's neck if I knew where to hit.'

'I'm goose neutral. No strong feelings.'

They sit in silence, regarding one another. She's wearing a tight blue-and-white top beneath a blue blazer, with figure-hugging jeans and kitten heels. Her blonde hair is unkempt, but in a way that suggests it has taken a lot of effort to make it look so carefree. Her lipstick is a deep red. She's wearing glasses, though the lenses are not prescription.

'Sorry about the Kardashian thing,' says her companion, pulling at his nose as if it were made of plasticine. He is a schoolboy in his mannerisms, forever fiddling, scratching, probing. 'Just came out.'

He's got a pint of lager in his hand. He's wearing a simple navy suit with a white shirt and gold tie. It looks wrong on him, but it takes some of the attention away from the state the rest of him is in. He's been dying for a while now. The man who came back is not the same person she gave up to save her an operation that she had given her entire self over to. For a year he hung in chains. For a year, bad men pumped him full of chemicals and poison and broke parts of him in turn as fancy dictated. By the time he was freed, he was something of a scientific experiment for the people who held him. How far could they push him before his will to live deserted him? That was the mistake they made. His will to live didn't come into it: desire to survive long enough for revenge was what kept his heart beating even as the rest of him gave out.

'You're bleeding,' she says, passing him a napkin. He dabs his chin, where pink blood is running from his gums and through the gap between his lips, a souvenir from when they dislocated his jaw and left it out of the socket so long they couldn't kick it back in. Such injuries do not seem to trouble him. The jaundiced skin, the open sores, the lesions to his scalp – he has never been one to complain. It is the things happening to his insides that are perhaps beyond enduring. His liver. His lungs. They are shutting down in stages. She's already made him a promise – if his brain starts to go, she won't let him suffer long. Such is the nature of their friendship. She may once have been his protégée, but she outranks him now. Outshines him in every way. And still she admires him. Still she looks up to him. Still he is the closest thing she knows to a real friend.

'I hate the Kardashians,' she says, pursing her lips. 'Not as much as geese, but close.'

'I don't think I even know what they look like.'

'Big feathery bastards.'

'Yeah? Which one – Khloé or Kim?'

She cannot help herself from mirroring his smile. They are sitting upstairs in one of the better restaurants on a quiet street in Shepherd's Bush. It's a relatively cosmopolitan area that boasts breakfast clubs and book groups, finger foods served on slate and bottles of Belgian beer. It's popular with the kind of clientele who call their children "guys" and reply with a variety of grape rather than just a colour when asked about their favourite kind of wine.

'You think he'll approve it? Seemed a decent sort. Can't imagine he'll be comfortable with handing over operational control to the fearsome ice maiden and her anonymous ghoul.'

'Ice maiden? Fuck off.'

'I called myself a ghoul...'

'Yeah, you did.'

He sits back in his chair. They are sitting on purple leather seats facing a table made of railway sleepers. There are only four other people in the restaurant. They stand at the bar, sipping exotic lagers from vase-shaped glasses.

'Places like this are putting real pubs out of business,' he says, shaking his head.

'You used to drink in a Wetherspoon's!'

'Shut up.'

She considers him from across the table. She still can't quite believe that she survived the fallout from what she has trained herself to call "the operation". She's always known herself to be good at what she does, but for her sins she had expected at least a little damnation. Instead it had worked out better than she could ever have imagined. Just five years ago she was head of the Drugs Squad with Humberside Police. Her mentor had been suspended for beating up a suspect in the cells, and she was surrounded by people who were either too good to be trusted, or too bloody stupid to be interesting.

She made some bad decisions. Fell for the wrong man. Got herself in deep and had to give up her associate to save her own skin. God knew he had long enough to plot revenge. And yet when he turned up out of the blue, when he stepped into the elevator and greeted her with a cheery "hello, Shaz", she had seen no malice in him. Sadness, yes. Hurt, certainly. But he didn't want revenge on her. He wanted revenge on everybody.

'You're ringing.'

She pulls the phone from her pocket. 'Oscar,' she says, rolling her eyes. 'Yes. Excellent. I appreciate that. You don't need to worry. No. Not as things stand. But of course, yes, given time. I'll forward the briefing notes. Yes. No. No.'

She hangs up. Looks up. 'We're on.'

Across the table, her operative nods, satisfied. 'Played him like a violin, love.'

She turns away from him, looking for a waiter. She can suddenly smell the cheap flowers. They remind her of something. Something sad. She wonders if they were the blooms at her father's funeral and realises she cannot remember. She'd had little to do with the service. As the baby of the family, it was not a duty that fell to her. It had been organised by her brother and sister, Scott and Geneva, and had been a predictably colourless affair. The service had been in the same church where he and Mum had married, forty-six years before.

She had been referred to during the service as a "happy accident". She'd been called that most of her life. There had been talk of naming her "Serendipity" but eventually, Dad decided that was a little too bourgeois for their part of Surrey, and settled on Sherilyn, instead.

She changed it to Sharon when she was seventeen and fell in love with a bad lad from Walthamstow. She couldn't bring herself to tell him her real name for fear he would make fun. She hadn't told him much about her home life. Not about the gymkhanas and the polo club and the special classes for gifted children that had been part of her life since she was seven years old. She didn't tell them about her dad, and the golf club, and the six-bedroomed house, or the riding rosettes or the brand-new Range Rover she received for her seventeenth birthday. She didn't tell him much about herself. Just said she was "Shaz" and that she liked the tattoos on his hands.

They were a couple for almost a year. It ended when her father found out. He took away the keys to the Range Rover. Took away her membership of the polo club. Made her choose between possessions and the bad boy who made her toes curl with ecstasy every time he stuck his tongue in her mouth and she tasted the hand-rolled cigarettes and beer on his breath. She chose possessions. She broke it off with him. Went to university, like a good girl. Dad had wanted her to join the family firm when she was finished. Instead, she chose the police. Then she chose to be something else entirely.

'I'll settle up,' she says, looking at her old friend. 'You got somewhere to stay?'

He nods. 'I always find somewhere.'

'Briefing at nine?'

'Fuck off, you can still taste the toothpaste at nine.'

'You've not got teeth.'

'I still like to suck the tube.'

'You are gross. Truly, you are a monster.'

'Yeah. Which makes you Frankenstein.'

II

Two days later, I've heard nothing from Bishop or the two men in the van. I have, however, got the latest on the *"plans"* for the castle. The information came from Theresa, obviously, who sat at the breakfast bar with her hands around a mug of quality coffee, and delighted in telling me everything she'd heard from one of her clients down at Strontian.

'Sparing no expense, apparently. Going to be one of those really fancy *"alternative medicine"* places as well as offering retreats and rejuvenations to the rich and famous. Done it well, don't you think – keeping it quiet, I mean. All sorted on the planning permission front, which must mean some palms have been greased. You know me, I try to keep my nose out of other people's business, but I couldn't help having a bit of a dig about online to see when it all went through with the authorities and there's next to nothing to be found, which means they probably aren't going to be advertising their services to the likes of me – much as I'd like to be tightened from the top.

'Company doing it is *A Thasgaidh Ltd*. Hope you don't think me nosy but I had a wee look and they're registered in Jersey. That's the Channel Islands, and I only hear their name when it's to do with something dodgy. The address given is a firm of accountants, but the directors are two women. An Alice McCall and an Ailsa McCall. I tell you, if I had my time over again I'd love to be an investigator. Either way, I'm hoping they need a cleaner…'

I drank it all in, bouncing Lilly on my knee and whispering the "giddy-up" song in her ear while she giggled and pretended she was on an out-of-control horse. Theresa had been delighted to hear about the posh cars I'd seen heading for the castle and even more excited to learn that one of the work vans had taken out the wall.

'We should go up there, don't you think? Go and demand payment and say you'll get the papers involved if they don't sort it out. In fact, I'll go. As your representative, like. Give them what for, and maybe have a poke around while I'm up there…'

I declined the offer. Sorting out the wall was low on my priority list. In fact, the only thing that seemed to matter right now was Bishop. He'd pretty much dropped off the face of the planet. It's not that I'm desperate to win his heart or to get some kind of answer for the cold-shoulder treatment – I'm genuinely worried. He'd wanted to tell me something the last time I saw him and I hadn't been in the mood for listening. I've tried to call him but his phone isn't connecting, and I sent a Facebook message to the mum of one of Atticus's school friends, who lives on the same stretch of property as Bishop. She reported back that she didn't even know the house was occupied, and that she'd never seen anybody matching his description, let alone noticed their absence.

I've had the same everywhere I've tried. The pubs

he's mentioned, the library, the canoe instructors down at Strontian that he told me he'd got to know pretty well. Nobody had seen him, and the canoe instructors remembered so little about him that I think they were only humouring me when they said they remembered him at all.

So where does it leave me? I mean, he's a grown man, and he briefly flitted into my life, and now he's gone again. What do you do in those circumstances, eh? I've thought about mentioning it to the community police officer but I can just hear myself trying to explain the situation and I wince when I imagine their face as I outline just how concerned I am that a man has dumped me and moved on.

So I do nothing. I play with Lilly. I look after the guest houses. I check my phone and try to find a way to stop Callum making good on his threats to come and visit the kids. I'm not ready for it. They're not ready for it. The wound is still too raw; too open. Whatever Lilly says, it's better for her to be kept away from toxic people.

I'm sitting at the kitchen table, enjoying half an hour of me time, listening out for the moment when Lilly will wake up and start shouting "booby", when I hear the first siren. I figure it for an ambulance at first. We hear them a lot. There are always people crashing into the loch or hitting trees, and the tree surgeons have a nasty habit of falling off branches at this time of year. But one siren becomes two, then three, then four, and in a moment I'm at the window, watching a full convoy of white-blue cars careering around the bend; blue lights casting eerie strobing shapes onto the silver-grey water.

Mr Roe is in the kitchen when I turn back towards the room. How the hell had he done that? The door was closed. Locked, even. I hadn't heard a sound. And now he's standing, perfectly still, looking at me, his head angled slightly to the right, as if he were a bird who has heard a worm beneath the ground. I feel gooseflesh rise all over my body. I realise how much he unnerves me. I don't know if it's his appearance or something more primal than that. He just gives off something that feels, well, wrong. It's as if he vibrates at a different temperature to any other person I have met.

'Oh, you scared me,' I say, beginning to gabble. 'Was there something wrong? Do you need something? I didn't hear you come in...'

He doesn't speak. I fall silent, staring at him the way he stares at me. I consider myself. Jeans, jumper, hair in a great bird's nest twist. If he's been beguiled by my appearance then he's done most of the work in his imagination.

He's breathing hard, as if he has exerted himself. He's wearing a battered raincoat over a padded shirt and corduroy trousers, but if he stretched out his arms he'd pass for a scarecrow. He's a dreadful colour; a shade that makes me think of uncooked chicken. And he seems to have cut his own hair. There are clumps missing; red patches on his scalp, open weeping sores. I thank God the kids are at school, while at the same time wishing, for the first time since I kicked him out, that Callum were here.

'What is it, Mr Roe?' I ask, some steel in my voice. 'I'd rather you didn't just let yourself in like this – you really did startle me...'

He raises a hand to his mouth. Puts his index finger to his lips.

'I'm sorry?' I ask, annoyed. I don't get shushed. Not in

my own bloody kitchen by a guest. Not a bloody chance. 'You're shushing me now? I'm not sure this is working out, Mr Roe. I'd rather that…'

He puts a hand in his pocket. Pulls out a mobile phone. Lays it on the table in front of him.

'I'm sorry,' he says, under his breath. 'Those coppers. All that racket. It's your friend.'

I narrow my eyes, confused. I feel my heart begin to race. There are jangling bells in my head. 'My friend? I don't understand,' I stammer, and start to move towards him. He picks up the phone. Flips his thumb across the screen and calls up a photograph. With a look akin to apology, he flips the phone and shows me the image.

I recognise the blue mesh of a lobster pot; the black, barnacle-encrusted bars; the orange buoys that dangle down one side. The contraption is set up on a strip of jagged rock; the background half sea, half sand.

Inside, a head, severed at the neck. Dark hair. A mouth hanging open, slack-jawed, tongue protruding like the tail of an eel. The eyes are gone. There is a deep slash to the left cheek, sugar-dusted with sand. And the top lip has been chewed away, revealing the top row of teeth.

Gold teeth…

'Jesus,' I say, and it takes an effort of will not to let myself start to shake. I look at Mr Roe uncomprehendingly. 'How? When…?'

He puts his finger to his lips again. Jerks his head towards the top floor. 'She sleeping? Little one?'

'Yes, went down a bit ago,' I begin, not understanding.

'Good,' he says, and puts the phone away. 'Then you've time for a walk.'

I feel the mean little smile twist my lips. 'A walk? Mr Roe, are you out of your mind? You're showing me a picture of a head... You expect me to just leave Lilly and come with you for a walk...'

He looks at me with something like regret on his face. Then he reaches into another pocket and pulls out a canister. It's black, and he has his finger over the nozzle. I recognise it from TV. It's CS spray.

'Yes,' he says, nodding sadly. 'Yes I do.'

12

On Ardnamurchan the fog closes in like a mouth. One minute the view is the quicksilver lake and the distant, purple-brown mountains across the loch. The next there is nothing but a stony grey darkness that moves in eerie, liquid swirls. Sometimes it seems as though some higher power has decided to simply change the channel and plunged our little world into static. I always expect something ethereal to emerge from the mist: a Viking longship, perhaps, or a collection of bedraggled Jacobites off to claim the throne.

I stand in the shadow of the back door, leaning against the damp wall, the door half open so that if Lilly cries I can dash to her side. My heart is thudding. I know people say that, but I'm not being overly lyrical. It really does feel as though somebody is thumping the pedal on a bass drum inside my chest. I feel all tingly inside my skin and there is a high, keening whine inside my head that makes my teeth hurt. I'm sweating, but I keep shivering, as if I'm running a fever.

Mr Roe is standing beneath the big ash tree, watching me closely. The spray has disappeared back into the pocket of his coat but we are both very aware of its presence. I know that the best thing to do is slam the door, lock it behind me, grab Lilly and call 999. I know there are police on the peninsula today and I doubt they would take kindly to a local being threatened by a holidaymaker – and an English one at that. And yet I don't really believe that Mr Roe will hurt me. Call me naïve, but I think he would only use the spray as an absolute last resort. And I saw how he looked at Lilly: a real gentle benevolence in his sore, weeping eyes. More than anything, I want to know why he just showed me a picture of Bishop's severed head.

I tremble as I think it, biting down on my lip until I taste blood.

'He's dead?' I ask, when the silence has become unbearable. 'Really? That's him?'

I see a sudden glow of red emerging from the fog and realise he has lit a cigar. When he exhales it's a vile, rasping sound, as if he is guzzling up the last of a milkshake through a straw.

'Be best if you just listen, love,' he says, quietly. 'I know you want to get back to the nipper and I'm in no state to be standing around shivering. So two ears, one mouth, yeah?'

I'm too pissed off to respond, and he takes my silence for consent.

'Your Bishop,' he says, accentuating the "B" so it sounds as if he's popped a bubble. 'I could ask you how well you know him, but I've been here a good few days now and it's pretty clear you don't know him at all. He's sweet on you, I can see that. Can't blame him neither – you're a balm to sore eyes, though I doubt you know it. I've known lasses like you all my life. Pretty as a sunrise and you spend your lives worrying about your hairstyle and your fingernails when all you've got to do to get whatever you want in the world is offer up a smile...'

I hear myself laughing, softly: a humourless noise that daubs the words "go fuck yourself" into the fog.

'Bishop and me, we come from the same sort of world. I'm not trying to be enigmatic – I'm too old for all that bollocks – but let's just say we've had one or two dalliances with bad people. And the thing about people like us is that we recognise ourselves in other people. I can walk into any bar and know which bloke knocks his wife about; which one to speak to about getting a knock-off TV; who to go chat with if I'm after a line of Charlie or want somebody's kneecaps knocking down to their socks. It's a gift, I suppose. And me and Bishop, well, we saw it in each other first time we clapped eyes on one another.'

'In my kitchen?' I ask, baffled, remembering the way the air had fizzed with toxic masculine tension as Bishop pushed his way past me that last day. A feeling rises up: a great surge of paranoia. Had Mr Roe followed him? Was that what had led to the grotesque picture: Bishop's head in a barnacle-encrusted cage.

'Wasn't the first time, love,' he says, and through the fog I can just make out that he is shaking his head. 'Bishop's the reason I'm up here. With you.'

I feel my heart beating harder. I don't have the first clue what he means. He's a holidaymaker. A paying guest. He's retired from some job in shipping and is on Ardnamurchan to practise his wildlife photography. I make out a change in the set of his mouth. He's smiling, watching me run through what I know about him.

'The van driver who did your wall,' he says, changing

the subject so quickly I feel as though I need to throw out a hand and grab hold. 'He told you what they're doing at the castle. I heard him say. Private hospital, yeah? Well, Bishop's something of a middle man on what will be a very lucrative venture. He's here to make sure everything goes smoothly before the first guests arrive.'

'He's in computer security. He said so...'

'He's into a lot of things,' says Roe, drily. 'He's a fixer, is Bishop. Whatever problem you've got, he'll find a solution. Need six brand-new Teslas by Friday night? He'll know a guy who can drop them off for you. Lady friend got footage on her mobile phone of you up to no good with her at the works party? He'll get it back. Got a shipment of contraband you want getting through the docks without inspection? He'll find a friendly face.'

I look at him accusingly. 'He's a drug dealer? And you were his inside man?'

He laughs at that. Laughs full and throaty, then turns away and spits something into the bushes. 'All sounds a bit melodramatic when you say it, love. But yes, we've encountered one another before. And we've both considerably improved one another's bank balances. Don't be calling him a drug dealer though. He's not. He's just good at helping drug dealers with their problems.'

I shiver, as a harsh gust of wind bends the branches of the trees and stirs the fog. For a moment all I can see is the hollows and contours of his face and in the half-light he is more corpse-like than ever.

'The photo,' I say, flatly. 'You showed me his head...'

'This morning,' he replies, inhaling smoke. 'Fisherman at Ardtoe pulled it in. Called the police once he got back to shore, and not before he took a few pictures for posterity. I'll say this for the Scots, you may be mean but you're eagle-eyed when it comes to a business opportunity. The fisherman was on to the news desk at the *Record* before he even rang the cops. Sent them this picture as an appetiser.'

'And how did it come to you?'

'I have friends in low places,' he says, and grinds his cigar out on his licked palm. He pockets the stub. 'Look, I don't know what Bishop's done to piss people off and I can't say for certain that it's definitely him, but it damn well looks like him and he sure as hell hasn't been answering his phone, has he?'

'You've been trying to contact him too?' I ask, trying to keep up.

'He's the one who brokered the deal, love. He's the one who's got a big chunk of my retirement fund and who's had me kicking my heels in your guest house since the turn of the year.'

'And you said it's to do with the hospital? The castle?'

I hear him sigh. It's as if he wants me to put the pieces together without him actually having to tell me anything.

'I'm not a well man, love. You've probably spotted that. I won't bore you with the details but my lungs are fucked and my liver's on its arse, which are both medical terms. And because I'm fifty-five and my blood's more pus than platelets, I'm a long way down the list of recipients for a transplant. I'll die before my name gets anywhere near the top of the list. And I don't think I'm ready to die just yet, Ronni.'

'How does that involve Bishop?'

'He fixes problems,' explains Mr Roe, softly. 'He can find you a donor, if you pay the right price. And I reckon another ten years of life is worth every last penny, don't you?'

I say nothing, letting all the tumblers slip into place. 'An illegal transplant? That's what this hospital is going to be offering?'

'Not on paper,' he says, and I hear a dry smile in the dark: a rustle of parchment touching flame. 'On paper it will be a private medical facility offering all sorts of holistic care; rejuvenation procedures and certain cosmetic surgeries. But for specialist clients, it will be offering up life.'

My stomach becomes a fist. I feel coils of wire around my guts. Everything seems too cold, too loud, too close. I find myself about to ask where the donated organs will come from. I stop before the words leave my mouth. 'You're buying the body parts?' I whisper, and it leaves a foul taste in my mouth. 'Buying organs from people who need money more than they need their insides?'

He shrugs, conveying in one simple gesture all that he seems to feel about the world and his place within it. 'You'd do it, wouldn't you? One of your kids was going blind, you'd buy a black market cornea if you had the connections to make the deal. Your Atticus needs a heart transplant, you'd sell everything you had to get him what he needed – even if you had to carve the heart out of somebody else using a spoon.'

I shake my head, protesting, but the truth of his words is inescapable. I know what I would do. I know what anybody would do.

'You can't buy a heart,' I say, petulantly. 'You can't donate a heart – you need a heart...'

He stands still, not speaking. I suddenly feel very empty, and terribly sad.

'Bishop,' I say. 'Why have you told me about what's happened to him?'

He moves quickly, appearing in front of me like a vampire emerging from theatre smoke. He gives off a reek of true foulness, as if something inside has rotted all the way down to mulch. 'There will be coppers here, Ronni,' he says, softly. 'Coppers asking questions. How well did you know him? What was the nature of your relationship? When did you last hear from him? And because you're a good sort you'll want to help. You'll be truthful. You'll be honest. And very quickly the coppers will find that he's been using you as a way to keep himself entertained while he waits for the first patients to arrive. And then they'll seize your computer and your phone and they'll start digging through every aspect of your life, and they might just find that a Nicholas Roe in Room 3 has a criminal record for all sorts of nasty shit, and then they'll get all excited and start digging around into my life, and that may just piss all over my one and only chance of getting the operation that will keep me alive.'

I cock my head, face twisting, unable to fully comprehend what he's saying. 'You want me to stay quiet so you can still get your transplant? Your illegal transplant! A set-up run by the sort of people who might just have cut a man's head off and thrown it into the sea? Are you insane?'

'The people behind the new venture – they aren't the sort to run and hide at the first sign of trouble. They've got half a dozen very well-connected people lined up for operations within the first few days. Myself included, though I'm nothing compared to some of the people who are buying themselves another slice of life. And if you tell the coppers about you and Bishop, you're setting them on a road that will end with me unable to get what I need. And without what I need, I'll die, love. And I don't expect you to care too much, but I have family, and mouths to feed, and sins to atone for. So all I'm asking is that you be as uncooperative as you can be, and I'll see to it that you're compensated.'

He moves closer, his yellow eyes boring into mine. 'The alternative is that I make a call to Bishop's contact and tell them that there's a loose end. And they will hate that, love. They'll really hate that.'

I stay rooted to the spot, unable to put into words just how much I want him to get the hell away from me and my house. Suddenly I want Callum. I want my lying, cheating ex to pull up on the driveway and tell me that I got it all wrong and that he loves me, and only me, and wants to come home and make everything right again.

'I hate this,' he says, his voice full of genuine regret. 'I think you're a grand lass. Clever, funny, tough. I can see something of the copper in you, truth be told, and for me to like a person with a copper's personality is not much shy of a miracle. I hoped we could be friends, but circumstances conspire to rob us of such luxuries, so now I just need you to say that you understand, you agree, and I'll go pack my stuff and be out of your hair before the morning.'

I hear my breath come in short, ragged bursts. I can't agree to what he's saying. I can't be a party to any of this.

And then one hand is around my jaw, pushing me back against the wall, and the other is holding the CS spray millimetres from my eyeball, his thumb hovering just above the button. His face swims in my vision. I see sadness in his eyes. Real, genuine regret that it has come to this. But I also see a willingness to do what must be done.

'I understand,' I say, in little more than a whisper. 'I'll do what you want.'

For a fraction of a second he looks as though he wants to tell me not to be so bloody stupid: to fight and scrap and knee him in the balls and do anything other than make a pact with this foul, corrupted demon. Then he gives a simple nod, turns, and walks away towards his room.

I slide inside the back door. Slam it shut. Bolt it, and slither down to the floor. I cry until my face is sore and my throat feels as if it has been cut with a blade.

When I finally look up, Lilly is staring at me, her petite little features a mask of concern.

'What matter, Mummy? Mummy cry?'

I reach out and hold her. Press her head to my own. Let her hold me, as if she were the mother and I the child.

At no point do I think about calling the police.

The deal has already been done.

13

A large house, stuck on the end of a terrace of tall Georgian properties. White-painted, like the others, with big sash windows and a door the same shade of green as the big laurel bushes which cling to the wrought-iron fence and which shields the bottom floors from prying eyes.

Inside, pure luxury. A basement has been converted into a games room with big glass doors opening out to a courtyard garden: a single mulberry bush serving as the focal point, accessed by a footpath of reclaimed sleepers and big glittering stones.

The members of the NCA Covert Strategy Unit are making themselves comfortable in the long, high-ceilinged room on the first floor. It's wood-panelled and two large black chandeliers hang from the ceiling, their light reflecting back from the lacquered wood and the big windows. The sun pours in to puddle in expensive corners – on the writing desk, at the foot of the Chesterfield sofa, slicing down on half of the reproduction George Stubbs equestrian portrait above the big open fireplace. One whole wall is given over to leather-bound books and the table at the centre of the room is so hefty and ancient that more than one visitor has wondered whether the builders erected the place around it.

The head of the unit is standing at the fireplace as if posing for a *Country Living* photo shoot. There are gold-framed mirrors and bowls of pine cones on the mantelpiece and though she has her back to the room she is using the reflections to survey the members of her team. She likes them to wait until she's good and ready. In other units where she has worked there has always been a surfeit of blokeish chatter: dirty jokes and silly comments and raucous laughs amid the belches and farts. Not in this unit, thank you very much. She's made that plain. She has no problem with people being boisterous and can hold her own in the smutty remark department, but the truth is she wants her team to be slightly in awe of her. Wants them to do what she tells them because they're afraid to do otherwise. And every time she gets to enjoy the sound of silence ahead of a briefing, she knows she's winning the game.

The three operatives are sitting quietly, their electronic tablets on laps or tabletops. Two women, one man. She knows their real names, knows more about their secrets than they know themselves, but she has instituted a strict confidentiality code since taking over and now insists that the undercover operatives refer to themselves entirely by code names.

She has few vices outside of a desire to become all that she can be, but she does have a fondness for opera. As such, she refers to her team members by the names of operatic composers. In the armchair is Verdi. She's got a Rubenesque look about her. Big bones, red hair, pale skin. She's still perspiring slightly from the walk from the Tube station.

At the table sits Smetana. Thin, sharp-eyed, always fighting off or coming down with a cold, she has a look of fragility that is utterly at odds with the facts on record. She's tough, determined and willing to go almost as far as it takes to get the job done. She was a detective sergeant with Thames Valley Police until she was seconded to the NCA.

Lounging in the wooden chair by the open window is Bizet. Forty-odd. Seen-it-all, done-it-all, he's a lugubrious, sick-of-it sort of soul who makes every tiny task seem like a Herculean level of effort is required to do it right. He's tall, too tall, and has developed a bit of a stoop through years of hunching over. He walks as if looking for a dropped coin. The boss doesn't like him very much, but she wants to keep him where she can make sure he's not causing mischief. He's a gifted hacker and she wouldn't put it past him to have already had a dig around in some confidential files looking for dirt on the team leader, and she knows, to her cost, that there is plenty to be found.

She turns into the room. Looks past Bizet, and out through the gleaming glass into the cold blue sky. Then she takes her seat at the head of the table, opens up the sleek little laptop, and hits a key at random. A moment later, the trio of tablets held by her officers light up with received information.

'One nine eight zero,' she says, without emotion, and the operatives key in the decryption code. Lines of nonsensical data and multi-coloured pictures delineate into confidential briefing documents, mugshots and witness statements.

'Item 1.9 in Bundle 3.3,' she says, looking at her own screen. She touched a tanned index finger to the relevant icon, and the picture becomes a grainy mugshot: a short, angry-faced man, with dark curly hair and sunken eyes. 'Operation Pontian.'

'Pontian?' asks Verdi. 'What does that mean?'

The boss eyes her coolly. 'We'll save questions until the end. Preferably after I'm gone.'

'Sorry.'

'I've no doubt.'

The space grows chilly as she glares at Verdi. Glares at her the way cats regard one another from opposite ends of an alley. Then she returns to the job in hand.

'This man is called Pope. Sometimes "The Pope". He's been known by that name since 1989, when some funny fucker said that he had such a charmed life it was as if he had a personal hotline to God. The name's stuck. Prefers it to his own, which we think was only ever an alias. Douglas Sturrock. Born in Paisley, 1955. One of seven children and the only one that his mum made no attempt to keep when the social services of the time took him into care. Children's homes, after that. Bad lad, getting worse.

'Ran away at twelve and didn't surface again until 1980, when he turned up with a tan and an attitude and a Foreign Legion bayonet, which he promptly stuck in the head of a retired caretaker from his old infant school. Didn't kill him, but not far off. Arrested, charged, then the procurator fiscal messed up with witness statements and he walked. Walked straight into the loving arms of Glasgow's favourite crime boss, Derrick Ovenden. Did his dirty work for him, and there was a lot of that to go around. Got himself a reputation for being particularly colourful in terms of teaching people a lesson. No simple kneecappings for Pope. Liked to snip your toes. Liked to scald your feet. Learned that one from Ovenden himself. And if you were going to die, he liked to get his money's worth out of the experience.

'We've got one report of him setting up a gladiatorial arena in an abandoned swimming pool. Sent three lads in there bollock-naked and chucked in a few weapons and said he'd let the winner out alive. There was no winner. They hacked one another to bits. He sat watching, drinking red wine and eating grapes. If there's no such thing as Caligula Syndrome, I'm going to patent it.'

She pauses. Takes a sip of water. Considers a cigarette and decides to save it until she's done.

'Fast forward to 1998. Derrick Ovenden is killed leaving a casino. His firm and another led by a couple of ambitious upstarts had been involved in an escalating series of confrontations. Two shootings, a stabbing and no shortage of slashes to the cheeks. Ovenden thought he was untouchable. He wasn't. Prime suspect in the killing was one Benjamin Moss – a teenage member of the Ovenden firm who figured he'd get himself in the good graces of the enemy by doing them a favour. He turned up two days after the shooting, banging on the door of his local police station and begging to be arrested. The locals obliged, but despite his best efforts he was released.

'They found him ten days later. Found some more of him the next day as well. Word was, Pope didn't see why his boss's death meant he should stop being loyal. With Ovenden dead, Pope took over, and the locals quickly learned that Ovenden had been the restraining force for many a year. With Pope in charge, the methods became more ruthless, the punishments for grassing became more severe, and anybody who threatened their territory was forced to suffer every kind of agony you can imagine.'

'I can imagine quite a lot,' says Smetana, quietly.

The boss allows that one to pass unremarked. 'You can read about it at your leisure. There are true crime books about all this too, and you'll be surprised to learn that it's not all bollocks.'

She takes another sip of water. Wets her lips. Clicks on an icon on the laptop. The image of a dark-haired man with gold teeth and a mocking smile appears on the screen.

'This gentleman goes by the name of Bishop. Whether we had that name before he got into bed with Pope, I'll leave you to speculate upon. He's a bit of a grey area for the intelligence units. We think he's mid-forties. Think he may be one Fraser Lockhart, who left university two terms into his second year to go and explore the world. Expanded his horizons you might say – geographically and chemically. Did time in a prison in Thailand and loved it so much he thought he'd try out a South American jail for comparison when he got out. Drugs offences, naturally. Refused any help from the British Embassy, hence the lack of information.

'Next heard of providing security services at a gold mine in Mazaruni, Guyana. Same man was rumoured to be involved in the illegal export of blood diamonds from Sierra Leone in 2009. A real world traveller, this one. Got a lot of connections and doesn't scare easily.'

She clicks on another image. This time the screen fills with an image of an emaciated man in ludicrously baggy football shorts, lying on a cot bed in what appears to be a khaki-green tent: mud and leaves at the base of the picture. He has bandages across his eyes, and a great curving wound across his stomach and sternum. One arm lolls off the side of the bed, trailing in the earth, but there is still a hint of life into the sheen of fetid sweat that clings to this dark skin.

'Illegal organ donation,' she says, straightforwardly. 'Top prices paid for anybody willing to put a price tag on their insides. Turns out we're worth a fortune. Corneas, lungs, livers, kidneys – there's a buyer for whatever you're willing to offer. And our Bishop here is connected to the same cartel that realised they were missing a trick when it came to despatching their enemies. No more dumping them by the side of the road, limbless and headless and bleeding. No, with a couple of health professionals and a few blind eyes turned – pardon the pun – then everybody who crossed them could be neatly repackaged as an organ donor. Up to and including their hearts.'

She looks up. Smetana is staring at her, nose wrinkled. Disgusted. 'This is Colombia, yes?'

'Among others. World Health Organisation has performed tissue samples on organs donated in the US, in Russia and a couple of choice European nations and the organs in question have been traced back to China, India, and most recently, South America. Some may have been willing donors. But not all.'

She touches another icon. Sits back in her chair as an image of a small, torpedo-shaped vessel appears on the screen. It cuts through the water like a shark surfacing to take down a surfer.

'This is a narco sub,' she explains. 'Not quite a submarine but not far off. Cuts through the water and is damn near impossible to pick up on radar or to spot from another ship. Hand-built, but not as basic as you might think. The cartels have been using them to get their product into the US for more than a decade but last year one was picked up not far off the coast of Spain. Point of origin, South America. These things can cross the Atlantic in the right hands. This one in particular had cocaine and heroin worth three million on board. That's a guess, of course. The crew followed orders and scuttled it before it could be recovered for evidence. For all we know it could have been ten times that.'

She pauses again, daring anybody to interrupt her. She gives a little nod. Clicks her finger on the screen. Calls up an image of a round-faced, unremarkable man with curly black hair and glasses. He looks like a junior school teacher: loud shirt, playful smile, a look about him that says: "I'm out of my depth but trying."

'Nine days ago, this gentleman was picked up by detectives in Greenock. Callum Ashcroft. As of late, he's been working in oil rigs and wind farms. He's a consultant drilling engineer, which is every bit as exciting as it sounds. He was arrested when the Drugs Squad raided a known hangout of one of the pubs with links to Pope. His face didn't fit. No record. No obvious reason to be there. Tried too hard when the officers took down his details and they saw through him in a flash. Took him to be interviewed at a separate station and told him they knew what he'd been doing. Not much of a strategy but it tipped him over. He told them the lot. Told them he'd got in further than he ever intended to.'

'Heard that before...' begins Smetana.

'He lives with his wife and children in a horribly out-of-the-way peninsula. I won't try and say it but it's in your documents. She runs a guest house and when he's not away working, he takes tourists out onto the lake.'

'Loch,' says Bizet, automatically, then winces, in apology.

'Okay, the fucking loch. He's a canoe enthusiast, though

it's hard to imagine why anybody would be enthusiastic about it. It's what he does to relax, apparently, and he's found a way to make it into a nice sideline. Chatty fellow. Always talks to the customers. And one day the customers were two lads from Glasgow. Nice as pie, or so he said. Chatted with him like they were the best of friends.

'It wasn't until they were all out on the loch that things turned. They had a proposal for him. They had cargo coming in from abroad – a shipment big enough to put most of Scotland into a stupor for a fortnight. But Border Force knew it was coming. They had to change their route at the last moment and ended up in the area off the Islay where the authorities are intent on sticking up an offshore wind farm. The crew were told to scuttle it in the event of being boarded, but they're a stingy lot, and couldn't bring themselves to. Before they headed for the lifeboat they wrapped as much of the product as they could in tarpaulins and oilskins and tied a trio of great underwater parcels to the channel markers marking out the proposed site.

'It so happened, Ashcroft was due to go and provide a surveyor's report at the self-same site three days later. All he had to do to make sure everybody went home happy, was take a different mode of transport out to the site. He'd had good links with one trawling firm, but this time he would go with a different pilot. He'd do the same job, but he'd turn a blind eye to whatever they got up to, and if anybody asked questions, he could flash his lanyard and his credentials and nobody would have a problem.'

'He agreed?'

'The way he tells it, they implied that it was only going to happen one of two ways. He was going to agree, or they were going to put a bullet in his head, then go visit his family at their little holiday home and kill every one of them where they sat. The alternative to that was getting richer, and having a favour in the bank.'

'Tough call,' says Bizet.

'Went well. Went without a hitch, in fact. And after that, the shipments started being left in the channel rather than brought inland, and every time they needed to be picked up, they had a tame consulting engineer who gave them cover to pick up. He got paid handsomely for it. He said he hated being involved, never wanted any of it, but once he was in he couldn't get out.'

She clicks back on the picture of Pope. Looks up and shakes her head at the unit.

'There's always a fly in the ointment, isn't there? And in this case, it's that Pope isn't immortal. Pope's a poorly man. Pope has cancer in his liver, in his lungs and in his pancreas. Pope is alive by the grace of whatever God he serves, and Police Scotland are rather pleased he is, because when he dies it will be open season as all the other gangs fight over his turf. He hasn't got a successor. He's only got one guaranteed right-hand man – colossal great bruiser whose party piece is smashing the pommel of a claymore into the heads of people who don't do as they're told. Likes to tell people he doesn't need the blade to kill with a sword. No photo on file, but we know he exists.'

'And where do we come in?' asks Smetana, as cautiously as she can.

'Pope controls most of the drugs trade in the West of Scotland and has a hand in almost every territory down as far as Manchester. The cartels have been using Spain and

Portugal as an entry point into Europe for their product. Pope has made the necessary connections to change that. He believes that the West Coast of Scotland is one big pearly gate for bringing cocaine, heroin, meth and fentanyl into the United Kingdom. And from there, on into the eastern European states. He has the connections to make sure people turn a blind eye at the right times, and the cartels certainly have the product to spare. They courted him, by all accounts. Sent their fixer to butter him up.'

'This is Bishop?'

'Yes. And Bishop found that the man who held the keys to the kingdom was dying. Doctors had given him months to live. Even if they could get him a donor for his liver, his heart was packing up. He was falling apart. And he wasn't ready for that.'

She stops. Breathes out, slowly, through pursed lips.

'He agreed to let them use his network, his connections, his entire bloody operation, and all they had to do was save his life.'

She looks at each of them in turn. 'He knew as much about Bishop as Bishop knew about him. Illegal transplants. Unwilling donors of everything up to and including a beating heart. That was his price. He wanted to live.'

'And Ashcroft shared all this?'

'Bishop had insisted on meeting Pope's contacts. Ashcroft had been wined and dined. Pope had grilled him. Wanted to know every conceivable problem they could face and needed to know who was reliable and who wasn't. Ashcroft chatted to him like he would any other business associate. Told him that he lived on the peninsula and that he had too much to lose if it all went wrong. Talked himself into his own problem but impressed Bishop. And Bishop insisted on Ashcroft being involved in future discussions. So he heard the lot. Heard he was now involved in human trafficking for the purposes of illegal organ transplants, along with everything else. Why do you think he spilled his guts when he got picked up?'

'And this is going ahead? They're flying him out to God knows where for a heart transplant taken from some poor bastard...'

'No. Pope doesn't fly. Only been abroad twice and didn't care for it. And he's on so many drugs to stay alive that he probably wouldn't survive a flight. No, it's happening closer to home.'

'In Scotland?' asks Bizet, taken aback.

She sits forward. Presses an icon. An image of a near fairy-tale castle surrounded by woods and water fills the screen. 'This, people, is on the verge of becoming a private hospital. It is six miles from Scotland's most westerly point, and close enough to the sea for people to smell the heroin. And this is where the likes of Pope will soon be able to purchase whatever body parts they feel they're lacking. The couriers bringing the product from South America don't know they're for sale as well. Three couriers per trip, one trip per week, only the captain making the return journey – his crew sold off for parts once they arrive. And those parts sold to the highest bidder...'

'That's grotesque,' says Smetana. 'What's our involvement? What's the objective?'

She nearly smiles at that. She does like enthusiasm. She nods to the back of the room, to where a scrawny man with bad skin and bleeding gums is leaning against a bookcase and regarding them all through a cloud of cigar smoke.

'Team, meet Puccini.'

Heads turn and eyes widen. It's as if God, or perhaps His opposite number, has crept into the briefing room.

'He's going to buy himself a life, just like Pope. He's in the market for body parts. He's our way in.'

He waves, lazily, at the troops. 'I know,' he says, sucking the butt of the cigar. 'Who'd believe it, eh? Me, with my Robert Redford looks...'

The boss considers him. Feels something so unfamiliar she barely recognises it. Feels a genuine warmth as she regards him, broken down and pained: dying in increments because of what he endured after betrayal. And for an instant, she wonders if this will work. If they can play it in such a way that not only will they get a result and stop some very bad people doing very bad things, he might just snatch himself a couple of spare parts along the way.

She touches the final icon on the dossier. Calls up an image of the man at the back of the room, taken in better times. Taken, when he was Detective Chief Inspector Colin Ray, and the world knew him as a hard-as-nails thief-taker who would do whatever it took to get a result.

That man died in the cellar. Died when he was betrayed by his number two.

She hopes that he likes the new character she has created for him: a corrupt shipping clerk and occasional gangster, unfinished business to attend to and morally ambivalent. It isn't much of a stretch.

'Team. Meet Nicholas Roe.'

PART TWO

14

It's a foul night: wet and dark and filled with the roar of the storm. Beyond the garden the trees thrash like fighting stags, the sound fighting for superiority over the suck and surge of the water against the shingly bay across the road and the churn of the rising river beneath the bridge. On such nights I cannot help but think of the crofters who used to make their home here: huddling together in a single room, arthritic fingers struggling to light a peat fire in the cold, black hearth. I know I am a child of my time. I sometimes wonder how much weaker we will become before we turn our backs on softness altogether.

Within our safe, warm space, the children glower at each other across ketchup-crusted plates, debating the great issue of the day.

'It's a skua! Skew-ah! Like, a skewer you put marshmallows on. Or eyeballs. You are so stupid, Poppy. How can you even...?'

'It's pronounced *squah*! Like, I dunno, "car" or "far" or "I hope Atticus gets attacked by a jaguaaaar" or something! Mrs Lewis said it!'

'Then she's wrong as well! Who'd call a bird a squaaaah? That's just dumb.'

'Ask Alexa, if you need proof.'

'I don't need proof, I already know I'm right. Tell her, Mum, tell her she's stupid.'

'Poppy not stupid. Atcus stupid.'

'Mum, did you hear what Lilly said? That's not on. No way. Lilly stupid!'

I've tuned them all out. It's like listening to the shipping forecast: a tapestry of random, indecipherable words that somehow provide a vaguely restful background hum. I only snap back in when Lilly picks up a cold chip from my plate and starts using it to clean her ear.

'Don't do that, baby – it's unhygienic.'

'What's 'ngenic?'

'It means it's dirty. Germs. Yuk.'

'Chips not yuk. Chips 'licious.'

'Not with earwax on them,' says Atticus, scowling. I glance at him. He looks so much like his dad that I want to turn away. I don't let myself. It's hardly his fault. I force myself to see the boy, and not the shadow of the man. It's not easy, with his jaw set as if he's sitting in a Friday night traffic jam. His fingertips are white where they grip the pages of his ornithology book. He and Poppy have been arguing since before I served up an evening meal of slightly overcooked chicken sticks, oven chips and spaghetti hoops. Atticus likes to think of himself as an expert in all things nature-related, having received the *Bumper Book of Birds* for Christmas, not much more than a fortnight ago. Poppy, on the other hand, likes to think of herself as the font of *all* knowledge, and has consistently been top of her class throughout her life. So far the debate has been relatively civil, though Poppy has definitely started changing her grip on her fork.

'Mum, you decide. Skewer or Squah?'

I look at my children, expectant expressions on their faces. I'm in an impossible situation and they know it. But I'm an experienced parent and know how to play this game. I can lie on demand. 'It's both,' I say, apologetically, as I busk like a jazz virtuoso. 'I heard it on the radio – a debate about this very thing. Turns out there's no correct way to say it, and the closest to the original dialect word is actually "squaw" like an Indian woman.'

They both look equally disappointed, though I'm rather pleased with the lie. Poppy doesn't take long to identify an opportunity to remind me that I'm well past my sell-by date as a human being.

'You mean Native American, I'm sure,' she says, primly. 'Indian is a term of oppression. It's like somebody calling you a Jock.'

'People did,' I say, sighing. 'At university, I was a Jock. The Welsh were Taffs. The poor sods from Liverpool were Scouse. Does it always have to be something to worry about?'

'Where would we be if people thought that about the N-word?' asks Poppy, and I find myself wondering, not for the first time, if Greta Thunberg's parents occasionally sent her to her room for being too bloody wholesome by half. 'Anyway, I'm not a Jock. I'm Scottish. A Hebridean, in fact.'

'Shut up Poppy,' grumbles Atticus, returning to his book.

'Yeah, shurrup, Poppy,' says Lilly, following her mummy's lead and spreading her criticisms evenly. She angles her head, looking up at me to see if she's in trouble. Then she does that thing of hers, putting a palm on my cheek and staring into my eyes as if she's been alive for a hundred years. It always manages to slow my pulse. She calms me as readily as she drives me mad.

I glance at the clock. It's 6.40pm. No police yet. No questions. Nothing on the news. The Ardnamurchan Noticeboard on Facebook has been relatively traffic-free, though a few residents further towards the headland have asked each other whether anybody knows the reason for the increased police traffic on the peninsula. I've been only half-present since Mr Roe made his absurd request of me. I've gone through the motions of my reality like an automaton, my whole consciousness devoted to trying to work out what to do. I'm normally pretty good at knowing what I think about things but in this situation I feel as though there are far too many grey morale areas to be able to act decisively.

Yes, Bishop and I were on the verge of being a couple. Yes, it saddens me to think he may have been killed. Yes, I find it revolting that he may have been involved in some criminal enterprise. Yes, I want the police to catch whoever may have done this to him. But no, I don't want to be involved. No, I don't want the island talking about me and my personal life. And no, I don't want to get on the wrong side of the people who may be using the old castle a front for illegal organ transplants. Who the fuck would?

Then there's Mr Roe. I grow irate whenever I think about him, but at the same time there is something about him that makes me want to help him to secure a few more years. He looks in such pain, inside and out. There's something in his eyes that speaks of agonies that nobody should have to withstand. And he showed affection to Lilly. Spoke to me with kindness and respect, right up until the point he pulled out the CS spray. I only half believe his story. Some of it sounds too outlandish, but then I know to my cost that sometimes, remarkable things really do happen to unremarkable people. If things had worked out differently, they could have happened to me. If not for circumstance, I could be somebody else entirely by now.

'What do you think, Lilly?' I whisper in her ear, nuzzling my forehead against hers. 'What's Mummy got to do?'

She seems to consider this. Gives it some intense concentration. When she makes her pronouncement, it's virtually profound. 'Biscuit,' she says, and nods, solemnly, in complete agreement with herself.

I'm laughing, cuddling her tight, when I see the yellow light flash through the darkened glass by the door. Headlights, pulling into the drive. Every cell in my body seems to clench: folding in on themselves like petals at dusk. Atticus gives me a strange look, and I realise I must seem horribly unlike myself. I've only picked at my meal and I've barely engaged with the ceaseless chatter over dinner. I'm a ghost at the feast.

'I'll get it!' yells Poppy, pushing her chair back from the table with a squeak.

'No!' I yell, and it comes out like a blast from a gun. Poppy stops, eyes wide, a hurt expression on her face. I feel so bad that I'd whup myself in front of her if it made a difference. 'Sorry, Poppy, that's way out of order... That sounded really harsh,' I mutter, and I realise my fingers are twitching, like the legs of a dying spider. I make fists, in mimicry of the clenched hand that bangs on the door. I try to make out the identity of the caller from the shape they cast in the frosted glass. They're tall. Wide. Burly, even. Dark coat, pale skin.

'Are you not getting it?' asks Atticus, looking puzzled. 'It might be one of the guests needing something. I'll get it, if you like.'

We stay as we are, frozen in some bizarre tableau. The knock comes again, harder this time, and then the shape at the door is joined by another. I watch as the person outside tries the handle, and I'm thankful that I chose to lock it again when the kids came back from school. Then, with mounting horror, I see the letter box flip open.

'Mum, are you going to...?'

'Ronni! Ronni is that you? It's Theresa. I really need to see you...'

My breath comes out so fast it feels as if somebody has stamped on my chest. I give a hurried nod to Poppy and she runs to the door, fiddling with the key in the lock. In my lap, Lilly gives a little yelp and I realise I've been holding her too tight.

'Sorry, baby,' I whisper. 'Sorry...'

Poppy pulls the door open and Theresa stands in the doorway like a drawing in a horror magazine. She's soaked to the skin. There's green slime on her trousers and up the front of her raincoat and her wiry hair hangs down her pale face like kelp. I begin to stand, to ask what's wrong, and I see the bruise on the left of her face. It's got a pattern to it: a series of straight lines, as if she has been pressed to a crimping iron. She's shaking: her whole being a strangled scream of pain.

'Oh, Theresa, what on earth...?'

Behind her, a large man appears in the doorway. His head almost reaches the frame and his huge barrel chest strains against the material of his shirt. He must be six foot seven at least and his arms look like skinny jeans stuffed with footballs. Theresa steps into the house and he ducks to follow her inside. As the light finds his features I see he's probably somewhere under thirty, and handsome with it. He looks a bit lost, as if he's embarrassed to be here. He's wearing a pale pink shirt under a sensible waterproof coat, and I realise that despite his size, he's not to be feared. He looks like a bear in a story for children, trying not to knock over anything valuable or cause anybody fright.

'Sorry, sorry,' mumbles Theresa, dripping water onto the floor. She lurches forward, moving as if her feet are nailed to the floor. 'This is Lachlan. He picked me up. Bodily, in fact! Helped me. Brought me here. He's got friends on Coll. Missed the ferry just for me. I couldn't ask him to take me all the way home... Told him to stop in here...'

'Found her by the forest,' says Lachlan, in a low, self-conscious growl. 'Thought she was a deer. She didn't want to go to hospital. Said to come here... She said that already, sorry...'

I look around for something I can offer my unexpected guests – something that might help the situation. I'm breathing heavily. I want to grab the kids and turn them away from all this. Want to turn myself too. I spot a towel drying on the radiator and put Lilly down so I can grab it and hand it to Theresa. She takes it gratefully. Up close I can see she's been crying. There's a cut on her lip and the bruise on her face is already swelling up. I look down at her feet and have to stop myself from exclaiming out loud. She's wearing borrowed boots – huge great walking shoes, their laces trailing. She follows my gaze, and I see her bottom lip give a quiver.

'They took my shoes,' she says, in a whisper. 'Lachlan loaned me these, to keep me warm.' She shivers, a great tremble that seems to shake every part of her. I find myself reaching out, an arm around her shoulder, pulling her in close. I feel an overwhelming sense of pity at seeing somebody so tough and indomitable transformed into such a pitiful, tear-streaked mess. I've known her since I arrived in this part of the world and she's not the sort to scare easily. Right now, she looks terrified. Looks broken.

'They?' I ask, sharply. I look up at Lachlan, who has his head bowed. Atticus appears at my side, holding Lilly, and Poppy slips in beside them, an audience to this strange play taking place in the kitchen.

'She wouldn't say,' rumbles Lachlan. 'I didn't want to ask too many questions. Not sure it's my business. But I couldn't leave her…'

'You did right,' I say, though I don't really know whether I believe any of what I'm saying. 'Theresa, come inside now. Let's get you warmed up and put some ice on that bruise, eh? Lachlan, do you need your boots back? Where are you staying? Theresa, put your weight on me. It's fine, it's fine…'

She's crook-backed, hobbling, as I help her to the kitchen table and she slips painfully onto one of the high-backed chairs. She gives a nod of thanks. 'A glass of water would be nice,' she says, looking up at me like a child. She slides her gaze to Lachlan. 'Your boots,' she says, dreamily, as if she's taken a bang to the head. 'Here, sorry… Thanks…'

She pushes the toe of one boot against the heel of the other, and I hear a noise like paper tearing before the boot hits the floor. And then she shrieks. It's a primal sound; a full-throated screech of pain, as if somebody has just torn grooves in her flesh with a dull blade.

I glance down at her feet. Raise my hand to my mouth.

Her feet are all blisters and glistening pink meat. Across the arch of her foot, the skin hangs loose: ruined flesh drooping low like popped bubble gum.

'Oh Jesus,' I say, and turn to the children. They are staring, disgusted and transfixed. Poppy's eyes are wide as saucers, and she reaches out for her brother as if he were a life buoy in rough seas. 'Go to your rooms, right now – go to your rooms!'

I look up at Lachlan, who's staring at the floor, his big face suddenly bloodless and sickly. 'She needs bandages, not your bloody boots!'

'I didn't know what to do,' he mutters, ashamed of himself. 'She wanted to get away from there. She was trying to walk – barefoot on the road. She wouldn't listen…'

'He's okay is Lachlan,' mumbles Theresa, in a voice filled with tears and pain. 'Let him go. He's got places to be. Thanks, lad. You needn't have stopped. Glad you did.'

He stands there like a naughty schoolboy and I realise he's waiting for me to dismiss him. I've got my hands on my hips, my hair falling in my face, my heart thumping as if it's going to pop, and suddenly all I want is to lock the back door again and drag the story out of Theresa. Who's done this to her? Why?

I answer my own question even as she starts to speak. I know where she was when these things happened.

'The castle,' she says, through gritted teeth. 'I went to talk to them about knocking your wall down…'

'Oh, Theresa,' I say, and I feel Lachlan move away towards

the door – the light shifting as his great big outline becomes smaller. I hear his shoulders rub against the doorframe. Hear the soft "snick" of the door closing behind him.

I turn Theresa to face me. Hold her gaze. I want her to know she's safe now. That whatever she has endured, it's over. And then I think about Mr Roe, and Bishop, and a severed head in a lobster pot, and recognise that any such utterances would be a lie.

'They told me not to tell,' she whispers, and she looks down at her ruined foot, regarding it as if it were something alien to her. The other foot remains encased in the too-big boot. Slowly, she reaches down and levers it off with her thumb. This time there is no scream. She simply starts to shake as she stares at what has been done to her.

Each toe is dripping with ink-red blood. The tips are missing their nails, and each is turning a gory blue-black, like over-ripe bananas.

'Theresa,' I say, and put my hand out to comfort her. She pulls back as if expecting a blow. She shakes her head, violently.

'I didn't mean to see,' she whispers. 'Didn't mean to make them cross. I shouldn't have peeked. I know that now. Shouldn't have peeked...'

I look up at her, all helpless pity and silent rage.

'What did you see?' I ask, my words coming out in a rush. 'Talk to me. Theresa, you're safe.'

'Men,' she says, turning terrified eyes upon me. 'Hooked to machines. Wires coming out of them like they were robots...' She stops talking as something surfaces in her memory. She shudders, her eyes brimming with tears.

'And eyes,' she whispers. 'Glass urns full of eyeballs, like gobstoppers in a jar...'

She folds in on herself. Gives in to the misery and lets me pull her toward me. And as she shakes and sobs and the pain in her feet sends knives of agony through her whole body, I find myself looking out through the darkened glass towards Mr Roe's quarters. And I feel my lip curl so that for just the merest moment, I am glaring out with bared teeth.

At once, my thoughts become absolutely clear. None of the other questions or concerns are important.

For this, somebody is going to pay.

15

We talk in the kitchen for an hour – Atticus in nominal charge of his two sisters and overseeing a hastily convened movie-and-popcorn evening, which involves the trio huddling around my laptop and arguing over which movie to watch until it's too late to watch any at all.

She tells me how the evening started, and how it has ended here, in my kitchen, with me slathering ointment into her blistered feet and trying not to gag as I look at the ruined stumps of her toes.

'You should be in hospital,' I keep telling her. 'They'll get infected. You could lose them, Theresa…'

She swallows three painkillers with a swig of tea, and gives me a look that could turn sand to glass. She'll go when she's good and ready. She needs to talk. Needs to get all the bad stuff out of herself before it festers and turns into something worse.

I ask questions at first, but soon I accept that I'm just slowing her down. I let her tell it her own way, and resist the urge to butt in until she's done. Only then do I let the angry tears fall, and bare my teeth in outrage and disgust.

★

'There were lights on at the castle. And I knew I should keep my nose out – just get myself home and leave things be. There was a north-westerly rolling in; the roads would be hard work. But I liked the idea of playing the hero, didn't I? Fair imagined myself coming to work tomorrow and telling you I'd got it all sorted. Those bastards in the van had seen the error of their ways and were going to be writing you a nice fat cheque to cover the cost of your wall. And I'll admit it, I didn't mind the idea of having a nosey about the place and a decent excuse to knock on the door. Posh private hospital, you said? Might have seen myself a film star, or seen Cher in there having her next facelift. So I did it on a whim.

'I thought I'd got lucky that the big gates were open. Pulled straight in off the road and was out front of the place before I'd even thought about it properly. I figured it would be a proper den of activity, if they're close to opening, but it's not much better than it was when I had a peek through the trees back in the summer. Still overgrown, still those nasty single-glazed windows, curtains hanging as if somebody's been swinging from them. And not a light in the place, saving the one that flicked on when I got out of the car. You know me, I'm not a scared person. I've buried three husbands and I'm not sure all of them were dead, and I don't let life give me the willies, and you can take that any way you want.

'But it was a bit scary, standing there in the dark in front of a big empty castle, and I wouldn't have knocked on the door if it wasn't for the fact that a big shiny black car had followed me up the drive. I don't mean they knew I was there, I mean they'd come in straight afterwards, and suddenly I didn't really want to be explaining myself to strangers in the dark on my own. So I got back in the car and figured

I'd leave it for another day. The car went past the front of the house and went around the back without ever noticing I was there, so I headed back towards the gates.

'Trouble was, the buggers had locked them after themselves hadn't they? So I was stuck. Padlocked the damn things, so all I could do was drive back up to the house and see if I could find some kindly soul to let me out. And that's what I did. Drove the way they'd gone, around the side of the house and around to what would have been the domestic quarters back when it was new. Two white vans, a big Porsche Cayenne, and a couple of fancy cars, all parked up in front of this big long building.

'I pulled in and got out and I swear my heart was beating like the clappers, and I had to do that thing where you want people to hear you but you don't want to startle them, so I was walking like my feet were wearing concrete slippers, and peering in between the curtains trying to spy somebody. Anyway, I tried a couple of doors and windows and even started shouting a few hellos, and finally I saw a light coming from a window right at the very back of the house. I don't know why but suddenly I was too frightened to make a din, and I just had myself a little look through the window so I knew what it was I was going to be disturbing.

'And I saw them. Two men. They were skinny and dark-skinned. I don't want to say the wrong word, but they were black without being really black, if you get me. Like, Asian, I suppose, but maybe that's not right either. But they were both laid there on these hospital beds. Do they call them "gurneys"? I'm not sure. But they were strapped down, and both of them had bandages around their eyes, and they had drips going in and out of them – I swear, it was like they were hooked up to something robotic. And the looks on their faces, Ronni. They were in such pain, and so scared, and as soon as I saw it I half fell over backwards, and I ran back to the car so fast you'd think there were dogs after me.

'Of course I was in such a state that I pulled out of the parking space like a lunatic and went straight into one of the big posh cars. And then I'm sitting there listening to this alarm going off, and lights are coming on, and the next thing this huge great brute with a face like a headstone is dragging me out of the car like we're mortal enemies, and he slaps me so hard across the back of the head that I felt my knees go. Next thing I'm hearing an English voice tell a Scotsman that he's over-reacting, it's not a problem, that I'll have friends and family nearby, and then they agree that I need to know how important it is not to tell anybody what I saw. And they did this.

'Told me my own life story, they did. I can barely remember what the nasty bastard looked like but he sat in front of me while I was squirming like a toddler on this rickety metal chair, and he tells me the names of my grandkids and my old mam and says that if I ever want to start causing them trouble, then what I'm about to experience will happen to them. And they won't be so nice about it. Then I just heard that sound you hear when you pour boiling water on an ant's nest, and then there's a thud-thud-thud and somebody I can't make out is hitting a hammer and a chisel against my toes, and I'm screaming in a way that would have my old dad spinning in his grave.

'And the next thing I'm walking down the middle of the main road, and that big handsome fella was picking me up, and all I wanted was to be here, because if I'm honest, love, this is where I feel most at home, and by Christ I'm going to make sure they get what's coming to them for this. I can't tell you what they looked like, but I know the cars and I know the way the big one smelled and the Englishman had a way of talking that sounded like he wasn't long for this world, and whatever happens next I want you to know that you don't need to ever blame yourself. You're a good lass, Ronni, and you might not always like people to know it but you've got a heart of gold under there, and I know to my bones you're hard as nails as well.

'Begging your pardon, but I think I'll spend the night. Is that okay? Those painkillers are kicking in, and it wouldn't do me any harm to have a rest. I'm not bleeding, am I? It's just that, the more I think on it, the more I remember this sizzle, after they were done – and this single red circle, like the lighter from a car. I think they stopped the bleeding. Why do you think they did that, Ronni? Why do you think they did any of it...'

Only when she's done, when she dissolves and lays her head down on her arms, do I decide what will happen next. She will stay the night. Tomorrow, we will go to the hospital. Go to the police. But tonight, now, I want to know if there is any part of Nicholas Roe worth saving. He's in the pub. That's his routine. His room's empty. Whatever truths he's concealing are there for the taking. He knows the men who did this to my friend. He wants me to keep my mouth shut so they can give him another chance at life. He has a picture of a man's severed head on his mobile phone, and he's desperate for me not to tell the police the little I know.

I need answers. And I'll do whatever it takes to get them.

16

When we bought the croft, we decided the barn was just big enough to be converted into three tiny guest houses. We bill them as "bijou", though I can't profess to really know what that means. They're cosy, one-bedroomed affairs: a bed, chair, a couple of sticks of furniture and enough room at the back for a toilet and shower cubicle. We do okay out of what people call the "boutique" market, though I've never understood why people are so desperate to leave their four-bedroomed houses to pay extravagant sums for a night dossing down in something not much bigger than a walk-in closet.

Mr Roe has been staying in Number 3. Beside him is Mr Paretsky and the Truloves are in the slightly larger chalet-style lodge at the far end. I've seen little of them since they arrived. I've heard from Theresa that they've taken to going to the Kilchoan Lodge on an evening and drinking gin and bitter lemon while playing Connect Four. Their breakfast dishes are always placed in the wicker basket as requested, though whether they eat the food or give it to the pine martens is anybody's guess. I don't have to guess with Mr Paretsky. He'd eat whatever you left out for him – up to and including deep-fried pine marten.

'Hello,' I say, knocking at the door just hard enough to wake any spiders that may be nesting in the keyhole. 'Housekeeping...'

Behind me, the house is all blackness and right angles; the doors and windows closed, the curtains pulled fast. The rain still comes in from a dozen different directions and I almost lost my fight as I ran across the lawn to the lodges, casting a huge silhouette as the security light flashed on. I'm soaked and shivering, but I'm not turning back. I know I won't sleep again until I feel as though I'm in control of what is happening to my life and my home.

'Hello,' I whisper, again, rubbing the soles of my trainers on the coarse welcome mat outside Number 3. 'Please don't be in...'

There's no answer from inside. I stand on the front step for just long enough to make it seem that I'm waiting for the occupant to make themselves presentable. I don't know if I'm being watched but I have a feeling I should behave from now on as though I am. And right now, at just gone 9pm on a weekday evening, I'm simply the owner of a guest house, popping in to one of the properties to make sure that the occupant has everything they need. The fact that I know him to be nine miles up the road getting pissed on cognac is neither here nor there.

Damply, coldly, I fiddle with the keys. The wooden door has swollen since it was first installed and every guest has complained about the difficulties in accessing their room. I fumble about for what seems like an eternity, wincing into the cold and the rain and the dark, before I feel the key turn in the lock and I half stumble into the cool, black room.

I reach out a hand and turn on the light, which takes a moment to flicker into life.

Even now I'm proud of what we did with the old barn. All of my guests are impressed when they first switch on the light. It's warm and snug and has a timelessness that speaks to the particular proclivities of whoever rents it out. To some it's a perfect spot for romance; to others a secluded get-away-from-it-all sanctuary tailor-made for creativity. To the couple who stayed last Easter, it was the ideal location in which to finally make good on eighteen years of office-based sexual tension – finally consummating their relationship with an abandon that threatened to shake the squirrels from their nests. Callum and I had heard them from indoors, and had taken their pleasure in one another as a reminder about how lucky we were to sleep in one another's arms most nights.

By the time they were done, we were just getting started. At the time, I'd felt brazen and lusty: delighting in the ardour my husband and I still felt when we reached out for one another in the dark. I've often wondered whether he was already fucking Kimmy at that point – whether he ever entered me still reeking of another woman's desire.

I close the door behind me. Lock it. Push my damp hair from my face and try to collect my thoughts. I need to know about this man. I find it impossible to believe that he has been truthful with me. His talk of Bishop – his candour about the nature of the new facility at the castle: none of it fits with what was done to Theresa. I need answers. Everything I've learned about Nicholas Roe suggests he's a chimera; a fantasy. And as for Bishop, I don't even know his first name. I suddenly realise that I've blundered into a situation that could have hellish consequences for those I love, and that it's already cost Theresa dear. If I go through his things, I know I'm likely to stumble deeper into whatever the hell this is, but some stubborn part of me needs to understand things before I decide how next to act.

I look around, wondering where to start. He keeps the place neat and tidy – that's for sure. It looks like it did when we first opened to paying guests: rough-plastered walls hung with great moody stag prints and maps of the peninsula. The light is set in a halo of pleached antlers and the bed is covered with a purply tartan throw. Mr Roe's solitary suitcase sits in front of the neat pine wardrobe and on the bedside table is a paperback book, its pages splayed open. There's a water glass too, and I remember Theresa telling me that she had seen Steradent tablets in the tiny bathroom cabinet, along with whatever else he was taking. I find myself putting the pieces together. He's getting ready for surgery. He's keeping himself alive until the operation happens, and in the event that it goes wrong, he's getting in his pleasures where he can.

I start with the suitcase. It's thoroughly nondescript: a grey-black without a lock. Inside, a slapdash collection of T-shirts, underwear and padded shirts, designed to keep out the harshest of Scottish winters. I rummage around in each pocket and find nothing more interesting than a forgotten packet of silica gel and half a ripped beer mat – its torn white edge showing three digits of a longer sequence: 078. What the hell am I meant to do with that? I turn it over and see if it's got anything more revealing on the rear. All I can make out is a lurid yellow and purple combination, together with a stencilled insignia. It means nothing to me. I take out my phone and snap a picture, just in case, then tuck the scrap of card back where I found it.

Under his bedclothes I find his pyjamas: a white T-shirt and a pair of black jogging bottoms. It makes me unexpectedly sad when I look at the label and see that they are for somebody aged thirteen.

The book is called *Necropolis*, written by one David Philip Lamb. It tells the story of Derrick Ovenden, a Glasgow gangster who ruled like a Sicilian godfather for the best part of forty years. I haven't read it, but I know the work. Callum devoured it in two sittings when it came out a few years back. Ovenden was definitely the real thing. He had a habit of crucifying his enemies and he ran his empire as if he were a branch of government – putting contracts out to tender and opening sealed bids from different assassins before appointing a particular contractor to take out his problems. I pick up Mr Roe's copy and leaf through it, holding it up to the light. I let it sit on my palm, letting it drop open on a random page. I read what Mr Roe pored over the last time it was in his hands, and feel sick as I realise what I am seeing.

'...when you mess with somebody's fingers or toes, you mess with their whole being. Don't get me wrong, when you slash a fucker's mouth you know you're messing them up for life, but if you hurt somebody's fingers or feet you know that even years from now, when they're trying to tie their laces on a cold morning, they'll look back at the mistakes they made, and wish it had all been so very different...'

I put the book back where I found it. Glance towards the door. I don't know what I'm looking for but there must be something that gives an indication of what sort of man I've allowed to stay in my home. Quietly, I start opening the drawers at the base of the wardrobe. Two pairs of socks, neatly balled, and a chunky, cable-knitted jumper. I pick it up, gently, and breathe it in. It hasn't been worn since it was last laundered – it smells of soap flakes and heather and the background whiff of stale smoke.

I look around me, wondering what the hell I should do next. I realise just how vulnerable I've left myself – how many strangers have passed through my home. Why haven't I asked more questions? He didn't arrive in a car – hasn't parked a vehicle anywhere nearby. So where are his other possessions? His camera, binoculars, his waterproof clothes? Has he made a friend who will help him store it all? Or has he decided to cut his losses and get rid of anything that may be stained with another man's blood.

I sit down on the bed, suddenly tired and pissed off. I think of Bishop, and find myself wondering whether I'm simply the victim of some elaborate joke. Maybe Bishop and Mr Roe play this scene out at guest houses up and down the country. Maybe this is how they get their kicks. I realise I'm fighting the urge to pray. I no longer wear a cross but my fingers are at my throat and would be pulling at my golden cross were it not at the bottom of my jewellery box on the dresser. In such moments, prayers are little more than wishes: directed at a deity instead of a genie. But they provide a comfort of sorts, and suddenly all I want is for Bishop to be okay and for none of this to have happened.

My gaze falls on the skirting board by the bed, just at

the place where the flex from the bedside lamp runs down to the floor. I have a landlady's eye for any imperfections. And there is a little smear of dark on the white-painted wood. Moreover, there is a fine, barely visible smattering of dust upon the floor.

I squat down. Flick on the bedside lamp and peer at the little speck of wrongness. I adjust my angle. The skirting board has been pulled away from the wall. Whatever has been used has slipped, streaking the paintwork. It has sent up a tiny cloud of paint and wood. Somebody has made themselves a hiding place.

I feel my pulse start to race, looking around for something I can use to lever up the wood. I can't seem to quell the impulse to dig deeper. Sense dictates that I pause; think things through – decide how best to act without causing myself more problems. But I've never been one for sense.

There's a teaspoon in amongst the tea-making facilities at the bottom of the wardrobe and I dart to the open door, retrieving it from the cup full of teabags and sachets of instant coffee. In moments I'm down on my knees again, wiggling the tip of the teaspoon into the tiny crack in the wall, giving a little grunt of satisfaction as it disappears into the space behind. I pulled and push, wiggle and yank, and then there is the glorious sound of a fixture coming loose, and the board is skittering away across the floor and I'm peering into a small black space behind it. There's a smell of damp and empty air; something that makes me think of abandoned cellars. I tilt the bedside lamp, throwing some light into the darkness, and give something between a grimace and a smile as I spot the bulging shape inside. I reach in, automatically. There could have been mousetraps, I tell myself, despairing. Could have been a bloody scorpion...

I look at my discovery. It's black and plastic and looks to my inexpert eyes horribly outdated – the sort of thing I'd have asked for as a Christmas present in my mid-teens. I turn it over in my hands, feeling the clunky buttons beneath my fingertips. As I do I feel a piece of the main casing come away and it falls through my fingers to the floor. I look down and retrieve the length of black plastic and realise it's a pen, of sorts: like something stolen from a book-keeper's or Argos. I fumble with the buttons on the side, trying to find some way to turn the damn thing on, and jab with the metal nib at what I take to be the screen. My index finger finds a small round cavity along the smoothest edge. I touch the pen to the hole, then to what must be the charging point, but it remains frustratingly dead in my hands.

Holding it to the light, I turn it over and over, searching for some indication that this belongs to the lodge's current occupant and hasn't been left by a previous guest. By the light of the lamp, I see scratches by the charging port: scratches left by a fragile or drunken person trying to make the connection. The same sort of evidence of pained fingers that left the scratch on the skirting board.

I turn the pen in my hands. Click my tongue against my mouth, a tick-tock of frustrated thought. I press the buttons in random sequences, two at a time, one at a time, but it remains steadfastly blank. I get back on my knees and scooch back to the hole in the wall. I reach in, feeling gooseflesh rise as I emerge, imagining all the different things that could scuttle out of the darkness. I root around, touching dirt, stone, thick twirls of cobwebbed dust, and then my knuckle touches something stuck to the inside of the remaining panel. It's small – no bigger than a postage stamp, and I have to prise it free with a nail. I pull it free between finger and thumb. It's a SIM card: old; black and gold – no shape I've seen before, but unmistakably some piece of technical wizardry. I look at the phone again, and tug at a tiny crack on the rim of the plastic. I put my nail into the groove and slide out a small panel, perfectly shaped for the card. I put it where it wants to go, and slide the panel back again. It moves slickly – far more than I would have expected from such a clunky piece of Nineties machinery.

The screen lights up; a soft grey, overlaid with green writing. It's code, a thousand different symbols and letters streaking across the display as if somebody has fallen asleep with their face on a keyboard.

Excited now, my pulse thudding, sweat greasing the backs of my knees, I jab with the pen at the screen. The digits stop scrolling. A cursor flashes, a simple icon waiting for a password. There's no keyboard I can make out, and the screen doesn't offer any obvious way to enter a code. I chew my lip, and wonder how long I have been out here. Should I put it back? Run home? Or take it with me? He won't be home for ages, surely. I could sit in the kitchen, think it through properly, lock the door. Could call Callum. The police.

I touch the pen to the screen. Distractedly doodle a shape on the glass. The lettering changes before my eyes. A warning sign flashes up. This is encrypted software, it tells me. I have three more attempts to get it right.

I want it to stop, suddenly. Want to hear a car pull up and give myself an excuse to throw it all back in the hole in the earth and run back to the house. I don't. Instead, I look at the nib of the pen. It's metallic. The screen is a hard glass. And when I doodled on the screen the machine acted as if I'd made an attempt at entering the code. I hold up the tablet to the light. Faintly, scored against the surface of the glass, I can make out a circle, and four straight lines: a child's drawing of a full, glowing sun. I copy the pattern with the nib. Hold my breath.

The screen fills with colour. Suddenly I'm staring at a series of document files, laid out neatly on a blue screen. They're dated: neatly labelled. I touch the pen to one at random, and find another series of files. I touch one at random. In a moment pixels become an image. A face. A pretty woman in her mid-twenties with dark roots and blonde hair and a stud in her top lip. She's talking on a phone, sitting outside a bar. There's water behind her. Posh flats. She's with somebody. He's facing away from the camera but there's a set to his jaw and a tightness to his shoulders that seems suddenly more than familiar.

I open the next image. See him. See him reaching out across the table, holding her hand, dark eyes staring into hers, a look on his face that I don't recognise, even as I stare into features as familiar to me as my own.

It's Callum. My Callum.

Holding Kimmy's hand.

The blood rushes in my head the way the floodwater surges over the bridge. What does it mean? Why does Mr Roe have a picture of my husband? Why does he have a picture of the skank I booted him out over?

Through the drawn curtains, a sudden flickering light. Somebody has activated the motion sensor.

Desperately, my fingers trembling, I shove the gadget back in the hole and wedge the skirting board up against the wall. I look around and know that I haven't left any signs of disturbance, but if it's Roe it won't make a difference. I'm in the room! And I don't know how to get out without being seen.

I hear the sound of a key in the lock. Hear the curses and grunts of an ungreased lock and a wooden door swollen larger than the frame by rain.

I brace myself. Then I hear the sound of objects being moved from the lodge next door. Paretsky. I let out a huge great breath of relief, and slip out the door, pulling it tight shut behind me and locking it all in one fluid motion. I move across the grass, my chest heaving.

Stop, dead, as I realise my mistake. The SIM card. I've left the SIM card in the device.

I turn back. Move back the way I've come.

From the street, a clatter of broken glass. Quickly, I creep to the edge of the house and peer round, looking through the trees to where the road disappears and the shingly beach begins. It's too dark and stormy to make any of it out tonight, but I can see the small, wiry shape that stumbles over the recycling boxes as he staggers his way home.

Mr Roe. Drunk as a skunk and a halo of grey cigar smoke around his head.

Silently, I unlock the back door, and slip into the kitchen, closing it behind me and leaning with my forehead against the glass.

At the kitchen table, Atticus sits chatting with a round, bald-headed man in Police Scotland uniform. I know him. PC Eoin Stewart. He looks up from dipping a biscuit in a mug of tea and his immediate reaction looks a lot like panic. He doesn't know what to say to me. Doesn't know what to do. And then a strikingly attractive woman in an expensive suit is walking through from the living room; her hairstyle more expensive than my car. And the expression on his face is pure relief.

'Mrs Ashcroft,' she says, with a smile that doesn't reach her eyes. 'I'm Detective Chief Inspector Emma Cressey. Do you perhaps have a moment?'

And suddenly, all I can hear is breaking bottles, and the thunder of my own rushing blood.

17

Ten weeks ago
Mount Alexander, Camaghael, Fort William

'**B**loody hell.'
The woman driving the blue Volkswagen Bora jumps forward in her seat. She hadn't known her passenger was awake. For the past ninety miles he has been doing an excellent impression of a shop dummy carved from discount ham. He's been sleeping with his eyes open, gazing deadly out of the grimy window as the urban landscape of Glasgow Central has gradually given way to greenery and soft rain. It has been a slow, tiring journey and she has kept the radio off in deference to the presence of her companion. She has had to fight an innate urge to chatter and to point out interesting sights.

Now, on the verge of reaching their actual destination, he has announced himself conscious, though she can see no obvious reason for the choice of words. They are down a dirt track, bounded on one side by a rusty chain-link fence and on the other by a scabby wall of trees and dead vegetation. The shortbread-and-thistles of Fort William's touristy areas are nowhere to be found in this out-of-the-way location on the very outskirts of town. In the distance, she can make out the snow-topped peaks of a jagged mountain range, but the immediate view beyond the glass is so dispiriting that the far-off panorama seems somehow unreal.

'Sorry?'

He shakes his head, readjusting himself and sitting up straighter. 'No. No you're not sorry. No manners now, love. No politeness. You're hard, right. You don't give a fuck. I say something you don't understand, it's not your fault, it's mine. Yes?'

She looks across at him. Dirty trousers, unwashed shirt, harlequin-patterned jumper and a greasy donkey jacket. She feels as though she's picked up a hitch-hiking tramp.

'Don't mumble, ya wee fuck.'

He smiles, showing mismatched teeth. The yellow ones are real. The gleaming white ones have been drilled into the bone, though they move around in his soggy gums like poorly hammered tent pegs.

'Was there a reason for the "bloody hell"?' asks the driver.

'Just occurred to me I'm in Scotland. With the Scottish.'

'What does that mean?'

'I've got a lot of Jock jokes. It's going to be a battle.'

'We can laugh at ourselves. You might get a few Englishmen-are-wankers jokes in return. Difference is, we won't be joking.'

'And you'd be right. We are wankers.'

'Takes the fun out of it if it's not news to you.'

'Take a coach trip to London. You'll find a load of arrogant pricks who still haven't been told.'

They turn a corner and the broken-down fence becomes something sturdier: a long line of corrugated iron panels nailed to big imposing posts. It points the way to where a low, pebble-dashed grey building hunkers down as if hiding from the wind, and which conceals the entrance to a large parking area. The surface is all craters and potholes: loose shingle and broken glass. Further ahead, another chain-link fence, barring access to a big flat space given over to dozens of wrecked cars – roofs smashed in, bumpers torn off: a mechanical graveyard full of metal bones and rusty innards.

'There,' says the driver, slowing down.

A dark-haired man is leaning against the door of the outbuilding, staring up at the sky as if in prayer. He still has his eyes closed as he turns towards them, delaying the moment for as long as he can.

'Not bad-looking. You might need to behave yourself.'

'Get tae fuck.'

'Not bad. Bit more spit when you talk though, eh? Bit more froth between the teeth.'

'I'm still being me.'

'Oh, right.'

They pull in to the empty parking area, bouncing over the pitted surface. A moment later, the back doors open and the man climbs in, announcing himself with a sigh.

'Don't start off like that, mate. Put a downer on proceedings. We've come a long way for this.'

'Sorry, I...'

'And don't start with a sorry. Can't stand apologists.' He turns in his seat. Gives him a once-over, then nods. 'I'm Nicholas Roe. I'm not, of course, but that's who the fuck I am for now. And you're Callum Ashcroft.'

A nod. He's pale. There's a darkness under his eyes. He's huddled inside his coat as if trying to disappear.

'This is Kimmy,' says Roe, nodding at the driver. 'She's a bad girl. Bad as they get. She's been working with one of Pope's rivals for a good while now but she's seen the light. She has special skills. She has connections. Connections that Bishop might need, and that Pope will appreciate. She's also your bit of skirt, and you're going to introduce her to the people you know.'

Ashcroft looks at Kimmy. She has her hair scraped back tight and there are gold studs in her dimples and top lip.

'You're a copper?'

Roe laughs, shaking his head. 'Well, you're going to be shit at this, I can tell. Should I just shoot her now and save you the bother? What's the matter, mate? Is it a syndrome, or something? There must be a name for it. I mean, nobody's allowed to say "moron" anymore, but it's the neatest fit.'

'I'm sorry… I'm nervous, I've never done anything like this before.'

'No, I hear you. I was the same up until I killed my first bastard. Figured it would be harder than it was. Now, take a breath, and do as I tell you. Say hello.'

'Hello.'

'Wrong. That's not how you talk to a Kimmy. Kimmy here, she's been through it. No time for soft soaping. No time for a gentleman or a romantic. She likes a man who bangs her head off the cistern when he's enjoying himself behind her – know what I'm saying? So, put some bass in your voice, mate. If you're going to be our way in, I need some faith in you and right now I wouldn't trust you to put your shoes on the right feet. Just take a breath. Get yourself together.'

Kimmy gives him what she hopes is an encouraging look. She's only partly in character. She can turn it on when required. Right now she's still mostly a detective constable, on secondment to the NCA. Even with the hair and the jewellery and the semi-permanent tattoos of former lovers' names tattooed on her left breast, she can't be Kimmy until she has to be. Every time she puts on the character it seems to eat a little bit of what lies beneath.

'I have a wife,' says Callum, quietly. 'She doesn't deserve to get caught up in this.'

'Wouldn't life be peachy if we only got what we deserved, eh?'

'Whatever happens, you have to keep them safe. You have to promise me that.'

'How would that help, lad? What's my promise worth to you? How about you make a promise to yourself instead. Promise yourself you'll do everything in your power to make things right. Promise yourself you'll do whatever it takes to put the bad men away before they can make good on their threats.'

For a moment, there is something like sincerity in Roe's eyes. Something flares: some spark of humanity. Then it is gone.

Callum turns to Kimmy. 'You all right, doll? That's some tan ye've got yersel'. Must have cost a fortune to fill a bath with that much Irn-Bru...'

Roe looks across at Kimmy, who gives a begrudging nod. 'It's a start.'

18

I keep a benign expression on my face: something that suggests I'm a little taken aback, but happy to help. Of course, Officer, not a problem, Officer – this sort of thing doesn't happen to nice middle-class ladies like me, Officer. I catch a glimpse of my reflection and realise I look more like a blow-up doll. I force myself to relax.

The cop is making herself comfortable, sitting down at the table and waiting for me to finish banging about with cups and saucers and the fancy milk frother in the kitchen. Coffee for her, tea for him. He takes sugar, she doesn't. I listen out for the sounds of conversation coming through from the next room but the only thing I can hear is the background static of the children: Poppy and Lilly arguing over who is the bigger idiot and who's the more amazing, interspersed with the occasional instruction from their big brother to shut up and move over.

Theresa is asleep in the room that used to serve as a study, and which is more of a junk room now. She's slumbering away beneath a couple of quilted blankets, her feet elevated with a mound of cushions and enough painkillers in her system to numb the agonies until morning. She was already slumbering when the police knocked at the door, leaving

Atticus to go completely against my instructions and let them in. If they know she's here, they're not saying.

'That one's yours,' I say, brightly, placing a poor attempt at a latte down in front of the senior officer and shoving a hand-painted mug towards the local. I sit down, pushing my damp hair from my face. Force myself to stay calm. I'm home. I've done nothing wrong. I've nothing to feel guilty about and I don't have to tell anybody anything if I don't want to.

'I saw a lot of police cars zooming past earlier on,' I say, brightly, talking to the PC. 'Wondered if it was an exercise or if there had been an accident or something. Weather took a turn, didn't it? And that bend at Kilchoan can be awful at this time of year...'

PC Stewart looks uncomfortable again. Shoots a look at the other officer, who's staring at me the way a botanist might consider a particularly interesting growth of leaf mould. I can meet most people's eyes, but the detective is both hard-faced and chillingly beautiful: a pearlescent blue iceberg in glacial water, entrancing and lethal. She has intensely green eyes and in the moment before I turn away I drink in enough of her appearance to be able to draw her from memory. She's cinematically attractive, and her eyebrows and teeth have clearly benefited from some serious treatment. She looks like she's just walked out of a salon, and her dark suit, pinstriped and slightly flared around designer kitten heels, has clearly been tailored. Her fingers are unadorned with any jewellery but her nails are perfect, and painted a deep shade of plum. She's tanned, and where her elegant neck disappears into the creamy collar of her blouse, a single gold rose hangs from the end of a fine chain. I wouldn't let Callum sit within five yards of her, and never downwind. She smells wonderful.

'Veronica Ashcroft,' she says, her hands folded in her lap. 'Ronni, yes?'

'Yeah, Veronica sounds a bit too formal...'

'Three kids, am I right?'

'Yes, Atticus, Poppy, Lilly...'

'You run your home as a guest house, yes? Three little lodges for holidaymakers out the back. Your husband, Callum – he did most of the work, so I'm told.'

'Well, I like to think I helped,' I say, determined to keep things friendly until I can work out what on earth to say.

'I understand your husband is working away at the moment,' she says, tilting her head and keeping her eyes fixed on mine. I fight the urge to look away.

'Don't be coy about it,' I say. 'You know this much, you'll know we're separated. I'm sure our local constable filled you in on all that. Can I ask why you're here?'

PC Stewart shifts in his seat. Slurps his tea and yelps, pained, as he scalds his lip and chin. 'The DCI here is with a different force, Mrs Ashcroft,' he says, wiping a big hand across his face. 'We have a responsibility to share information...'

'So you'll know he's had a fling and I've kicked him out and that I burned his clothes in the front garden, yes? You'll know I'm considered a bit of a nutcase by one or two locals?'

A little smile creeps across the DCI's face. 'Yes, I heard. None of our business, really, and I can't condone criminal damage. But well done.'

I'm not sure how to respond. Is she on my side? When

will she mention Bishop? What do they know? It's taking all my energy not to start jiggling my legs up and down on the spot.

'I understand you've made a new friend recently,' says DCI Cressey. 'Jim Bishop. Newcomer to the area. Is that correct?'

I look from her to PC Stewart and back again, my mouth dry. 'Jim, is it? He's never said. Just Bishop. Yes, we've had a couple of drinks together. Why? Is he okay?'

'Could you tell us about the nature of your relationship please, Mrs Ashcroft?' asks PC Stewart, while Cressey continues to stare. She's so still, so poised, it's like there's a Greek statue at the kitchen table.

'Well, it's not a relationship. We got talking at the beach a few weeks back. Had a couple of drinks, like I said. Nothing serious.'

'Is it a romantic relationship?' asks Cressey, and she rolls the word "romantic" around in a way that some people would be willing to call a premium phone line to hear.

I stop myself from replying. Take a moment to compose myself. Give her a look that is all apology. 'Can I ask you what's going on please? I don't want to be awkward but the kids are upstairs and they'll be needing bath and bed and whatever may have been happening between Bishop and me has pretty much fizzled out, so I really would appreciate you telling me what's going on.'

Cressey purses her lips. Sucks on her thoughts. 'We're concerned for Bishop's welfare,' she says, at last.

'You are? Why?'

'Well,' she says, stretching out her hands and inspecting her cuticles. 'Somebody's cut his head off.'

Beside her, PC Stewart sprays a mouthful of tea. He starts dabbing at his nose with the back of his hand. Cressey hasn't moved. She's staring at me in a way that is all challenge. She wants to see how I'll react. What I'll say when rattled.

I start laughing, nervously, grinning a silly grin and unable to work out how to hold my hands. I look from one to the other. Outside, the storm is raging. The rain is hitting the front windows like fistfuls of grit. I have a sudden image of Mr Roe: picture him face-down by the dustbins. I wonder how things will play out if the coppers run over him as they leave.

'You are joking, yes?' I ask, at last. 'Cut his head off? Tell me you're joking. Of course you are. Even if it were true you wouldn't tell me that. It's a joke, yes? Some sort of English humour that's lost on me. Where is he? Really? Are you actually looking for him or has he done something bad?'

'Why do you ask that?'

'Because you're the police, and you're here asking me questions, so it has to be one or the other.'

'Does Mr Bishop have any enemies, Mrs Ashcroft?'

'I don't know,' I say, a note of panic in my voice. 'I don't really know him. He works in cyber security and has a place near the ferry terminal. We've chatted, but he was more of a listener than a talker. And it sort of petered out.'

'You made several calls to his mobile phone number on Tuesday,' says Cressey, smoothly. 'Quite a lot of texts too. Texts sent from what appears to be a position within Glenborrodale Woods. Which, coincidentally, is very close to where Mr Bishop's telephone received them.'

'No,' I say, shaking my head. 'No, you're getting it wrong

– I was supposed to meet him and he didn't turn up and that was the end of it. I knew it wasn't going to last, and I'm okay with it.'

'Mr Bishop hasn't been seen in several days, Mrs Ashcroft. And today, as-yet-unidentified human remains were discovered at Ardtoe.'

I put my hand to my mouth. Everything seems to be buzzing. There are spots dancing in my vision. I need to be alone – need time and space to process everything. 'That's horrible,' I say, looking at PC Stewart. He's a little green around the gills as he remembers what he has dealt with today.

'Yes, just a bit. And the reason I'm here is because I have reason to believe that your Mr Bishop was connected to organised crime. Mr Bishop was a mid-level player with at least two known cartels and has connections to a crime syndicate that my unit has been investigating for some time.'

'Bishop? No – he works in security. I told you…'

'What do you know about the man staying in your guest house?' she asks, rubbing her wrists together as if spreading perfume.

'I don't know what you mean,' I say, and my throat sounds dry as scorched paper. *This is it*, I think. This is when she tells me they know all about the castle, the new owners, the service they'll be offering. This is when they ask me to provide a statement that pitches me into the middle of something I can't imagine a way out of.

DCI Cressey leans forward. Her perfume is dry and fruity, like a good white wine. She looks at me the way I've seen fighters stare at one another from across the ring.

'It's a school night, Mrs Ashcroft. It's dark, and cold and

you've no doubt had a difficult day. I'm going to give you a little time to think about things, and then we'll revisit this conversation. We'll need a formal statement, and once that is done, it will be very difficult for you to come up with a new narrative somewhere else down the line. So you'll be wanting to tell a story that sits right. That you can live with. Because I had to spend several hours on a pissing helicopter to get here, Mrs Ashcroft, and I'm staying in a hotel that offers milk in little plastic containers. So my patience is a little thin. I would use this evening to make good decisions, Mrs Ashcroft. Perhaps take a really good long look in the mirror and ask yourself what sort of person you want to be. We'll pick this up again another time.'

She stands up so quickly that it feels like we're about to have a brawl in a saloon. Then she smiles at me. Extends a hand. I take it in mine, and don't let my eyes betray me as I feel the piece of paper she has pressed against my palm.

'We'll be out of your hair, then, Ronni,' says PC Stewart, looking hugely relieved to be leaving. 'Theresa Gunn does some cleaning for you, doesn't she? If you happen to see her, let her know we could be doing with a wee chat when she has a moment.'

I glance up at DCI Cressey. She's smiling as if she knows.

I stay seated until they've closed the kitchen door and I hear the roar of their car disappearing down the driveway. There are no sounds to suggest they've squashed any slumbering drunks.

In my palm, a doubled-over piece of paper. I unfold it as if it might explode.

Eight digits, and six more separated by dashes. An

account number and sort code. *My* account number. *My* sort code.

Underneath, a single question mark. I'm no fan of puzzle games, but I think I know how to solve this one. I'm being made an offer. But by whom? To do what?

Then I fold my arms and lay my head down on the table. Drift into a dream full of severed heads, and stolen hearts.

19

Seven weeks ago
Alexander Street, Clydebank

The pub is next to the railway bridge just off the centre of Clydebank. It's a big sandstone affair, with red paintwork and dark windows and as Nicholas Roe mooches through the diagonal rain towards its uninviting façade, he experiences the overwhelming sensation of coming home. He has spent his life in such pubs. Has made friends and enemies and drunk himself blind with both in equal measure. He understands the men, and occasionally women, who find their sanctuary within. He does not believe himself to be an alcoholic as he never truly craves alcohol, but he yearns for such warm dark spaces the way a rodent might hunger for the familiar dankness of its burrow.

He checks his watch as he nears the door: 3pm. The streetlights haven't been switched off at any point today. Sunrise has been dismissed as a nasty rumour. It's dark and damp and thoroughly miserable and absolutely perfect for his needs.

He pauses at the entrance. Two plant pots are filled to

overflowing with cigarette butts. He grinds out his cigar on the doorframe and pockets it. If the men he is pursuing are as well connected as he has been led to believe, they would have the capacity to DNA test any forensics left behind. Such precautions are not paranoia. He knows, to his cost, that in these halcyon days of budget cuts and operational streamlining, the people he pursues are better resourced, better informed and better advised than the police officers who chase them.

Inside, no surprises. A threadbare red carpet, beneath a half dozen round wooden tables and hard chairs. Ripped beer mats on sticky tabletops, woodchip on the walls. Black-and-white pictures in cheap frames and fruit machines flashing neon. Two and a half customers today. An old boy sits at a table offering the best view of the door, halfway down a pint of heavy and with a faraway look in his yellowy eyes that suggests he has been searching for answers at the bottom of pint glasses since he was a boy. At the other end of the room, a scrawny man with a prominent Adam's apple pushes a stroller back and forth with his foot while fiddling with his mobile phone and eating crisps from an open packet on the table.

A stout, matronly barmaid emerges from an open door behind the bar. Gives him what passes for a smile. He returns it and surveys the signs on the bar taps, then glances at the optics behind.

'Pint of that,' he says, nodding at a pump. 'Double Auchentoshan. Drop of water.'

'Drop of water? We don't do cocktails.'

Roe licks his lips. Gives her a once-over. Black top. A couple of gold necklaces disappearing into a crevasse of cleavage. Illegible iodine tattoos on freckly forearms. A tooth missing in her top row. She has a landlady look about her. If there were time, he could be persuaded to propose.

'That an English accent?' she asks, flicking the tap on the real ale.

'Would it be a barrier to our friendship if it was?'

'Not necessarily. I mean, you're starting with a disadvantage.'

'In that case, get one for yourself.'

'Kind of you. Cheers. Just a half, I won't take the piss.'

'You were well raised, I see.'

'Oh I'm pure angel, I am.'

Roe sips a couple of inches of his pint. Hands over a twenty-quid note. It's English currency, and she looks at it cynically.

'That's legal tender,' says Roe, smiling. She returns it. Nods, their friendship cemented.

'Meeting somebody?' she asks, serving herself and plonking herself down on a stool behind the bar.

'Aye, soon enough.'

'Here for anything in particular?'

'Holidaymaker, love. Here to see the sights.'

'Fuck off, no you're not.'

He grins. Takes another three inches off his pint. 'On my way further north, as it happens. I think they used to call it convalescing.'

'You've not been well?'

He gestures at himself. 'Do I look well?'

She shrugs. 'Seen worse. Seen better. None of my business. Where is it you're off to?'

'Out Mull way. Highlands and Irelands. Get some proper air in my old lungs.'

'You'll like it. Good for the soul. They should prescribe it on the NHS. Cheaper than antidepressants.'

'Yeah? There's room in the car. You should pack a bag.'

'Not sure Suzanne would like that?'

'Suzanne?'

'The wife.'

Roe feigns colossal disappointment. In truth, he knows all about Gaynor, the landlady. She's not yet fifty, has three grown-up children, and though she's on to her fourth marriage, this is her first to a woman. The woman in question, Suzanne, works at a bridal boutique in Glasgow. They met when Gaynor was trying on the gown ahead of tying the knot with husband number three.

She seems about to impart some other confidence when her expression changes. Somebody has silently entered the bar. Somebody huge. Where he stands, Roe feels as though a black cloud has just passed in front of the sun. He turns, slowly, and finds himself face-to-chest with a colossal man. Although he wears an unremarkable suit and has combed his wayward red hair into a neat side-parting, he looks to Roe as though he would feel more comfortable in breastplate and sitting astride a shire horse: hooves the size of dinner plates and muscles like its rider.

'Fucking hell,' says Roe, by way of greeting.

'Yeah, I bet that a lot.' His voice is soft – a low rumble.

'Can I get you a drink? Or a packet of crisps? I worry about your blood sugar.'

'Funny.'

'Drink, big man?' asks Gaynor.

'Do you have milk?'

'Just for my coffee,' she says, apologetically.

'I'll leave it then.' He looks at Roe. Wrinkles his nose. 'Drink up. Car's outside.'

Roe grins, moving one of his wobbly teeth back and forth with his tongue. 'Cut the roof off, have you?'

'You and me are going to fall out,' says the big man. 'We haven't even become friends yet and already I can see it going wrong.'

Roe feigns contrition. Leans against the bar and sips his whisky. He needs this man to know that he's not afraid. That he's dealt with bigger men than him. That he's the real deal. He can afford what he's trying to buy. He's a friend worth having.

'Are we going somewhere pretty?' he asks.

'Maybe around the block. Maybe out to the woods. We'll see what you buy yourself with that mouth of yours.'

Roe shakes his head. 'I'm flattered, but you're not my type.'

The big man leans down. 'If I held you up by the ankle and shook you, what would fall out?'

Roe finishes his whisky. 'Try it. See what happens.'

The air between them is heavy with unthrown punches. Roe knows he is all bravado. He barely has the strength to wring out a tea towel most days and if he were to throw a punch at this monster of a man he fancies it would be like hitting a roll of carpet. But he is aggressive by nature and has not yet adapted to his physical frailties. He still talks like somebody who knows how to hurt.

The big man reaches into his trouser pocket and pulls out a mobile phone. He types out a quick message.

'Updating Facebook?' asks Roe, draining his drink.

'Asking permission,' he says.

'Need a piss, do you?'

'I'd like to hurt you a little bit.'

'Keep me posted,' says Roe. 'Same again, please, love. And a Chupa Chups for my friend.'

The phone vibrates. The big man looks disappointed. 'Another time,' he says, and turns his back. He walks back to the door. Has to turn sideways to leave.

'I wouldn't do that again,' says Gaynor, cautiously, putting down his glass. 'He's important. And bloody massive.'

Roe shrugs. 'I'm not easily intimidated.'

'I can see that.'

She considers him again. 'I think we can do business,' she says, at last. 'If you can afford it.'

'I can afford it.'

'And you know what you're buying?'

Roe nods. Downs the whisky in one. 'Time's ticking away. |Look at the state of me. There's no waiting list in the country that I'd meet the criteria for. This is my chance.'

'It's not me who makes the decision. I'm a representative, that's all.'

'The way I heard it, you're the gatekeeper. You're a good judge of character. I get past you, I've got a chance.'

'The big man – he'd have pulled your head off. Nailed your feet to the floor.'

'I'm dying, love. What the fuck do I care?' he sucks his teeth. Tastes blood. 'Who was it he asked permission from?'

'The boss. He'll have sent him down to get a look at you.'

'Isn't that what you're for?'

'I'm for a lot of things. The big man's just got one job. He does it well.'

'So, we're moving forward? Look at me. I've got weeks.'

She looks through him. Weighs him up. 'You'll get instructions. Where to be, and when. Don't die before it happens, otherwise your family still owes. Preparations will begin in good faith.'

He raises his pint glass. 'Your health,' he says, his eyes briefly glistening. He looks for all the world like a hard man trying not to cry grateful tears.

Gaynor nods. Pours herself a shot and downs it. 'And yours.'

20

A little after midnight I drag myself up the stairs to bed. The kids have all flaked out in front of the laptop and I can't bring myself to move them, so I head to Poppy's room and lie down under her Dora the Explorer bedspread and turn on the little music box that casts the shape of multi-coloured unicorns onto the wall. My head's pounding. I know I need to eat something, drink something, but it all seems too much fuss, and my brain is still chewing away at itself with echoes of the dream. In the nightmare, it wasn't Bishop's head in the lobster pot. It was Callum's, his teeth gleaming gold. I saw myself, too: chest splayed open, ribs sticking out like teeth, my whole torso emptied. My eyes remained open, blinking rapidly, as I stared up from a hospital gurney, and a figure with a scalpel approached my face. I hadn't screamed as I woke, but the urge to run had been very, very real.

I pull the covers over my head. The bed smells of Poppy, all fusty and lovely: wet grass and cereal. I breathe it in. Try to get comfortable and realise that my phone is digging into my hip. I roll over and pull it free. I haven't looked at it in hours. Haven't trusted myself to. I want to call Callum. It's eating away at me, making my insides fizz. Why has

Roe got a picture of him with Kimmy? Where were they? Does he know Roe? My paranoid mind conjures up a dozen different scenarios in which they could be connected, and none of them appeal. I want the truth, not some palatable version of it.

I switch it on. Wait for it to warm up. Close my eyes as the picture flashes up. My family, in happier times, wrapped up in kagouls and wellies and splashing through the shallows at Sanna. We're all grinning, and nobody's faking it.

There's a missed call from Callum and two more from numbers I don't recognise. I've got one new voicemail: an enquiry from a well-to-do Dundonian enquiring about last-minute availability in the Easter holidays. I delete the message, angry with her for not being Callum.

I look at the time: 12.14am. He might still be awake. And if not, if he happens to be dozing beside his fancy piece, then I'm not going to shed a tear for spoiling their beauty sleep. I think I deserve some answers.

My eyes begin to close before I can decide what to do. I'm tired to my bones. I feel all warm and languid and somehow, despite all of it, there is a little bit of mania in there too. I feel alive. Scared, yes; unsure what to do, certainly. But there's a vitality to all this – a feeling that I'm involved in something that threatens to show me a world that I'd previously thought only existed in books and movies. Bad people have been doing bad things, and somehow it's washed up at my door.

I slide my phone under the pillow and let sleep take me again.

*

I wake to the smell of crushed earth and stale ash. It's pitch black inside the warm pink bedroom, but I know immediately that I'm not alone. It's a presence: a sense of wrongness that tells me without any possibility of contradiction that there is somebody here, in my home, in my daughter's bedroom – watching me sleep.

I shift position. Pull the covers down to expose my face. Whoever it is may have let their eyes grow accustomed to the dark. This is Poppy's room. Whoever stands at the foot of the bed may not be expecting a grown woman.

I control my breathing. Run through the possibilities. It could be the kids, looking for Mummy. Or Theresa, lost and high on painkillers, trying to find her way back to the cluttered guest room.

That scent again. Something foul. Something bad.

Mr Roe.

'You were in my room,' comes a voice. It sounds like a saw blade moving across sandpaper. 'Helped yourself to a little look-around. Thought I would return the favour.'

Slowly, fighting the urge to cry out, I pull myself upright. Reach out and flick on the little unicorn lamp. Look at him through eyes that aren't yet ready for the light.

He looks worse than I've ever seen a human being. He's rotting. It's as if lightning has struck a random grave and the decades-dead resident has clawed their way to the surface and come looking for a room. The skin beneath his eyes hangs down, exposing weeping red sores, and the scabby blisters in his hair make me think of barnacles and rockpools. There's a heat coming off him: a greenish pestilence that makes me want to burn every item of clothing and furniture he's ever touched.

'What do you think you're doing?' I ask, and I hear the fear in my voice even as I aim for defiance.

'Told you, Ronni. Told you exactly what I'm doing. I'm having a little nosey, poking around. I'm riffling through the drawers, love – I'm moving the pictures and having a sneaky peek behind. I'm sticking a spoon in the skirting board and rooting around for whatever I can lay my beady eyes on.'

He's standing at the foot of the bed. He's got a dirty fawn raincoat over jeans and an old-fashioned stripy shirt – the sort that might be a pyjama top. I can see the bones peeking through his chest. Can see the great tracery of blue veins on his flesh: seamed like ripe Stilton.

'You talked to the police,' he says, and I notice that he's leaning against the footboard. He's wearing gloves. 'The pretty one. The one who acts like butter wouldn't melt. You talked to her.'

'They were here!' I say, in an angry whisper. 'What am I supposed to do? None of this is anything to do with me!'

He shrugs, not caring. 'It is, love. Well done on working out how to open the Palm Pilot, by the way. Took me a bloody age.'

I screw up my eyes, confused. 'Palm Pilot?'

'Bit of technical wizardry that you found in the skirting board, love. Don't pretend.'

I pause before replying. Panic rises as I begin to wonder how long he may have been here. Where else he may have strayed before finding me.

'My friend, Theresa…'

He wrinkles his nose. 'Didn't have to happen that way. Poor lass. It won't be much consolation but heads will roll.'

He gives a twitch of a smile – something that may be a wink. 'No pun intended.'

'I don't know what to do,' I say, and it sounds pitiful to my ears. Roe sits down at the foot of the bed, the blankets pulling tight at my lower legs. He looks at me for several long, awkward seconds.

'You should call your Callum,' he says, at last, and he begins to fumble in his pockets, pulling out tissues and receipts and the stubs of smoked cigars. He finds one, still-moist butt and holds it to his nose, breathing it in like the head of a newborn baby.

'Why would I do that?' I ask.

'Because you saw the picture. Him and his fancy piece. You want to know how he knows me.'

'And if I asked you?'

'I'd tell you the truth.'

'But how would I know it was the truth?'

'See,' he says, with a smile that shows off long, ratty teeth. 'Knew you had a bit of copper in you.'

I pull the blanket around me. Look at the vile, broken-down specimen oozing smoke and corruption in my daughter's room, and somehow I still feel some twinge of sympathy for him. He's dying. He's got one chance at life. And circumstances are conspiring to take it away from him. And then I think of the suffering that has given him his second chance. Think of the sort of people who have given him this opportunity – an opportunity he has only earned through dirty money. I don't know whether to pity him, hate him or turn my back and hope he leaves.

'What did she ask you?' he says, quietly. 'The boss?'

'The boss?'

'DCI. What name did she give you?'

'Emma Cressey.'

He nods at that. 'Good. Solid. What did you make of her?'

I find myself answering even without understanding why. 'Expensive. Full of herself. Sharp as a blade. Ruthless. I wouldn't want to take her on.'

He smiles properly, a father hearing praise about a favoured daughter's gifts. 'Aye, that's not far off. She tell you about Bishop?'

'Wanted to know the nature of our relationship. Told me he'd had his head cut off, just to see how I'd react. Said I should sleep on it before deciding how to proceed. She knew I was holding back.' I stop and eye him, accusingly. 'She asked about you.'

He looks taken aback. 'Did she?'

'The man in the guest house. That's what she said. Asked if I knew the sort of man he was. The sort of man you are. She gave me a piece of paper with my bank details on it. Like she was trying to bribe me? But do the police do that? For information? I mean, I know you have informants and stuff – Callum's into his true crime books and knows all this stuff, but...'

'It's not a bribe for information, love. It's a bribe for silence. Somebody wants you to keep your trap shut.'

'But she was the one asking questions!'

'Keeping up appearances, love. For the local plod.'

'I don't know who to believe!' I say, and my voice cracks.

He shakes his head. 'Ronni, you don't know the half of it.'

I swallow what's left of my pride. Look at him with eyes

full of pleading. 'Why do you have a photo of Callum? What's he into? Are we in trouble? I feel, so lost, Mr Roe. I don't think of myself as a brilliant person or anything but I don't know whether I deserve to be in the middle of all this.'

He sucks on his lower lip, an eel slurping at its own tail. 'I'm just a sick man asking you to let my operation go ahead. That's what you need to remember. Bishop was a man you briefly knew, and you can't help anybody out with information about who might have hurt him, or why. And as for what happened to your friend, that's bad business and it disgusts me and I'll make sure people will pay. My advice is to feather your nest the best way you can. If there's money in it for you, take it. You've got kids. A decent future, if you play it right.'

'I'm not that kind of person.'

'We're all that kind of person,' snaps Mr Roe, a sudden flash of temper in his face. 'We're a disgusting species, Ronni. We're a plague. My body is a planet and all the things eating at me are tiny human beings. That's how it feels. We're all rotten, but while we're here we may as well be the best we can be. I've got stuff to make up for. Everybody does. My operation is in three days. Just bite your tongue until then. I can make it all right.'

I close my eyes. Breathe. Hope that when I open them again he'll be gone. 'Why do you have a photo of Callum? I need to know.'

I hear him sigh. 'There's a lot you don't know about your husband, love. Not your fault. Not his either. Some of the best relationships are built on secrets. But I won't do business with anybody I don't trust, which means I do what I can to find out chapter and verse. Bishop brokered this deal, but Bishop's just one man. Bishop has associates. He has people in his life. He's very well connected.'

'What's that got to do with Callum?'

He's shaking his head at me, almost pitying. 'Not him, lass. The girl. She's one of Bishop's connections. One of his brokers.'

'No,' I say, shaking my head. 'No, she's just some bimbo – some tart who's got her claws in my husband…'

'No, love – she's a very clever operator who works for one Derrick Ovenden.'

'The gangster?'

'The same. Very important man, Mr Ovenden. Great fucking horrible one too.'

'And Callum just happened to get caught up in all this, did he?'

'I've told you – ask him for yourself…'

There is a sound on the stairs, a creak outside the bedroom door, a shifting of weight on a creaky board.

Mr Roe is off the bed and reaching into the pocket of his coat before I even have time to register the sound.

Two figures, rushing through the doorway, a hiss of CS spray and the sudden blue volt of a Taser, and then Mr Roe is on his back and a young woman is screaming, her hands at her eyes, and in the doorway, holding a plastic Taser, glaring at the figure on the floor as if he were the very devil, stands my husband.

He fixes me with a look I don't remember seeing before, then pries the woman's fingers away from her tear-streaked face. Even through the grimace, I recognise her. Kimmy.

She growls. Swears. Crosses to where Mr Roe lies, convulsing, on the floor, and pulls the two electric volts from his chest. He opens his eyes and stares up at her. Manages a twitch of a smile.

'Hello…'

She brings her fist down, hard, on the bridge of his nose, and he drops back to the floor, blood running down his cheek. She stands up, smearing her hand across her face, and looks at me. Looks me up and down, and decides I'm not worth her time.

'Callum?' I ask, quietly. 'Callum, what's happening…?'

He looks at me. Through me. I could light a cigarette on his eyes.

'Get dressed,' he says, coldly. 'We've got a lot to talk about.'

21

Six weeks ago
A small, damp flat on Dempster Street, Greenock

'Slow down...'

'I said she's kicked me out! Burned my clothes on the front lawn! She saw the messages. Me and Kimmy. What do I say? How do I tell her?'

'You fucking don't, lad. You take it, for her sake.'

'No, she thinks I'm sleeping with her!'

'Let her think it. It's better than the truth.'

'But I need to be here! That's why we did it this way, isn't it? So I can be here. To keep them safe, to oversee things, to deal with Bishop...'

'Yeah, but you've fucked that up. How did you let her find it?'

'I don't know, my brain's all over the place. I can't remember half the lies I've told; I don't know who I am. I've been talking to her like she's Kimmy – being such a bastard. She deserves so much better...'

'Stop whingeing. Slow down. We can work it to our advantage. You and Bishop have got a good relationship.

You've already got Pope on your side. Kimmy's in – she's doing a good job. Tell Bishop you're shacking up with Kimmy, you won't be around to make sure things go smoothly at the castle. He'll have to come out of hiding himself. He's a fixer. He'll either send somebody else or do it himself. We might get the lot of them.'

'How can you say that? My life's falling apart and all you care about is the operation!'

'You've made your bed, son. You have to lie in it.'

'And if I don't? If I just tie a weight to my feet and paddle out into the loch and let my problems slip beneath the water…'

'Then you'll be leaving your wife and kids to pick up the pieces. And you'll lose your one ally.'

'My ally?'

'Me, son. I'm on your side, believe it or not. Do what I tell you, and we can all come out of this with what we want.'

'That's what Bishop said.'

'Don't listen to Bishop. Don't listen to Pope.'

'I should listen to you, should I? Who are you, God?'

'No, son. I'm the fucking devil. But I'm a devil on the right side.'

'Please, Mr Roe…'

'Don't call this number again. Go. Do what she wants.'

'But I love her!'

'Stop it. You'll make me cry.'

22

Callum picks up Mr Roe with little visible effort: scoops him up and carries him like a groom holding a new bride. Blood runs down Mr Roe's face and drips on the floor: a trail of droplets guiding my way as if I were a plane looking for landing lights.

'The children,' I say, following him past my bedroom door and towards the stairs. 'They'll want to see you... Callum, they'll want to see you...'

Kimmy, leading the way, looks back over her shoulder and gives a shake of her head.

'Not now,' says Callum, shifting his position. Mr Roe's jacket slides down his arms and I see more of the blue-veined skin of his chest. I suddenly find myself terrified that this man is going to die, and die in my family home.

'Callum!' I say, raising my voice. 'Why are you doing this? Why are you here?'

He jerks his head, telling me to follow, and I grind my teeth in frustration as I move down the stairs and into the living room. The fire has died in the hearth and the large, high-ceilinged room is bitterly cold. Kimmy flicks on a lamp and a pale yellow light illuminates the space. Callum lays Mr Roe down on the floor. Kimmy, in the process of sitting down on the sofa, tuts at him and crosses over to where he lies. She turns him onto his side, classic recovery position, and shakes her head at my husband as she shoves past him and plonks herself down on the couch.

Standing by the door I give her proper consideration. Older than I'd thought, definitely. Maybe thirty. Bad skin. Hair pulled back in a greasy ponytail to reveal a lean, sharp face: her profile hard enough to split timber. She's got a row of studs up her left ear. She's wearing stonewashed denim jeans and tasselled suede boots, and when her Puffa jacket falls open she reveals a belly button stud peeking out from beneath a ribbed pink-and-black polo neck. She sees me looking. Opens her arms wide.

'I would say take a picture, but I reckon you don't need one. Reckon I'll stay in your mind quite a while.'

'Kim, don't…' begins Callum. He's standing over Mr Roe, looking down at him as if surveying the pattern of a newly purchased rug. He doesn't look like himself. He's shaved his hair right down to the scalp and he's got a few days of stubble covering his face. When he's home he's always clean-shaven. Neatly turned out. He likes polo shirts and chinos. He looks wrong in his black camouflage trousers and tight-fitting bomber jacket. It seems as if the man I've been married to for the past twelve years is playing dress-up.

'Callum?' I say, again, and suppress a shiver as he turns to look at me.

'That all you say, is it, doll?' asks Kimmy, smiling. 'Callum, Callum, Callum. Christ, no wonder he's sick of your voice.'

Temper flares, despite it all. 'What did you say to me?'

'Oh, that was so sweet.' Kimmy grins, mockingly. 'A

real flash of character. Go on, do it again. In fact, show me another emotion. How about shock? Or sexy. See if you can do sexy. Callum says you used to be quite the looker.'

I feel as if somebody is reaching inside me and running sharp nails over my heart. I want to smash an elbow into this hard-nosed bitch's face, but I need answers more than I need satisfaction. I look to Callum, trying to convince myself she's not here.

'You said you wanted to talk. I reckon now's the time.'

He looks at me, scratching his face, his eyes dispassionate. He's frightening me. Pissing me off too.

'Look, Callum, your kids are asleep upstairs. Theresa's in the office. I don't know what you want with Mr Roe but nobody's going to be hurting anybody I care about, I tell you that much. You've stayed away, like I asked, and I don't think you've suddenly turned up just so the kids can meet your new fancy piece, so just tell me what's going on before I call the police and get shot of all of you...'

'You won't be calling the police,' says Callum, shaking his head. 'Even if you did, they'd be no help.'

'I don't know what that means,' I say. My temper snaps. 'Bugger this – you can just get out. Take him with you if you like. I don't want any part of whatever you've been up to. And I don't ever want my kids being around somebody who carries a bloody Taser! Where did you even get that? And where did you meet this...' I gesture at Kimmy, who gives me a warning look.

'Choose your words carefully, doll.'

'I told you weeks ago – it's not what you think. It's a business alliance, nothing more.'

I roll my eyes, disgusted. 'I saw your messages! Saw the

way you talk to each other. I saw a bloody photograph of you holding hands down by the water!'

He looks at Kimmy. I follow his gaze and see that she's curling her lip. 'I bloody well knew it,' she mutters. 'Go on, fucking stick him now.'

'No,' he says, shaking his head. 'This is my home. Our home. I want to have something to come back to.'

'You don't do as I say you won't be going anywhere. It'll be years in Barlinnie, and every one of them will hurt.'

He glances at me and for a moment I see the man I married. There's a sadness to him: a hurt. He's got the beaten, hangdog look of somebody who's tried so hard to do right that he's doomed himself to disappointment. For a moment I want to put a hand on his face and tell him that it will be okay – that I know he's a good guy and that whatever the problem is, we can work it out together. But there's a dying man on my floor and a skank on my sofa and it doesn't seem the right moment for a display of affection.

'Can I have a drink please, Ronni?' he asks, quietly. 'A Scotch. Just to get the taste out of my mouth.'

'Aye, open a bottle,' says Kimmy, putting her feet on the coffee table. 'I'm as dry as a nun's gusset.'

I push my hair back from my face, trying not to tug it out by the roots. Outside I hear the gale howling through the thrashing, broken trees; hear the rain hitting the glass like pennies on a drum skin. I find myself heading to the kitchen, finding glasses, reaching into the back of the drinks cupboard for the Lagavulin. Out of habit I fill a water jug and put three tumblers on a tray; walk back through to the living room like the good little hostess and fill everybody's glasses while fighting the urge to spit in two of them and smash the third directly against the temple of whoever looks at me next.

'Your health,' says Kimmy, and takes a gulp. She winces. 'It'll do. Prefer a voddie, but needs must.'

'Thank you,' says Callum, and breathes in the golden, peaty scent. He closes his eyes. Takes a sip. Then he crosses to what used to be his chair: a burgundy recliner angled to stare out through the glass doors and across the lake. He turns it back in to the room and gives me his full attention. I situate myself on the stone of the fireplace. I sip my own drink and enjoy the tingle and burn. Through the base of the glass I notice the big logs in the basket: the poker by the fire. I flick a look at Mr Roe. He's making an ugly snoring sound, as if his throat is constricted.

'What do you know about this man, Ronni?' he asks, quietly.

'No,' I say, shaking my head. 'You don't get to ask me questions. You're the one who has the story to tell. For God's sake, there was a copper here today asking me questions about a severed head! And Roe here is begging me to stay quiet about what I might or might not know so he can get the operation that will save him. And then I see he already knows you, and apparently Bishop does too, and as for the delightful Kimmy here, well I'm just none the bloody wiser, so if you ever want to have anything to do with your children you start talking!'

On the sofa, Kimmy gives a snort of laughter. 'Christ, she's okay when she gets het up, Budge. You were right.'

I flash angry eyes at her, then the name she has used causes my thoughts to grind together like broken cogs. 'Budge? You haven't been called Budge since school! This your midlife crisis is it? What's next, a motorbike? You've got your younger woman, got a chance to play the hard man. Making up for lost time, are you?'

'I need you to shut up, Ronni,' he says, his teeth together, the glass in his hand. 'Shut up and listen.'

'Shut up and listen? Are you out of your bloody mind, Callum?'

'Bored now,' says Kimmy, in a sing-song voice. 'Can we hurry things along? He's not accustomed to waiting.'

'She needs to know,' begins Callum, giving her his attention. 'She can't say the wrong thing. You know that better than I do.'

'And you think you can get her onside in the next ten minutes, do you? I've told you, just get her and the kids in the car and get them away from here for a few days. They can come back when it's all wrapped up. You too, if you've played ball.'

Her tone changes as she talks. There's less malice in her voice. Her accent changes. It's as if she's somebody else entirely.

'He's already said!' hisses Callum. 'If he doesn't meet her, it's all done. All off. Then nobody gets what they want. She can do this. She was a probation officer. She's cleverer than either of us. And if you want your result you'll listen to me. I know him – you don't...'

I look from one to the other, squeezing the whisky glass in my hand. 'See who?' I ask, quietly. 'You're scaring me, Callum.'

He rubs his forehead. Pressed his glass to his brow. Looks at me as if his eyes are heavier than he can stand.

'I'm not what you think I am, Ronni. I've made some

mistakes. Got involved with the wrong people. And if I want to get out of it I have to do some more things I don't want to do. Like deliver Mr Roe here. And prove that my wife isn't going to spoil the party. You need to meet a man who's going to ask you some hard questions. And every single thing depends on getting the answer right.'

'Who?' I ask, and it feels as though there is icy water dripping on my skin.

'You don't say his name. Not out loud.'

Kimmy looks at me, something like sorrow flashing in her eyes. 'We call him "Pope".'

'Why?' I ask, and it feels as though my bones are vibrating with an electrical charge.

'Talks to God,' she says, directly. 'And has a hotline to the devil too.'

I look back to Callum, hoping that he'll tell me that this is all some elaborate joke – that he's just having an affair and that everything since is something he's cooked up to distract me. I can see in his face that he's not lying.

'Theresa can stay here with the children. You need to come with us.'

'Come with you where? Theresa's off her head on painkillers. She needs to be in hospital! Where are we even going? And do you know what they did to her? At the castle? Do you know what they're doing up there? Is that what you're involved in...?'

On the floor, Mr Roe coughs, and opens his eyes, staring up at me like a corpse granted one last look at the world. Nobody else notices. He closes one eye, a lazy wink, then retreats into the very picture of unconsciousness.

'Whatever happens, I want you to know, I did what I thought was right.'

'They'll carve that on your headstone,' says Kimmy, pulling herself up. As she moves, I spy the gun in her inside pocket. It feels as though there are cold stones dropping into my guts.

'There won't be a headstone,' he mutters. 'If it goes wrong, there'll be nothing left to bury.'

23

Four days ago
A large hotel on the banks of Loch Lomond

'Can I buy you a drink?'

She looks him up and down. Shrugs, exposing three-quarters of an expensive breast. 'I don't know. Can you?'

'Are you a costly round?'

'Yes. But I'm worth every penny.'

'I've no doubt. What is it you're on?'

'Gimlet.'

'A what now?'

'And you were doing so well.'

She's sitting in a high-backed tartan chair, letting the glow from the open fire cast interesting patterns on her bare legs. She's wearing a white robe, and wearing it well. She's spent the past hour enjoying the hotel's spa facilities. Half an hour in the pool, fifteen minutes in the sauna and then an icy dip in the plunge pool to seal her pores. She's paid for her own accommodation: topping up the meagre allowance permitted by the NCA, and is making sure she gets her money's worth. She hadn't seen the point in getting dry after her dip. Just pulled on the complimentary bathrobe and padded through to the lounge. Her bag is leaning against the chair, laptop and case notes vying for space alongside towel and sodden swimming costume. The other occupants of the bar are taking it in turns to look at her: some disapproving, some with so much admiration that it stops on the verge of drool.

'Go on, honestly, tell me what a gimlet is.'

She looks up at her suitor. He's okay on the eyes. Quite well put together. Blue shirt, tweedy jacket with a little stag's head lapel, neat chinos and stylish brown brogues. Thirty, perhaps. His ears stick out a little but she has forgiven worse handicaps, and she's not averse to having something to hold on to. She glances at the clock above the fireplace. It's a little before 5pm. She could find the time for him, if she felt the urge.

'Depends whom you ask. It's essentially gin and lime juice, but some cocktail waiters like to add their own little touches.'

'And how do you like it?'

She licks her lips. Gives him a moment's attention. 'In my mouth.'

There's something dispiritingly predictable about the way he reacts. He gives her a grin, all silly and boyish, and hurries off to the bar, almost tripping over one of the low tables as he goes. The barman, polishing glasses and looking suitably splendid in tweed waistcoat and purple bow tie, gives a tiny nod of his head: one professional to another, marvelling at a job well done. He's seen it all, and the blonde in the bathrobe is easily the most confident, self-assured and icily fanciable woman he has ever seen.

She watches the fire while she waits for her suitor to return. Occasionally, she turns her gaze towards the big windows at the far end of the room. The darkening sky is smudged with a riot of pastel shades: pinks and purples and crocus-yellow adding flecks of colour to the surface of the loch and lighting up the yachts that bob in the harbour. She can see the silhouette of the seaplane, and if she were to squint she would just about see the mountains beyond.

She tuts at herself as the earworm surfaces in her brain. She's been singing about the bonny bonny banks of Loch Lomond since she arrived three days ago and every time she thinks she's killed it off with a blast of an aria it finds a way to creep back into her skull.

'One Gimlet,' says the man. 'Do you mind if I...?'

'If you what?' she asks, feigning bemusement.

'Sit down.'

She frowns. 'What?' she looks at the chair opposite. 'Here? With me?'

'Yeah.'

'I'm not sure. I mean, I'm sitting here looking for some peace.'

Little ripples of annoyance show on his face. 'I got you a drink.'

'Thanks. Appreciated.'

'So can I sit down?'

'Why do you think one thing naturally leads to the other?'

He looks genuinely baffled now, as if some infallible law has been broken. 'Are you being shitty with me on purpose?'

She turns away from him, already bored with the game.

She has very few hobbies but toying with feeble men is one of her favoured leisure pursuits. People make such assumptions about her she feels it is almost a duty to put them right. For all the things people say about her, she is not promiscuous. She uses what she's got and her ambitions have no limit, but the idea that she would loan herself out to somebody for the cost of a gimlet strikes her as faintly insulting. If he does get to enjoy her it will be only after she has spent so much time tearing him to pieces emotionally that it will be all he can do not to weep on her shoulder. She learned such techniques from the men she has fallen for, and if she ever has a child she intends to teach them that some old adages really do hold true. Treating people mean keeps them considerably keener than one might think.

'Do you want me to just go? It's okay. I'll go…'

He looks sad, suddenly, as if she's told him he can't come to the party. He puts the glass down on the table in front of her. As he moves past her, she raises her left foot and strokes it down the back of his leg. Smiles, and gives him a little wink. He isn't sure how to react, and it delights her. As he straightens up, she shoves him backwards. He gives a feeble yelp and topples into the neighbouring chair, spilling his drink down his front. He looks up, angry and confused, and she is smiling at him, slyly: the way a praying mantis might before devouring a partner.

From the depths of her bag, a low vibrating; in the periphery of her vision, a soft blue light.

The man is forgotten. All else is forgotten. She plucks the phone from the satchel and turns her back on her companion, holding up a hand to mask her lips as she softly says "hello".

Her face doesn't change as she listens. She's too practised at deceit to betray herself so cheaply. But beneath the glacial façade she feels a colossal surge of panic for her oldest and best friend. She may have once been willing to let him die, but those were different times. She's a different person now. Not exactly better, but she serves her very worst for those more deserving.

She's up and heading for the door without a goodbye. She needs to be in Ardnamurchan, and fast. There's a head. A severed head, in a lobster pot...

'I'll be Emma Cressey. DCI. Stay tight. Don't drink more than you have to. Keep her safe. For God's sake, keep her safe...'

24

Inside the car the darkness presses in like gloved hands. I'm in the passenger seat, with Callum driving. In the back, Mr Roe lolls, a melting mannequin, getting closer to where Kimmy sits with each turn in the road. It's not Callum's car. I spotted an Audi badge as we climbed inside but if it is, it's an old model I'm not familiar with. He wouldn't let me wake the children. I could see it pained him to be so close to his kids and not permit himself to go to them, but he was being as strict with himself as he was with me. I roused Theresa as gently as I could. Told her she would have to keep an eye on the children if they woke. And then we were wincing into the teeth of the gale, watching cloud stir itself in great roiling Möbius strips as the three-quarter moon found its likeness in the phosphorescent silver of the loch.

'He'll want reassurance,' says Callum, as we head west towards the point. On the landward side the trees are a static army: charcoal-black spears held in claws by straight-backed soldiers. There are broken branches in the road. Something dead and furry lies in a brown-and-red smear by the entrance to the boat house. Further along, a dead bird, its neck snapped, lying on the verge like a broadsheet newspaper.

'I don't have anything to tell him!' I say, my voice a hiss, like interference bleeding from a car stereo. 'I'm not involved. I don't know how you're involved, Callum!'

'I never wanted this to happen,' he says, quietly. I see him move his hand from the steering wheel and for a moment I think he's going to put his big palm over mine. I flinch away, and he squeezes the wheel.

'How bad is it?' I ask, staring at the side of his face. 'Roe said they're bad people. They did awful things to Theresa just for looking in. She saw men. Wires coming out of them, bandages on their eyes...'

'No she didn't,' says Callum, urgently. 'No, Theresa saw some lights on at the castle and went to investigate and some passing bad lads gave her a seeing to. She hasn't told the police. Won't tell the police. And she's only told you the bare bones.'

'Callum, who are you protecting?'

'You!' he spits. 'Us! Just trust me, please.'

I say nothing. Rain spatters the glass. There's no other cars on the road. It's 2.50am and I can think of no good reason for anybody to be out in the dead of night.

'And Mr Roe?' I ask, quietly.

'A holidaymaker. A weirdo. Got overly fond of you and started making advances. Telling you all sorts of silly stories. You woke up to find him in the house. I gave him a seeing to, and then persuaded you to come with me to see a man I know who'll make sure it all goes away. You're an innocent. Naïve. You don't know what's going on.'

'I bloody don't,' I mutter.

'And the English copper. DCI Cressey. She came to speak to you about a missing man. A man you'd had a couple of drinks with, but you had nothing to tell her. You'll continue to have nothing to tell her.'

'How is this man involved?' I ask, tension pounding in my temples and gripping my jaw. 'Surely I can busk this better if I know what not to say. Who was trying to bribe me?'

'What do you mean?' he asks, glancing at me.

'She gave me a piece of paper with our bank details on them. Somebody was trying to get me on their side.'

He grinds his teeth and flashes a look in the mirror at Kimmy. She's saying nothing. Glaring through the window, through her own reflection, watching the white caps on the water. Tension is coming off her in waves.

'You don't mention it unless he does,' he says. 'She might be in his pocket. It might have been him making the offer.' He hits his palm on the steering wheel. Shakes his head.

'It doesn't seem like you have any of the answers either, Callum,' I say, and hear my voice catch a little. I can't stand this. I could handle hating him when I thought he was screwing somebody else. Grief softens the heart but anger gives it steel. Now I feel equally lied to, but I don't know how far the virus of his deceit has crept into our relationship. I don't know where we could go from here. It all seems too momentous, suddenly. I want to leap out of the car and run into the woods. Want to sprint back into the real world, where things like this don't happen.

'We're here,' says Callum, and up ahead I see a gap in the treeline. I've seen it countless times before and never wondered what might lie beyond. The road is full of abandoned properties and half-ruined crofts. All I know is that we're only a couple of miles from the castle at Glenborrodale.

Callum rolls the car slowly through the gap and we're quickly enclosed in thick forest. He slows down and slides down the window, peering out at the muddy track beneath the wheels. He turns back to Kimmy. 'Two vehicles at least. Heavy.'

'Fuck,' mutters Kimmy. Beside her, Mr Roe gives a groan. 'What will happen to him?'

'I don't know,' says Callum, and we move forward into the dark of the wood, the lights turned into a dancing black mesh by the movement of the trees. He glances at him. Shakes his head. Looks at me as if he wants to tell me something and clamps his mouth together to stop it coming out. 'He got himself into this. I wish it could be different.'

We carry on up a dirt track, claw-like branches skittering against the windows and bodywork, and then we're emerging into a clearing, where a small white-painted cottage sits halfway up a slope, its near side sheltered by a semi-circle of trees. A Porsche Cayenne and something that looks like a London black cab are parked side by side on the small patch of shingly drive, blocking the view of the front of the house. All I can make out are dark windows, and the top of a red door. Through Callum's open window I can smell something incongruous and nostalgic: the mingled scents of comfort, of home. A peat fire, salt air, damp earth.

I look at Callum and it feels for a moment as if we're young lovers again, sneaking away to a countryside bothy for a night of passion. I remember the time before the kids. Before life started pulling him down. He'd been vibrant, once. So full of self-belief. Maybe Bishop had reminded me of him, a little. The cocksure certainty that everything would work out. The years have chipped away at him:

reduced his confidence, his self-belief. Humbled him. There have been times I've thought it was for the best – that his arrogance was an ugly thing and something we shouldn't be holding up as laudable in front of the kids. But I miss it. I miss him telling me that I worry too much; that he's got a plan, that he knows a guy who knows a guy and he can get what I want a bit cheaper than on the high street. I've acted so bloody holier-than-thou. Taken the shine off every one of his mad schemes. And now he's done something that's so far beyond our world I don't know if he'll ever come back.

Behind me, I hear Kimmy open her door. She takes Roe under the armpits and drags him out after her, letting him drop to the hard, mud-streaked ground. He gives a groan. His eyes stay closed.

'Whatever happens, you have to trust me,' says Callum.

I get no chance to reply. He opens his door and slips outside. As he moves, I see the knife, sheathed, stuck in the back of his jeans.

I climb out of the car. It's cold. We're higher up the mountain here and I know that if the sun were out we would be able to see across to Coll and Mull through the gaps in the trees.

'Get his arm,' says Kimmy, and I realise she's talking to me. She heaves Mr Roe to his feet. I slip an arm around his waist, and together we drag him across the long grass and scattered stones to the front of the house. I see a wisp of smoke rising from the chimney. As we squeeze between the two cars, the drawn curtains at a downstairs window twitch, and a moment later the front door creaks and opens inwards, a warm yellow light briefly illuminating the curious quartet on the doorstep.

The man who's opened the door is huge. Six foot seven if he's an inch. Huge. Introverted.

'You're the one who brought Theresa…' I begin, and stop myself as I feel Kimmy's fingers squeeze my wrist.

I glance down at his hands. He's got something metallic wrapped around his fist. Something cold and black. I realise it's the pommel of an old sword, guarding his big fist like an iron cage.

He stares through me. Looks at Mr Roe, then at Kimmy, and finally gives his attention to Callum.

'Two minutes early,' he says, in a low growl.

Callum shrugs, his manner completely transformed. 'Want me to go kill some time in the woods? Think I saw your mum up there, grazing.'

He doesn't rise to it. Looks at me. 'She okay? The lady?'

I don't know how to reply. Is this him? Is this the one who they're all terrified of?

'He's in, yeah?' asks Kimmy, beside me. 'It's just, this dying bastard's leaking all over me and I wouldn't object to a place by the fire, if you could shift your big arse.'

The man I knew as Lachlan is about to speak when a voice drifts out from behind him. It's Glaswegian; dry and breathy, like the crackle of a dying fire.

'Bring them in, big man. Fierce fucking night. Fierce. And there's a lady present, I'm told. Two, if you count Kimmy, and plenty of people have counted Kimmy. Make room, lad. Let's get this over with, eh?'

Callum looks up at Lachlan, daring him to contradict the instruction. Slowly, like a rock being rolled away from a tomb, Lachlan steps aside, and we shuffle into a small, whitewashed corridor. A wooden door stands open to our right, and the warm peaty smell is drifting out. Callum leads the way and I hobble in behind, finding myself in a room that smells of peat and whisky. Something else, too. Something chemical. Medicinal.

It's a small, comfy room. Seventies carpets. A low, Ercol sofa and matching armchair. Open fireplace, peat smouldering away. The walls are flock wallpaper. Gypsy horse brasses and a couple of Rembrandt reproductions hang lopsided on single nails.

By the window, his back to the fire, sits a small man. He's completely hairless: not so much as a smear of fuzz on his head, eyebrows or chin. His eyes are sunk deep, like belly buttons in a plump gut, and there's a malformed lumpiness to his features, as if the bones in his face have shifted like tectonic plates and made bumps and ridges where there should be none. He's sitting in a high-backed rocking chair, his hands in his lap, dressed in comfortable loungewear and a too-big jacket. He could be fifty. Could be ancient. I don't want to be harsh, but my first thought is that he looks as though he's wearing a stocking over his face. My second, perhaps unkinder, is that he looks like a penis wearing a condom three sizes too small.

'How you going?' asks Callum, in front of me, as I slip my arm from Mr Roe's waist and Kimmy gives him a shove. He topples into the centre of the room and lies there as if dropped from a great height. The man in the chair stares at him for a moment. It's hard to read his expression, with the deep-set eyes and the perfectly bald features. But when he looks at me, he's smiling: a big red curve of a thing, a livid slash of colour in the pasty features.

'You'll be the missus,' says the man, and he reaches

down to his sides. There's a clinking of metal and he rolls forward. I grasp what I'd mistaken for a rocking chair is in fact a vintage wheelchair: the sort of thing old ladies and gentlemen would employ to take the air at a spa town in Victorian times.

'Like it?' he asks, staring up at me. 'I'm a slave to the old ways. Born into the wrong time. Nobody makes things properly anymore. Sorry, where's my manners? I'd stand to greet you, but my body's not co-operating. Takes me an age to get out of my chair and I can never be sure I won't have embarrassed myself – much as the big man at the door there does his best to save me from such petty humiliations.'

I look to Callum for guidance. He's chewing on the inside of his cheek, listening to the man as if he were the greatest orator of his time. Beside me, Kimmy rubs at her eyes.

'Boring you, am I, love? I see you've had a wee weep. Or did our pal here get off a shot of the CS before you brought him along?'

Kimmy doesn't speak. I stand awkwardly, unsure what to say.

'I'm Pope,' he says, and there's that smile again. 'I understand you've been unnecessarily ensnared in a business transaction that I have an interest in. A gentleman of my acquaintance has gone and got himself disappeared. There's talk of a nasty nick to the neck. Talk, too, of a fancy English copper coming up and making waves. I'm not a well man, Ronni. You can see that for yourself. And I don't need aggravation at my time of life. That's what I told Callum here. I said, Callum, I'm not so young as I was, and I suffer with my nerves. Do me a favour and go round up your pretty wife and ask her to come see me. We can chat.

Set the world to rights. Explain a few things. And while you're there, how about you pick up that zombie-looking prick who's been staying in the guest house. We can get together. Light a fire. See how the land lies…'

'Mr Pope,' I say, and the tremble in my voice isn't forced. 'I don't really know what's going on. Callum and I are separated. As far as I know he's with this lady now, and I don't know why they're here, or why you wanted to see me, and it's all a bit much with the kids at home. As for Bishop, I don't really know him, and I just hope he turns up safe and sound. I'm really rather out of my depth, if I'm honest.'

Pope doesn't alter his expression. Up close, I can see that his eyes are an unsettling blue, and as he stares into me the pupils expand and dilate and seem to form new patterns, like ink dropped in water.

'You've coached her well, Callum,' says Pope, still looking at me. 'You said all that without moving your lips. Trouble is, I'm a bit neurotic. Paranoid, even. And I still get this horrible feeling she's going to hold a grudge about one or two things, and she's going to make a fuss. The big man there told me what the delivery boys did to your friend's feet. A liberty. A genuine liberty. It will be repaid, I promise you that. You can watch if you want. But I need you to respect an old man's wishes and keep your own counsel for a few days more. I can arrange that in several ways.'

I feel the presence of the big man in the doorway. Look down to Mr Roe. An expression of genuine pity ripples across my features and I see a flash of delight in Pope's own, mangled expression.

'Fond of him, are you? Aye, he's a character. Done some good turns for a lot of people over the years and it's a pity he's spending his final days on this earth looking like something thrown together from old animal bones, but there's never been much justice in the world. He'll have told you, I'm sure. Told you why he's here.'

'He's taking wildlife pictures,' I say, trying to please.

'Yeah, course he is. And Bishop's just a nice man passing through, and you didn't get the note from DCI Cressey, and all of this is such a dreadful misunderstanding. Am I right?' He shakes his head, then looks up at Callum. 'I can't believe you brought her, son. If it were me, I'd have had it away in my toes. Got her and the kids and pissed off somewhere safe for a few weeks. I mean, I'd have found you, but I'd have appreciated the chase, and a corpse looks so much better with a tan, don't you reckon?'

'Leave off, Pope,' he begins, and the man in the chair holds up a hand.

'Mr Pope, please. I liked the way she said it.'

'Fine, Mr Pope. We're good. There's no spanner in the works, no fly in the ointment. We've got everything the way it needs to go. Supply sorted, demand sorted, route sorted. You're safe. Give yourself this chance. Trust the people who've never let you down. Ronni and me, we're going to have a long talk, but you can trust her as much as you trust me. As much as you trust Kimmy here, or the big man at the door.'

Pope grips the wheels of his chair. Moves forward and back, the tyres leaving grooves in the carpet. At length, he looks at Mr Roe.

'He's not died, has he? I wouldn't like that. He's paid for a product. Paid for a certain standard of care. I don't like the idea of him snuffling his last in this piss-poor croft in the middle of nowhere.'

I move towards him. Bend down to put a hand under his head and help him up. Pope raises his hand: Caesar holding back a baying crowd. 'No, let Kimmy show her maternal side,' he says.

Beside me, Kimmy gives a little snort of laughter. Moves forward to help him up.

Pope stares at her. Waits until she's on her knees, both arms under Mr Roe's arms, trying to haul him up. Then the shape behind me detaches itself from the wall and moves past me with the momentum of a runaway train. Callum turns too late. Lachlan smacks his right fist into his jaw and there's a crack like the breaking of a branch. The metalwork surrounding his huge hand glints in the firelight as he raises his arm like a club, and brings it down on the back of Kimmy's neck. Pope doesn't move.

And I'm standing stock-still, my hands at my mouth, and Pope's eyes are staring up into mine.

'Now,' he says, licking his lips and wheeling himself forward. 'Let's try it all again, and without the lies.'

'You've killed her,' I mumble, staring at the broken shape on the floor, laid out over Mr Roe like a shawl. I look to Callum, unconscious on his side, a great purple swelling on his left cheek. 'Why did you do that? What have we done?'

He laughs. It's a dry, snickering sound: a cartoonish, unpleasant snuffle. He shakes his head. 'You really don't know, do you? Don't know what you've got caught up in. Who I am.' He gestures at Mr Roe. 'Who he is.'

'No,' I say, shaking my head. A tear spills, and I cuff it away, angry with myself. 'I just want this to be over.'

He looks disappointed. Then he turns to Lachlan. Shrugs. 'Go on, lad. You heard the girl.'

And the big metal hand comes at me like a cannonball.

PART THREE

25

S he isn't often lost for words. Her life has seen no
shortage of luxury. She knows the best restaurants in
Monaco, where to get the best gimlet in Tunis at 3am on a
Tuesday morning. She's made love inside a mummy's tomb
and fucked her knees bloody in a private box at the opera
house in Palermo. For a time she spent her nights living
aboard a yacht in South Dock Marina, Southwark, only
venturing onto dry land when the need for fresh champagne
superseded the desire to stay naked upon silk sheets and
rose petals with a very bad man. But the view that greets
her as she sits up in bed is enough to make her pause and
do nothing but commune with something that, though she
hates the word beyond measure, cannot be thought of as
anything other than sublime.

A big golden sun is rising over a perfectly aquamarine
lake; the sky swirled with pinks and purples, flashes of
gold. The mountains beyond are impossibly perfect – great

tartan pleats of heather and rain-sodden green, clinging to sheer rock and folding politely inwards to make room for waterfalls that cascade like spilled sugar.

She spent last night in a comfy "eco-cottage" looking out over Loch Sunart. It's a home built of curves, the turf roof and driftwood exterior conspiring to render it near invisible from the road. It has been designed to resemble a seashell and there is not a single straight line within. It's unashamedly romantic, and she had felt a distinct frisson of something akin to loss as she sat in the big slipper bath drinking her Prosecco and Chambord and watched the stars fill the sky.

She leans back. Winces. The bed is made of reclaimed driftwood and looks better than it feels. She reaches over and retrieves her phone from the nightstand. It's coming up to 6am. There should be missed calls. Should be voicemails and updates. But the phone service is at its patchiest here. Instead she goes straight to her email – the connection guaranteed by satellite Wi-Fi, the dish carefully masked by a screen of trees in the neatly tended garden outside.

She scrolls straight to the last missive from Oscar Parkin, the man who thinks he's her boss. He sent it just after 2am – a demand that she update him first thing, or face consequences that could, he fears, be "severe". She grinds her back teeth, bunching up her left cheek like a fist. Quickly she logs in to her personal email, looking for the message she knows, to her bones, will be waiting. It's another from Oscar, sent ten minutes later – from his personal account.

So sorry I had to go through the motions and tear a strip off. You know it's just for show. Really need to hear from you though. Last we got was that you'd left the accommodation at Loch Lomond and that you'd banked a favour with the local plods about not releasing the details of some accident? A body part found at sea? I've acted like it's a matter of operational integrity that I don't share the information but I'm feeling a bit of a mug, all things considered.

Are you okay? When will you be making the decision to go in? Remember, you have all the resources we can muster but we need to be in the loop. Christ I wish I was there on this one. I know you're doing something important so I'll try and butt out. Just remember I'm thinking about you. I'm always thinking about you... xxx

She climbs out of bed, her bare feet pleasant against the wooden floor, already starting to grow warm from the increasing sun. She crosses to the window and stares out. In her head she is moving pieces like a chess champion. She cannot let any of the agencies get their hands on what she's got. For her unit to get the glory for any collar to come out of this operation, there can be no doubt as to who put things together. And yet she has a nagging suspicion that things are moving faster than she can deal with. The last information they received from Kimmy indicated that Pope's operation was at least a fortnight away and that the couriers delivering the shipment through Callum's route have not yet left Guyana. They had believed themselves to have time to muster at least enough intelligence to put together a proper arrest team.

Bishop's death was a shock. He'd been the arrest she was really looking forward to. She'd entertained fantasies of flipping him – persuading him to open up about the endless networks he has helped establish globally. She imagined striking a bargain, in which he would only agree to talk to her. Her, and her alone. That would bring her to the attention of the right people. And then, well, who knew?

Now she finds herself on this barren, rugged stretch of coastline, waiting to hear what the hell is going on and posing as Detective Chief Inspector Emma Cressey. The last she heard from Roe was just after midnight. Ashcroft had been in his room. She'd found the hardware. She might already know about her husband's real betrayal and not just the so-called "affair" with Kimmy. He was going to have to talk to her. He was going to have to tell her the truth.

He'd already rung Callum to warn him that he was taking such a dangerous step, and Callum had begged him not to. Said she would find it easier to forgive infidelity than the notion he had got his family caught up with murderers and drug smugglers. Roe wouldn't be moved. He had that old iron in his voice: the cold fury of somebody who has made a decision and is willing to damn the consequences. He's got a soft spot for Ronni – she can tell.

Sir, full briefing before COP. Matters in hand. Assets 1, 2 and 3 still in play and no operational compromises. Radio silence to be maintained. Concerns appreciated but not necessary. Best, SA.

She sends the email, then makes her way to the kitchen and fills a glass with water. She gulps it down, wipes her chin, then picks up the landline, sitting snugly in a cradle on the kitchen table. She rings the number from memory, rehearsing a little speech in her head. She's sorry to ring so early. She needs to come and talk to her again. She understands that the picture has become a little clearer and that Nicholas Roe has revealed the actual nature of his sojourn on Ardnamurchan. She can offer protective custody, provided she cooperates. She can make it all work out, provided she stays quiet a little while longer and gives her a chance to make an arrest that will cement her legend, and stop some very bad people doing even worse things than she has done herself.

She already feels as though Ronni could be an asset. She'd expected some reaction to the passing of the slip of paper – the amateurish attempt at bribery. Ronni has not reacted like a person out of their depth. Has neither reported her, nor jumped at an opportunity to feather her own nest. She is somebody with a decent mind, and perhaps, a touch of integrity. Once upon a time, she might have made a decent copper.

'Hello, this is DCI Emma Cressey. Am I speaking with Ronni...'

She stops talking. The phone has been answered by a child. A boy. He sounds frightened.

'This is Atticus. I don't know where Mum is. She's not in her bed, but we slept in that. Theresa stayed here, and she'd been hurt. She's in the spare room and there's blood on the bed. There's blood on the stairs too. I think somebody was here. I heard noises in the night. Poppy said she had a nightmare about Dad. The house smells funny too. I don't really know what to do...'

She feels her stomach clench. Has a vision of her friend, manacled, bleeding, being hurt the way he was hurt before: the first time she betrayed him, the first time she gave him up in a bid to prove she would make the hard decisions when they were called for.

She makes sure there's some steel in her voice when she talks.

'Atticus, listen to me. This is what I want you to do...'

26

Sickness comes: a greasy tongue, licking at my thorax and probing at my throat.

Scent, now. Damp. That cold, grey-green fustiness of outbuildings and empty bedsits. Something else, too. A high, chemical sort of smell. Antiseptic. Something fruity, underneath. And there, beneath it all, the low hum of ammonia.

Slowly, like a story made of shredded pages, I begin to remember. Those last hours. Theresa. Waking up to find Mr Roe at the foot of my bed. Callum and Kimmy. Violence. Lies. Then the journey through darkness to the house on the hill. The big man, with his metal cage of a fist. And Pope. He'd given the order. Told them to hurt me. He had. Done his master's bidding and more besides.

Pain, now. Pain that sings. It feels like the worst hangover I've ever had. Every cell in my body seems to be coming apart at once: grinding against one another with saw-toothed edges. My head feels as though something two sizes too big has been squeezed into my skull and the pain across my back and neck and shoulders is so intense that I wonder, for a terrifying moment, whether I have been deposited at a hideous angle: my spinal cord taut as a guitar string, my vertebrae bunched against one another like stones beneath the hull of a wooden boat.

I can't see. There's nothing covering my face so I know that the room is dark. Not quite black, but I can't turn the lumps and bumps in the charcoal gloom into anything familiar.

Then the surge of it: the great crescendo of panic and pure unadulterated terror as I see the faces of my children swim in my mind's eye like moonlight on a choppy sea.

All other thoughts fade away.

Atticus.

Poppy.

Lilly.

I see them waking up in a house that has no Mummy. No Daddy. Just Theresa, with her tortured feet, and that lingering whiff of violence and loss.

I force myself to stay calm. I try to make sense of my surroundings. Attempt to sit up. I roll, drunkenly, clattering onto my face. I can't work out up or down. I feel rough cord against my face. Carpet. Dusty, damp-smelling carpet. I begin to reach out, to put my hand down for support, and I realise with horror that I can't make my limbs do what I want. There are jagged white lines in what passes for my vision and a terrible tingling in my arms. It's like a migraine. Worse. I wonder if something has been knocked loose in my brain – whether the little bones in my inner ear are shaking around like dried peas in a tin.

And finally I am aware of myself. The fog clears in a way that makes me think, incongruously, of suddenly finding the right station when searching through the radio channels. At once, I am aware. I'm lying on my side, knees drawn up and my legs bound at the ankles. My hands are behind me, tied tight at the wrists. As I try to lift my head there is a grotesque moment of connection and I realise that the clammy blood on my face has briefly adhered me to the carpet.

I lick my lips. There's no gag in my mouth, thank God. My mouth is horribly dry and it takes an age to work some spit into my mouth. I clear my throat with as little noise as I can, and try my voice. I can croak. Can whisper. Talk to myself, alone, bound, terrified beyond words.

'Hello... hello, is there anybody else there? It's Ronni. Can you hear me? Callum? Callum, we need to get to the children. Will he hurt them? He can't, can he? What does he want? People know us! He can't just make it like we don't exist. We have lives. People care...'

I stop talking. The words come back from far away. I'm in a room with a high ceiling and a dusty, damp carpet. I roll forward, wriggling on my elbows and knees, commando-style, waiting for the moment when whatever is tethering me in place snaps me over backwards. It doesn't come. I'm not tied to anything, save myself. Whoever dumped me here must have expected me to stay unconscious until they returned. How long could that be? Who had tied me? Bundled me up? Dropped me on the floor like a roll of old carpet?

My heart starts to beat faster in my chest. I can see the children's faces again. Cruel, unhelpful images begin to flash in my mind like photographs ripped from an album of the grotesque. I see Poppy waking to find the big man leaning down over her – his huge metal hand closing over her mouth like the legs of a great crab. I see Lilly, waking to the lingering aria of her father, her Daddy – searching the house for the man she adores and misses so much, and instead finding Theresa dead, her mangled toes sticking out from the end of the bed.

I push forward, elbows and knees, feeling the rough carpet abrade my skin. I stop as I feel the faintest whisper of draught. The chemical smell is stronger – so too that dirt-and-tree-bark smell that I know as well as any local might. I can smell the forest. I can smell the dawn.

My head bangs against something hard. I rock back onto my haunches and stroke my face against the obstacle. It's rough. Exposed brick and ragged, dusty plaster.

'Please,' I whisper, to myself and the air and to the whole horrible world. 'Please…'

I shuffle around, putting my back to the brick. I don't know which direction my captor might come from but I know that whatever I do I have to do it quickly. Feeling like a fool, half tempted to give in to some mad giggle, I start rubbing whatever binds my hands against the roughest chunk of brickwork. I have a sudden memory of Saturday afternoons watching cowboy films with Dad. There would always be a handy piece of glass or a smouldering campfire upon which the hero could test their bonds. But brick would do. Brick would definitely do…

It happens quicker than I'd imagined. One moment my hands are bound together at the wrists and the next they spring apart as the hard plastic that had bound them gives way. At once I feel the blood returning to my fingers, my palms, my wrists, and it feels as though my fingertips are filling with ground glass. Awkwardly I change my position and pat the floor with my half-dead hands, looking for something that might allow me to cut the bonds at my ankles. I touch something cold and curved and metallic. Paint-pots. A stack of them, piled haphazardly against the brick wall. And then my hand closes upon a length of something hard. Thin. Unyielding. Covered in something congealed. I begin to hack at the tie-wrap that holds my feet together. My fingertips touch bare skin and I experience a hard, ugly memory. Theresa's feet. Her snipped toes. The things they did...

The bonds spring apart and I sprawl on the floor as if released from a trap. I shudder, exhausted, and realise that the pain has subsided as surely as the adrenaline has flowed through me. I want to sit still, to gather my breath, to take stock of what the hell to do, and then I am shuffling back against the wall as I hear the unmistakable sound of footsteps, and muffled voices.

It takes me a moment to tune in to their frequency, and then I am turning snatched words into sentences, as I hear the two men come closer, moving towards a spot directly in front of where I sit and cower and clutch the paint-streaked object as if it were a blade.

'...lost his fucking mind, mate. No talking to him anymore. Whatever's in his innards is in his brain too. He's gone, man.'

'I hear you, but what choice is there? If it all goes his way he rules the roost for another God knows how many years, and if we're the ones who've been with him through the bad times then it has to be good for us. And even if it goes wrong, loyalty will look good with whoever comes next. I don't want the job but I don't mind being close to it.'

'You're just shitting your pants in case the big man loses his temper with you.'

'Fuck off. And anyway, he doesn't lose his temper. That's what's so scary about the big bastard.'

'So we're doing it, yeah? Nothing fancy. She's probably closed her gills already.'

'Closed her gills?'

'You know. Died, like. Swallowed her own blood. She was snoring like her throat was full of hacksaw blades when I dropped her. She might have done us a favour.'

'You got your gloves?'

'Come on, the tide…'

'Billy, put your pissing gloves on…'

Emotions crash against one another within me: rival tsunamis that twist and rise and threaten to suck me under. There's fear, yes. But it's rage that fills me more than any other emotion as I sit, coiled, in the dark and wait for these two bastards to stop discussing whether I'm dead or alive and the best way to remedy the situation if I happen to be breathing.

Desperately, praying for any kind of help, I cast around for something I can use as a weapon. As my eyes become more accustomed to the dark I realise that I'm in what I take to be a disused bedroom. There's a headboard and mattress against the far wall – pasting tables set up in front of a high window hung with ragged drapes. The object I'm holding is the aerial from a radio, coated in thick, dried paint. I reach out and close my hand around the lid of a large tin of paint. I lift it. Half full. Heavy as a dumbbell. Heavy enough to swing.

The sound of a key turning in the lock.

The sudden square of yellow light spilling in a great rectangle into the tatty room.

Two men, their shadows long and dark, stepping lazily into the space as if expecting to find a dead woman.

I spring forward from where I crouch, swinging the tin of paint like a mace. It makes a perfect arc, an inch-perfect upswing all the way from the floor, and I give a primal shriek as I deliver the blow. The tin catches the nearest man just below the hinge of his jaw and makes a noise like a frying pan striking a wall. His feet leave the floor. I feel the tremor all the way down my arm. I swing it again, catching him on the temple, and one side of his face caves in like soft fruit.

'*Fuck, Billy! Billy – move! Hey! Hey, Billy!*'

As the one called Billy crumples like somebody sinking into the earth, I lock eyes with the other man. I recognise him as the driver of the van that hit the wall, but the realisation seems to come in some far away point in my mind, where reason and common sense still play a part. Here, now, all that matters is the need to be free. To be with my children. On his eyeballs I fancy for a moment that I can see a tiny reflection: see a half-naked, blood-soaked woman, face in rictus, teeth bared, swinging the paint pot down like a club.

He raises a hand to protect himself. I feel the bones shatter as the metal hits flesh, and then I feel warmth on my hand and on my stomach and my legs and I look down to see that the aerial I have been holding in my other hand is buried in his gut all the way up to my hand.

His eyes bulge, mouth frothing, teeth mashing down upon his tongue as it slides from his open mouth like a dead sea slug, and then he is falling backwards and I'm standing over him and bringing down the paint tin again and again on his head.

Exhausted, drenched with rapidly cooling blood, I slump backwards, gasping, chest rising and falling like a racehorse.

None of it matters, I tell myself. Not the dead men. Not the thing you just did. You need to get home to your children. You need to make sure they're safe. This is what you're for.

Billy is wearing white trainers. I slip them off his feet and try them on. They're a size too big, and still warm. He's got a black coat on, and I drag it from his shoulders as if stripping the children for a bath. In the pocket, a mobile phone. The key-pad is locked.

Cursing, I check his other pockets. Check the other man's too. A wallet. Cigarettes. A strange, hard object that I discover to be a roll of coins tucked into a long black sock. I pull on the jacket. Use the hem of Billy's T-shirt to wipe the blood from my face. Pocket the phone, and the cosh. Put my back to the doorframe and push both big, heavy men into the room with my feet.

In my pocket, the phone rings. It sends a shudder through me as surely as if a cold hand has reached up and touched my neck. I retrieve the phone. The number doesn't come from a known contact – the screen instead filling with the digits of a random mobile phone. I feel an overwhelming urge to answer it. Perhaps whoever is ringing is from a different world to the brutal one in which I find myself. Maybe all I need to do is tell them that I'm in danger, that people are going to be hurt – that they need to send the police, and fast. My finger hovers over the phone and finally, I stab at the screen and raise it to my ear.

'Billy? Job done, mate?'

I say nothing. Just listen to the unfamiliar voice.

'Aye well, when you're done we'll need you on the ward. One of the donors is kicking off and the doc can't get near him. I can't get down there. Having a ball with our friends right now. If you pass the van, pick me up the secateurs, would you? Cheers, lad.'

He ends the call. I'm left looking at a locked screen. As I begin to put it back in my pocket my fingertip brushes the screen and a message flashes up, saying the print isn't recognised. I realise, adrenaline surging through me, that it works on fingerprint recognition. Grimacing, hating the feel of the clammy skin, I manoeuvre Billy's cold fingers and press each in turn to the screen. It flashes into life and I sit grinning madly to myself in the dark.

I should call 999 – I know that. Instead, I call home.

'Ashcroft residence.'

I know the voice at once. The English detective. The impossibly beautiful, cold-eyed copper who had pressed the note into my hand.

'This is Ronni!' I gasp, the words shooting out in a breathless rush. 'Are you at my house? Of course you are, sorry, sorry. Are they okay? Are the kids okay? I don't know where I am! They've got Mr Roe, and I think they might have Callum and the woman he's been seeing, and Mr Pope talked about an operation and giving himself another chance, and I just smashed two men to bits with a tin of paint...'

'Calm down please,' comes the reply, cool as ice. 'Yes, the children are well. Yes, I'm at your home. Medical help is on the way for your friend. Now, tell me about Nicholas.'

'Nicholas? Mr Roe? Yes, he was with me. Callum tasered him! I don't know what's happening.'

The line starts to crackle and cut out. I curse. Repeat myself. I want to shake it until she drops out of the receiver and starts being some bloody help.

'You said the operation was going ahead? Was Nicholas in the vicinity when that was said? Or Kimmy?'

'Why are you asking this? What's happening?'

'Mrs Ashcroft, it's vitally important that you stay precisely where you are. Take whatever steps you need to remain out of sight and do not be tempted to try and find…'

I'm left staring at a dead phone as the signal drops out. I want to scream, but I swallow it down, and let myself think of the children. Safe. Safe at home, with a police officer. A police officer who knows more than she will tell me, and who tried to buy me off…

I need to get away from here. The knowledge is absolute. The door is open. There must be a way out, wherever the hell they've brought me. I recognise the scents of outdoors and know the nearness of home. There is no question of waiting here – waiting in the dark for whatever comes next.

I slip out into the corridor and close the door behind me. I know at once my suspicions were correct. I'm at the castle. At Glenborrodale. I'm in a long, cold corridor lit only by flickering bulbs, moving quickly across a threadbare carpet with a Seventies pattern: loud and ugly and torn to shreds in places where a convoy of equipment has been dragged across its surface.

I run without knowing where I'm going. Run in the only direction I can. Sprint down the corridor past open doors and closed doors and as lights flick to life above me.

All the while, I see my children. See them tied to gurneys. See them being opened up with sharp blades and leering men stuffing cash into their guts as they pull out their intestines like flags from a clown's pocket.

I reach the top of a staircase. Scurry down the curving stairs, one hand slick on the bannister, feet thundering on the stairs. I catch a glimpse of the dawn: a shaft of sunlight spearing in from a gap in the curtains at the base of the stairs. I know I'll throw myself through if I have to. Know I'll do whatever it takes.

And then I hear him. Hear him screaming as if somebody were drilling into his bones.

Callum.

27

'Warm enough, Mr Roe? Comfy? I can get you a blanket. Man in your condition should take care of himself...'

Roe is strapped to what he takes to be a full-size snooker table. He has been pinned out like Vitruvian man: like a rat ready for dissection. He cannot feel much beyond his knees and wrists so cannot tell whether he is being held in place by bonds or whether something has been driven through his wrists and ankles. He cannot see who speaks to him. The voice comes from somewhere towards the back of the room. It carries no trace of accent. No trace of emotion either.

Nicholas Roe is all too familiar with the different ways that people behave when they sense the nearness of death. Some scream. Others beg. A certain type will adopt a kind of posturing bravado: a refusal to give in to the crippling fear that courses through them. He has met a handful of psychopaths in his life and has always found himself begrudgingly impressed by the absence of fuss they make in times of suffering.

He knows himself to be among their number. He can hold out in the face of pain for a very long time. He endured every conceivable form of suffering when a captive of the criminal syndicate that took him to the place between life and death and who returned him there at their pleasure. He kept his fight for a long time. Never let them think they had destroyed him. He kept his eyes on them as they brought the hammer and chisel down upon his bones. He dredged up every last insult he could think of and spat it in their faces as they went about the business of disassembling him.

But eventually, the will to fight bled out of him. Eventually, he felt the first stirrings of defeat. He experienced a whispered, disloyal urge to beg. To plead. To ask them to stop hurting him, just for a moment. He never acted upon the impulse, but by God he had wanted to.

Here, in the big, red-painted room towards the rear of the castle, he takes comfort in the fact that there is nothing that can be done to him which hasn't been done before. It is no effort for him to affect an air of bravura. He isn't afraid.

'Would it be horribly predictable if I told you to fuck off?' asks Roe, raising his head and looking down at the bits of himself on display. He's gladdened to see he has trousers on. His feet are bare. Chest too. He squints into the semi-darkness. Sees the length of flex around his left foot and feels a moment's relief. Cord, not nails. That had to go down as a win.

'I fear you're not happy with the service you've paid for,' says the voice. 'I should imagine this isn't your idea of a professional transplant and care service in the relaxing grounds of a luxury private hospital. Would I be right?'

'You're here for the bed bath, are you?' asks Roe. 'Crack on then, son. Balls could use a wipe.'

'We find ourselves in something of a quandary, Mr Roe,'

says the voice, and it seems to have altered position. It's coming from elsewhere in the room now. Roe tries to get a sense of his environment. High ceiling – the scent of stale cigars and spilled whisky; the baize beneath his skin. He's in the games room, he realises. Still on the peninsula; not far from the loch. He thinks, fleetingly, of Ronni. He allows himself to hope that they left her where she fell. He cannot put any weight behind the fantasy. The big man hit her hard enough to crack a thick skull. He feels a great wave of regret surge within him. He had thought that by being close to her, he could keep her safe in Callum's absence. It had been a contract of sorts: an unspoken agreement between himself and her husband. He would make sure nobody harmed her or his children, and he wouldn't pull out of the operation.

'Quandary, is it?' growls Roe, licking his lips. 'Sorry, son, awful big word that. Are you saying you've fucked up? Looks like it to me. Looks like you've taken my money and knocked me about like a piece of meat, is what it looks like. I've paid for a second chance. I'm due a new liver and lung. I've taken my meds. I've let you take your samples. I've kept my mouth shut and done whatever you've wanted me to do. And now I'm pinned out like a kite!'

'It's not ideal,' says the voice, ruefully. 'And if it's any consolation, this is very much against my judgement.'

'And you are?'

'Unimportant, for now,' comes the reply, smoothly. 'Suffice to say, I am the one who will decide whether you get the service you paid for, or whether it would be best to put a line through your name.'

Roe feels hope unfold like the petals of a rose. There's

still doubt. They might not yet know who he really is. He could still put things right.

'What have I done wrong?' asks Roe, raising his head. There's a stab of pain across his shoulders. He hears a grotesque crackling sound as he tries to catch his breath. Tastes blood.

'Pope is not an easy person to do business with,' he says, wistfully. 'He has whims. Enthusiasms. He can be impulsive. This entire venture is questionable in terms of risk-to-reward ratios. I fancy we are causing ourselves more problems than we are solving. The supply chain that he controls is an obvious asset, but the use of couriers as donors is only going to lead to difficulty in finding new couriers. Word does get around, I'm afraid. And there is something distasteful about the work we will be doing here. I'm not squeamish, but those who become medical professionals surely do so out of a desire to help and heal. I fear for the integrity of the individuals we have been forced to recruit to perform the opposite service.' A pause, and a long, slow exhalation. Roe smells cigar smoke. His own brand.

'Are you smoking my cigars?' he asks, and sucks blood through his teeth. 'One liberty too far.'

'I must say, Mr Roe, you are not doing much to help your case.'

'And what charges am I facing?'

'Pope thinks you're a cop. I do not. Others within his employ do not. I don't wish to be rude, but I cannot see you as anything other than the near-dead specimen who so desperately thrust his money into the hand of our salesman and begged for a new liver and lung. You are a dying man, that much is clear. You don't wear make-up. There are no affectations. Your teeth really do slip in the gums and your eyes have the look of somebody who sees things that might not be really here. It is my recommendation that we return some of your money, carry out your procedure as requested, and allow you to go about your life without any of the unpleasantness that Pope has requested.'

Roe hears his breath stutter as he tries to breathe in. The man hears it too.

'Your medical notes say that a transplanted organ could buy you years. Not a lifetime, but years. I have had your background checked and triple-checked and everything I have learned reinforces my believe that you are who you say you are.'

'But...'

'The trouble is, though I can see from your demeanour that you are not unfamiliar with high-pressure situations such as these, the man who brought you to see Pope does not have your fortitude.'

Roe closes his eyes. Thinks of Callum Ashcroft. Knows immediately what he has done.

'He's told you I'm a cop,' says Roe, without emotion.

'He has. He is proving quite a disappointment, all things considered. He is begging for his life, and the life of his pretty wife, even as you and I talk like gentlemen. We have not even had to particularly hurt him. Fear of what we will do has been enough to persuade him to talk.'

'To say anything you want to hear, you mean,' spits Roe, temper in his voice. 'I don't know him from Adam. His wife runs the guest house I've been staying in. Pre-emptive convalescing, getting fit ahead of the op – saying my goodbyes. He turned up last night. Pulled a Taser on me.

Next thing I'm in front of a sick man in a wheelchair and a bloke the size of Giant Haystacks is hitting me with his big metal hand! I've paid money to you people. I'm dying! What's he even accusing me of? What am I here for? Who am I chasing?'

There is no reply. For a moment, Roe wonders whether he has been left alone – whether the speaker has slipped out and left him to his own worst imaginings. And then there is movement. A shadow falls across his chest, and he angles his head. Looks up into dark eyes, and gleaming gold teeth.

'Me,' says Bishop, softly, in his ear. 'I think you're chasing me.'

Roe looks up into the dead man's face. Gives a quiet little laugh.

'The lobster pot?'

'Not a difficult trick to pull off. Nobody sees past the teeth – least of all when the flesh is half eaten away.'

'I paid you. I did what you asked me. That prick who brought me in would say anything to save his skin...'

'I realise that. Which is why I'm giving you an opportunity to state your case. Tell me you're not a copper. I'll make my recommendations to Pope. He may be agreeable. He is currently being prepared for surgery. He is rather jubilant. I believe he and I will do business together for some considerable time – or at least, as long as it takes to persuade his contacts that they are better served by my other associates. And then, well – I shall have to repossess that which doesn't belong to him.'

Roe pauses. Swallows, painfully. 'His heart?'

'His fucking heart.'

'And you'd do that, would you? You'd turn on him? Kill

him? Put your own South American buddies in control of all the narcotics flooding in to northern Europe…'.

'He will live because I have procured him a heart, Mr Roe. He will die when I take it away.'

Roe sucks his lower lip. 'Can I have a tug on that cigar?' he asks.

Bishop smiles. Puts the stub between Roe's lips and lets him take a long, comforting drag. He breathes out a plume of grey.

'The woman who was with him. Hard-faced. Kimmy, was it? Who's she?'

'According to Mr Ashcroft, she too is a police officer. My colleague is currently questioning her just as I question you.'

'And the woman. Ronni?'

'Alas, I fear that by now she will have been disposed of. This isn't her world. She could not be called upon to keep her own counsel about what we are doing here. Her friend may yet try and tell the authorities that she was ill-used here at the hands of Mr Pope's rather brutish associates. She cannot be permitted to validate that story, or to give any information that could lead to Mr Pope's rather sizeable enforcer. I'm sure you see that.'

'Where?' asks Roe, quietly. 'Where is she now?'

'Physically?' asks Bishop. 'An upstairs bedroom, I think. The hotel is getting rather crowded. Our couriers from Guyana are being kept as comfortable as possible ahead of the procedures. The fight has quite gone out of them and they are enjoying the benefits of our hospitality. If they know what awaits them, they haven't spoken of it aloud.'

'They're alive?'

'Of course. Even now, your new lung inflates and deflates

in the chest of a small, dark-skinned man called Ignatio. I hope you will take care of it, should it make its way into you...'

Roe looks up at him. 'Big mouth, ain't you?'

'I feel that you and I have an understanding. We are alone here. If I allow you to go ahead with the operation, you will be in my debt and in my confidence. And if not, you will be dead and no threat of any kind.'

'There's a third option,' says Roe, craning his neck so he can put his face directly in Bishop's eyeline.

'And that is?'

'Third option, is that my colleagues have overheard everything you've just said. The third option, is that I'm transmitting this whole conversation back to the team leader with the National Crime Agency.'

Bishop smiles. 'With what? You have a tracker in your balls?'

Roe returns the grin. Feels the pressure relax in his left hand as the knot he has been clawing at with his long yellow nails gives way as if chewed through by a rat. 'No, lad,' he says. 'It's just below the skin of my bottom rib.'

'Fuck off.' Bishop laughs, but he glances down to Roe's navel. Considers the wickerwork of scars and half-healed wounds.

Roe closes his hand around a billiard ball. Lurches forward and cracks it, as hard as he can, across Bishop's cheekbone. It caves in like hard pastry, and he falls backwards with a grunt – slipping onto his back and his head cracking off the floor with a sickening thud.

Roe looks at the ball in his hand. It's pink. He grins to himself as he starts unpicking the ties that hold his other hand. Decides, on balance, that when he writes the report, he'll say it was black. He has a reputation to maintain.

Moments later, he slithers down from the table. He's in pain everywhere, but that is nothing new. His clothes are in a neat pile at the rear of the room. He retrieves his jacket and searches for the tiny, pill-shaped piece of metal sewn into the seam of the lapel. Presses it hard. Sits down, and catches his breath, as it begins transmitting. Painfully, arthritically, he climbs up on the pool table and fumbles around on the dusty light until he finds the recording device. Voice-activated – the best money can buy. There are a dozen of them scattered around the different wings of the castle. He got lucky the day he decided that the games room should be on the list of locations. He knows enough gangsters to have no doubts that it would be somewhere that bored men might congregate and let their guards down. Then he searches Bishop's pockets and finds a slim, black mobile phone. He reaches over and pulls down Bishop's blood-caked eyelid and points his eyeball at the screen. It comes to life. He dials the number without preamble.

When she answers, her voice is a balm for his wounds. He tells her what he has. What he needs. Then he tells her not to delay, and hangs up.

'See you soon,' he whispers.

Then he dresses himself and heads for the door. He stops, his hand on the handle. A selection of old-fashioned games and bits of sporting equipment are in a rack by the door. A smile crosses his lips as he picks up the croquet mallet.

'At last,' he whispers, as he feels its pleasing heft. 'A chance to look sophisticated...'

28

O scar Parkin is just leaving his apartment when his mobile phone gives a soft chirrup in his trouser pocket. The ring tone is the one that marks the caller out as important. It's the one he's been waiting for – the one that has kept him up until 3am and which he had begun to fear would not come.

He looks at the screen. The caller ID is not shown but that is through choice. He uses an NCA encrypted telephone and the caller display unit shows only the most basic information, lest prying eyes are watching through a long lens. He knows it's her. Even though she cannot see him, he automatically stands a little taller. Across from his apartment door there is a large mirror, angled to show anybody approaching down the long corridor. He walks three paces and stands in front of it, examining his reflection. Blue tie, knotted fat. Blue suit, white shirt flecked with little speckles of orange. Big glasses, head shaved down to a billiard-ball gleam. If this is the moment; if this is when it all goes to shit, he wants to at least feel prepared for it. His reflection tells him he can handle this. He's good at what he does. He needs to stop worrying, and allow himself to hope that things have gone right.

'Hello.'

He watches himself in the mirror as she talks. Matters have moved far quicker than they had anticipated. The first of the transplants is happening today. It's Pope. The man himself. It all simmered over last night. Ronni Ashcroft discovered that Nicholas Roe was concealing his true identity and he'd had no choice but to break cover. Her husband and the unit's other undercover asset both did their damnedest to keep the operation on track, but to do that meant involving Mrs Ashcroft. That led them to Pope. And Pope hadn't believed them. Now, Roe, Mr and Mrs Ashcroft and the other undercover operative are being detained by Pope at the castle on Ardnamurchan. And somehow, near-miraculously, Roe has managed to alert her to the presence of the resurrected Bishop. All the players are in one place.

She needs tactical support, and needs it urgently. This could be a career-making operation. It could lead to the arrest of Pope, his deputies, and Bishop, not to mention the smashing of a new smuggling route and the saving of several lives in the form of unwilling organ donors. But he's the only one who can make it happen. And it has to happen now.

Parkin runs a hand over his face. Takes off his spectacles and rubs them on his tie. He says nothing for a moment, just looking into his own eyes and weighing up the odds.

'If it goes well, it's a huge result. If it goes wrong, that's me done. And no doubt you step into my shoes. Not a bad position to find yourself in, eh?'

She doesn't respond, and her silence irks him. Her whole tone irks him: that entitled, arrogant way she has – even as she informs him of a major balls-up in her operation, she acts as if she's doing him a favour and this was the plan all along. She should be on her knees. Should be pleading with him. Instead, she sounds like she's giving him one last chance to do something right.

He stares into his own eyes and feels briefly disgusted with himself. He's better than this. He's a good man who wants to do the job correctly and stop people getting hurt. There are people in danger. Officers. Civilians. Poor unwitting drug mules. To delay through self-interest would be the act of a bastard and he knows, having met plenty, that he is better than that.

'Stay in a signal zone,' he says, breathily. 'I can get you a unit. Tactical support, based at Argyll and Dunbartonshire. I primed them last night. They're waiting for the nod. You make the arrest. Then we'll make all the pieces fit.'

She has the grace to say one small word before she hangs up. It's barely a whisper, but it makes him feel good.

'Sir...'

29

I can smell fresh paint. Through the double doors at the end of the long corridor I find myself in an area of the castle where workmen have made progress. There is little light, but the walls gleam a moonlight white and the carpets have been ripped up – showing a wood floor beneath. There are dust sheets down in places and against one wall are big open boxes. I peek inside. It's full of tasteful art prints and self-assembly frames. A smaller box contains glossy leaflets, advertising the new "*Convalescence and Rejuvenation Spa*", opening this spring. I find myself wondering how many of the rich and famous guests paying for detox sessions and facial peels will know that in another wing, men from the far side of the world are being sliced open and having their organs removed for transplant. That their reward for crossing the sea to bring narcotics into Scotland is to become little more than a suitcase full of cash.

I hear it again. The screech of it – the high, agonised wail of pain. Callum.

I don't feel like myself anymore. I can't seem to make my hands do what I want. I'm groggy, ham-fisted. There's a numbness spreading through me. I can't hear properly. There's a dull bloom of warmth across my back and it feels as if parts of me are falling asleep in turn. I shake my head, willing some life into my legs, and half run, half stagger down the white-painted corridor towards the sound of the shriek.

What are you doing? I demand of myself. *Stop. Stay safe. Hide! Think of the children. You can't just blunder in. What can you do?*

I ignore the voice. Push open a wooden door and suddenly I am staring through a glass panel into a long, brightly lit room. I scrabble backwards before anybody can see me, and try to make sense of the picture before me. At the back of the property, through the last wooden door, is what I can only think of as a field hospital. Whatever purpose this room used to serve, it has been transformed into a long, white-painted space. The doors that shut it off from the main house have a glass panel midway up, and light spills out along with the noises of suffering and pain that have called me here from the relative safety of where they left me.

Crouching low, half afraid to move, I force myself to scurry forward and to peer through the glass. I have to bite down on my hand as I see what lies within.

There are four hospital beds, side by side. Strapped down, lashed like patients in a Victorian asylum, three dark-skinned, emaciated men. They stare at the ceiling, slack-jawed but chests heaving – drugged into some kind of paralysis. One man has gauze pads taped upon his eyes. He's hooked up to a drip. Somebody has placed a blanket over him but shivers still rack his frail body.

And beyond, in the fourth bed, the woman I know as Kimmy. She's on her side, in what I take to be the recovery position. She's been stripped. Bruises cover her back where the light catches her pale, scrawny form, and a colossal purple patch blooms on her cheek. She's not tied down. She's not moving.

I turn my head. Duck down. In the corner of the room, enormous in a too-small chair, is the big man. The one who hurt me. Who hurt all of us. He's talking into a mobile phone, his face inscrutable.

I raise my head again as I hear another anguished yell of pain, and then a door opens at the far end of the room and a tall, white-haired man in surgical scrubs pushes through from a darkened space beyond. He's shaking his head. Grumbling. The big man stands as he approaches. I press my ear to the door, but I can only catch snatches of words.

'Not ready... can't work like this – too many unknowns, not even sanitary, let alone sterile...'

The big man doesn't want to hear it. 'Make it work,' he says. 'He dies, you die.'

'It's not like that. It's not wishful thinking, it's medicine...'

'You've been paid. Do your fucking job...'

And then that scream again. It's an animal thing: the screech of something hurt beyond enduring. Head down, showing as little of myself as I can, I watch as the big man pushes past the man in surgical scrubs and barges through the doors into the room beyond. I bite down on my wrist as he returns, moments later, dragging Callum by one bloodied foot, his fist wrapped around his ankle, hauling him out like a sack of rubbish. He's naked. His face is swollen all down one side and his fingers stick out at different angles like the stakes in a broken fence. All the toes are missing from his left foot. Blood bubbles in his mouth as he yells, despairingly, and as I watch his lips move, I realise that the scream is not some unintelligible cry. It's a word. A name. He's shouting for me. He's shouting Ronni, as if he's a child who wants his mother.

I feel parts of myself begin to dissemble. I'm overcome with such pity and love for him that it almost saps me of my fury. It comes back in a tsunami. How dare they! How dare they do this. To him. To me. To any of these poor bastards in the beds. I have to fight with myself to stay where I am – to not push through the doors and beat my hands bloody against the back of the great beast who has taken my husband apart.

I sense a presence behind me. I turn, braced for impact, coiled to run.

'Don't,' says Mr Roe. 'Don't go in there.'

By the light of the window I make out his features. He's at once the man I know and somebody else entirely. The illness that has haunted his features seems to have melted away like yesterday's snow. He walks taller. Carries himself stronger. Years have fallen away from him. He puts a hand on mine and I see blood on the backs of his hands. He looks at the blood on mine.

'They're on their way,' he whispers. 'Police.'

I look through him. Make sense of it. 'Police like you?'

He nods. 'Yes.'

'How long?'

'Soon.'

My face creases with fury and frustration. 'They're going to kill him.'

He peers past me. Takes in the scene. I hear the dull thud of big meaty hands hitting flesh, and know that fresh harm is being done to my children's father. I look at the big wooden object that he holds in his hand. It's a mallet: a big round head on it.

'Give it to me,' I beg. 'I'm quick. I can hit him, and you get Callum out of there.'

He shakes his head. 'He'll be armed. He's doing this to entertain himself. He could already have killed him if that was the instruction.'

'You're the police! You can't do nothing and let him die.'

He looks into my eyes, trying to get me to understand. 'I'm not scared of him, love. But if I go for him and can't take him down, he tells Pope what's happening. And Pope will do what all cowards do when they feel the walls closing in. He'll scarper and burn the place down. And there's no back-up, love. Nobody here to make sure those poor sods on the gurneys get free…'

'And no result for you, eh? No arrests, no glory?'

'Fuck glory,' he spits.

We both hear the big man's voice. Both hear the words, clear as the sky above the loch. '…think you'd have had enough now, Callum. Think it's time to put you down. Doc here says you've got a few bits and pieces in you that haven't ruptured. Maybe we'll find a buyer for your eyes, eh?'

Sadness shows in Mr Roe's face. Acceptance too. The decision's been made.

'Been a blast,' he says, and one bony hand closes around my arm. He yanks me away from the door with such force that I tumble into the wooden doors across the hall, and then he is pushing through the swing doors, barrelling into the brightly lit room: the mallet in his hand, becoming a poleaxe as he changes his grip.

I scrabble forwards, trying to follow. The door clatters into me, knocking me backwards, but through the strobing in my vision, I see.

The big man is down on one knee, blood gushing from a wound to the crown of his head. The man in surgical scrubs is on his back, both hands between his legs, blood gushing from his crushed nose. And Roe is leaning over Callum, trying to get an arm beneath his head…

'No!'

The big man is back on his feet. He grabs Roe by the head – his whole hand closing over his skull like a basketball player clutching the ball, and he drags him backwards as if he were a child. He throws the other hand as if it were a hammer, and Roe only just manages to wriggle free of the grip in time to duck the lethal blow. He kicks out, booting the big man between the legs, but if it pains him he doesn't show it. I watch, in stasis, as he throws another great haymaker and I see Roe swing upwards with the mallet. It hits the giant in the chest and he staggers backwards, half stumbling over Callum.

I charge forward, unable to help myself, and Roe, gasping for breath, throws the mallet towards me. I catch it as I move and in one fluid motion I bring it down, hard, on the big man's forehead, as if on a fairground strongman machine. He grunts and slides sideways, and I rush to Callum, who blinks, bloodily as I swim in and out of his vision. 'Oh God,' I say, and it's all I've got. 'Oh God…'

I don't see the big man move. Just feel the sudden agony of a hand closing around my neck. I leave the floor, feet kicking, gasping for air, and my vision spins and swirls and eddies as he dangles me high in the air. I see him stand over Callum. Kick out frantically as he raises his huge boot above his skull.

In the doorway, a flash of light. Blonde hair, blue eyes, an absolute absence of feeling in her impossibly perfect eyes.

She holds the gun with both hands. I see tanned skin. Perfect nails. See her lips move, and some part of me heeds the instruction. With my last surge of strength I reach down and claw at his eyes, feeling my index finger slip into the warm, gooey softness of the eyeball.

He drops me, and I spill to the ground.

And then Mr Roe is covering me with his lean, powerful body, and all I can hear is the muffled bang-bang, and then the ground seems to shudder as the big man falls like a tree.

A moment later, I am being pulled upright. Roe is checking me over for wounds. And from somewhere nearby I hear the sound of shouts and running feet and the roar of revving engines.

She's standing in front of me. There's not a hair out of place. She's just killed a man and there's nothing there – no tears, no twisted lip.

I think of myself. Feel the blood on my hands. Those men, I think, suddenly. I killed those men…

'Get him?' asks Roe, softly.

She nods. 'Lovely guest room in the east wing. Paisley pyjamas and a bottle of Lucozade. He's still up there, if you want to go take a piss before we take him in.'

Roe shakes his head. 'And Bishop?'

For the first time, she smiles. 'Oh yes,' she says. 'We've got Bishop.'

'Alive?'

'Just about.'

'You think he'll talk? Tell us what we want to know?'

'Yes. And I won't even need to touch his toes.'

I stop listening. I'm on the floor, cradling Callum, stroking his forehead, the blood on his skin and the blood on mine mingling like spilled paints.

Roe moves to the far bed. 'She's got a pulse,' he says, of the woman I know as Kimmy. 'She's hard.'

I hear his knees crack as he bends down and looks into my eyes. He gives me a nod.

He puts his hand on mine – the one that covers Callum's brow. Then, so softly as to be almost inaudible, he says "thank you."

Then he stands, turns, and walks out the doors, and I'm left with the woman who just put two bullets in the man who was trying to kill us all.

'Who is he really?' I ask, my mouth dry.

She shakes her head.

She'll never tell.

And I'll never ask again.

Epilogue

Now...
Somewhere near Chelmsford, Essex

Agreen-and-pink canal boat, tied up at a shabby marina on the Chelmer and Blackwater Canal. Dirty lace curtains cover dirtier windows. Over the rail, black water holds a sickle of moon and gaudy puddles of coloured light.

Inside, Nicholas Roe. He looks well, all things considered. He sits at the small galley table and pours a glass of good red wine into a brandy glass. Sniffs it. Holds the aroma, then takes a sip.

'You've got no class,' says the woman, returning from the bathroom. 'And that toilet is disgusting.'

'Don't blame yourself, love. I'll open a window. We all get tummy troubles from time to time.'

'Fuck off.' She smiles, sitting down.

He toasts her health with his glass, and hands her a proper red wine glass that he has been hiding beneath the table. She smiles, indulgently, and takes it. 'Barolo?'

'Could be. They were in a case on the deck of another boat. Twelve of them. An invitation, wouldn't you say?'

'You just took them?'

'No, I whistled and they followed me home.'

They sit in companionable silence. The clock above the sink says 9.03pm. She may yet stay the night. He might yet invite her to. Perhaps tonight they will finally talk things through. What she means to him and what he means to her. It will never be physical – it is a bond beyond that. She kept him alive even as she sentenced him to death. She's turned him from one thing into something else entirely. Whatever he is, she has created. She is his redemption, and he is hers.

'Everybody happy, then? I saw the press conference. Jesus, Parkin was tumescent.'

'That's hard, yeah? Erection.'

'You know it is. You don't have to play me, love. I know you're cleverer than I am – don't pretend to be less than you are.'

'Sorry, old habits.'

'Die hard.'

'Yeah, you do. And yes, they are. Bishop is talking. We've got new friends in enforcement agencies all the way across Europe and the Feds are literally wanking themselves silly over the information he's providing.'

'And he'll only talk to you, yes?'

She sips her wine. 'Yes.'

'You've got it safe?'

'The recording? Yes. To be used only if he stops cooperating, or threatens to talk to somebody else.'

'And the organ donors?'

'A bit fucking confused. Home Office is offering asylum but they still want to go home.'

He shakes his head. 'Nowt as queer as folk.'

'Go on,' she says, eyeing him. 'Ask.'

'About what?'

'About her. Mrs Perfect.'

'Ronni? What are you implying?'

'Not a thing. But yes, she's doing okay. He's not. Injuries aren't healing any time soon but he's not facing any charges and we'll be dipping into the discretionary fund to provide financial assistance.'

He sucks his lower lip. Roots around for a cigar. Lights it, slowly, and states his case.

'She's good, don't you think? Clever. Tough. Dogged. Could run a safe house without batting an eyelid. Middle of nowhere…'

'And she'd do it?'

He shrugs. 'I think she could do anything.'

'Pope's got days,' she says, changing the subject. 'They're readying for war in Glasgow. We've probably caused more problems than we've solved.'

'That's the job, love.'

They stay quiet for a time. Drink, and think, and let words unsaid dance on the air between them.

'You saved my life,' he mutters, at last. 'He'd have torn my fucking head off.'

She looks away. 'Least I could do.'

'Yeah, probably.' He smiles.

She looks around her. 'I can't believe you bought it. This was the scene of a major arrest. An asset, recovered under the Proceeds of Crime Act. Do you really plan on staying here?'

He shrugs. 'Nowhere else to go, love.'

She drains her glass. 'The unit's the toast of the NCA. You're in line for a QPM. Me too.'

'Oh,' he says. 'Goody.'

'So you can take some time, if you want. Take a real holiday. Actually convalesce. Get well.'

He smiles at her, knowingly. 'I'm not going back to Scotland. The air's too fresh. I had to suck an exhaust pipe just to get my breath.'

'So where?' She pulls a flier from her back pocket. It's neatly folded down the middle. She opens it up and shows it to him. It's a spa, in a little town in Madeira, Portugal. 'They offer all sorts of services,' she says. 'Some of them aren't entirely legal. You might benefit from what they have to offer. I have the discretionary fund, like I said.'

He takes the leaflet. Gives a nod of thanks, and pockets it.

'You want to stay?' he asks. 'The sofa pulls out. I could make it up, if you want.'

She looks around. Makes no attempt to hide her distaste. 'No,' she says, flatly. 'No, that would be fucking horrible.'

He grins, delighted with her. 'Do you want me to talk to her? Ask her about the safe house idea?'

She nods: the Ashcrofts already half-forgotten. She has her eyes on bigger prizes. She's learned an awful lot of things from her conversations with Bishop. Knows more than any police officer should – especially one willing to take a life for the right result.

'You're thinking of the next op,' he says. 'What have you got for me?'

She looks him up and down. Wonders whether her love for him will ever be enough to stop her putting him in harm's way. Decides that, on balance, he probably doesn't mind.

'When you're away, don't top up your tan too much. We need you pale and interesting.'

'Oh yes?'

'Yes. You're going to Guyana.'

He drains his glass. 'That's a song, I think.'

She considers him. Gives a moment of absolute honesty. 'I'm pleased you're not dead, Colin.'

He can't help but smile. He hasn't heard his name spoken in such a long time he'd almost forgotten who he used to be.

'And I'm pleased you're still a bitch, Shaz,' he says, in return.

Then there is just the sound of boats kissing damp timbers on the black waters, and the familiar laughter of two old friends.

About the Author

DAVID MARK spent more than fifteen years as a journalist, including seven years as a crime reporter with the *Yorkshire Post*. His writing is heavily influenced by the court cases he covered: the defeatist and jaded police officers; the competent and incompetent investigators; the inertia of the justice system and the sheer raw grief of those touched by savagery and tragedy. He writes the McAvoy series, historical novels and psychological suspense thrillers.

Dark Winter was selected for the Harrogate New Blood panel (where he was Reader in Residence) and was a Richard & Judy pick and a *Sunday Times* bestseller. He has also written for the stage, for a Radio 4 drama (*A Marriage of Inconvenience*) and has contributed articles and reviews to several national and international publications. He is a regular performer at literary festivals and also teaches creative writing.

David also starts to get all squirmy and self-conscious when he looks at stuff like this, so we'll leave it there.

@davidmarkwriter www.davidmarkwriter.co.uk